D1176228

The Oxford Library of Italian Classics

GENERAL EDITOR: ARCHIBALD COLQUHOUN

ITALIAN REGIONAL TALES
OF THE
NINETEENTH CENTURY

ITALIAN REGIONAL TALES
OF THE NINETEENTH CENTURY

Selected and introduced by

ARCHIBALD COLQUHOUN *and* NEVILLE ROGERS

and translated by

BERNARD WALL · ARCHIBALD COLQUHOUN
LOVETT F. EDWARDS · ISABEL QUIGLY · CONSTANCE HUTTON
NEVILLE ROGERS · ANGUS DAVIDSON · W. J. STRACHAN
ADELINE HARTCUP · ANTHONY RHODES
GEORGE ARTHURSON

LONDON

OXFORD UNIVERSITY PRESS

NEW YORK · TORONTO

1961

Oxford University Press, Amen House, London E.C.4

GLASGOW   NEW YORK   TORONTO   MELBOURNE   WELLINGTON
BOMBAY   CALCUTTA   MADRAS   KARACHI   KUALA LUMPUR
CAPE TOWN   IBADAN   NAIROBI   ACCRA

PRINTED IN ITALY BY
OFFICINE GRAFICHE FRATELLI STIANTI
SANCASCIANO VAL DI PESA (FLORENCE)

CONTENTS

INTRODUCTION

The aim of this volume is to present some of the best Italian short stories from a period little known and from which few examples have been translated into readable English. Italian was richer in short stories during the last half of the nineteenth century than it had been for three hundred years, and the first problem of the editors was to find some kind of map to help the reader across little known country. Since most Italian writing of the Risorgimento period and immediately after was 'regional' in one way or another, this seemed to provide the most effective framework. The idea of a composite picture of the peninsula and its islands in terms of stories selected from the principal regions seemed both convenient and attractive. But such simplifications take no account of the mysterious processes of literature. The wind bloweth where it listeth and seeds do not grow up in equal abundance on every soil. A selection on a territorial basis might have had illustrative charm and geographical coherence, but it would have involved a confusion between quality and content, a rejection of good material which happened to come from one of the more productive regions, and the inclusion, maybe, of inferior work from less prolific ones.

To ensure that the 'regional' arrangement should be a convenient framework and not an arbitrary and inconvenient frontier we have everywhere put considerations of quality before those of geography. The demands of our material also imposed on us a liberal interpretation not only of place but of time. For just as writings refuse to group themselves geographically to suit editors, so do writers fail to accommodate their life-spans to arbitrary chronology. Though all our authors were born or produced their best work during the nineteenth century, and though all most certainly belong to it in spirit, some continued writing well on into the present century. In terms of timespan writers such as Deledda and D'Annunzio belonged less to the era bounded artificially by the years 1850-1900 than to a phase which ended with the Second World War and could almost be called 'From the First to the Second Risorgimento'.

Italian regionalism, of varying kinds, is of course by no means dead even today. One striking example may still be sensed in the air of little capitals preserved by so many towns throughout the peninsula. Beneath this lies often a depth of local feeling seldom taken into account by the casual visitor; it exists still, and is so stubbornly ingrown, because incomparably more ancient than the sense of belonging to a United Italy, which is, after all, not yet a hundred years old. Perhaps it was not a paradox but a natural result that the 'Regionalist School', in the text-book sense, did not appear until after the official unification of the country. Such a shock would surely make any organism more conscious of its component parts.

One wonders if in spite of recent changes the basic local behaviour has altered so very much, either in outlying country districts or even in the heart of great cities from whose warren slums have sprung, like lilies from mud, dialect poets such as Belli and Trilussa in Trastevere, Porta in Milan, and Di Giacomo from the Neapolitan *bassi*. In Sicily there must be a connexion between the birth there of the local regionalist school of *'Verismo'* (powerful enough to be a decisive influence on modern Italian literature even now), and a conduct pattern that is clearly traceable today and seems to have expanded rather than contracted. Communications on the island may be a little easier—though country roads are as deserted as in Edwardian Ireland— the post may arrive more regularly from immigrant relatives in America, but the same compulsions, the same strange tensions can be seen at work now as described by Verga, Capuana, De Roberto, and more recently by Brancati and Tomasi di Lampedusa, (in Pirandello's plays all but the tension is transmuted).

This lack of basic change in Sicily is characteristic and perennial. Both Danilo Dolci, a Sicilian by adoption, and the bandit Giuliano, seem timeless figures, like Rinaldo and his knights of the puppet-shows and carts. The Mafia is a part of Sicilian life that has spread and flourished in its transplanted state while never losing its home roots; and the chief of Los Angeles police has a map of Sicily on his office wall to help trace ramifications of feuds begun in Sicilian villages and still producing their crop of murders all over the Americas.

But banditry is only a tiny percentage of Italian exports, and the extent to which ordinary southern Italians still group themselves abroad according to origins is seldom realized by visitors to, say, Soho in London or San Pietro in California, where a few years ago every inhabitant of certain streets came from fishing village on the island of Ischia. The very difficulty of translating '*il paese*' indicates a concept and feeling for which we in England have no exact equivalent (for 'our part of the world' is both vaguer and somehow class-conscious in its detachment). In essence Italian local loyalty abroad is deep-rooted and sincere, whatever its outer form. Recently in America the father of a family that had left Italy some two generations before was being congratulated on the excellent husband recently acquired by his daughter. '*Si*', he replied '*È molto simpatico, molto buono. E poi ha anche soldi, ma non è del paese*'. ('Yes, he's very nice, very good. And he's got money too; but he's not from *il paese*'). The bridegroom's grandparents had been, maybe, Milanese, instead of from the same group of Calabrian villages as those of the bride's father and mother.

Such bonds are as tenacious as that other form of local

and personal pride, the omnipresent 'bella figura' or 'face', whose origins would be worth tracing throughout the Mediterranean and further. That veil of self-deception which can bedevil small-town Italian life and is open to such sad political exploitation, leads all too swiftly, via regional feeling, to a narrow provincial pride amounting to nothing better than local *sciovinismo*. Fucini shows the links between this *bella figura* and false pride, particularly when combined with *il paese*; thus his village in the Maremma must have a monument because every wretched hamlet around has one, though the local worthies have no idea who it is to be for; and in another cruel little tale he describes the reactions of a village mayor bamboozled into thinking he is to entertain the local Prefect.

This deep south of the Maremma still exists, much as it was except for crop changes, though scooters take lads and lasses to the local dance. It is a Tuscany quite unconnected with Renaissance glories, tea on the Via Tornabuoni or Ruth Draper's sketches. Can witches still be consulted there as they certainly can in Lucania? Here, anyway, in the tales of Tarchetti, Fucini, and Deledda (for each was steeped in a characteristic local life) are views from the inside of the oft-quoted 'paganism' displayed all over the southern mainland and islands. Such writers treat it with respect, though the Tuscan's approach is of one interested in the pathology of human credulity, while the Sardinian's is of one convinced of a manifestation of truth. (Southern Tuscany, it may be worth noting, has always been a breeding-ground for messianic deviations, as far apart as early Fascism, 'historical anarchism', and a local brand of communism). Here we glimpse the Church in its historic role of canalizing paganism. An old woman in Fucini's story prays to God and the Virgin Mary to help her family now that they have made a real effort to help themselves—by calling in the local witch-doctor. How easy is the transition from faith to credulity! Then the same family decide that the medical doctor is quite mad at proposing 'iron tonic and sea air' as treatment, but see nothing untoward in the witch-doctor's terrifying mumbo-jumbo with Holy Water and a hen's feather. How equally strange is the relation of credulity to incredulity! Is there some connection, maybe, between this southern witchcraft and the poltergeists which hop around Christian missions in Africa and the East, 'like rabbits', as recently described by an authoritative Carmelite friar? But even within the walls of the Albany they are not unknown.

Much of what these stories describe may be typical of peasant life everywhere. When the peasants in this same tale think that the witch-doctor has effected a cure, they already see the baby as a fine strapping youth driving his furrow. Life is hard, they live close to the soil, and the tragedy of losing a *piccola creatura* is not only the death of a child but the earthly end of a son who will help them wrest a living from nature, particularly when they are old and unequal to pursuing the struggle themselves. Such attitudes must have parallels in many peasant economies still—in the remoter parts of Ireland, in odd corners of Europe and even in America.

We have a tendency to project upon Italy certain primitive manifestations of human behaviour as if they were typically Italian. The idea that the whole country is a kind of native reserve of quaint old Frazerish cults and superstitions must be just as irritating to Italians today as the attitude once so prevalent among cultured foreigners, and not unknown still, that it is one vast museum of dead-and-gone works of art (combined, at times, with a living market of native flesh). This may partly explain why to many young Italians, *folklorismo* in the arts is almost a term of abuse, though, amid the mazy dialectics of Italian criticism, the attitude is traceable to more sources than one.

One favourite approach to primitive life in the Mediterranean is through myth, and there have been some promising attempts at mopping up leavings from Freud and Marx, while hitching on to Jung and his pupils theories that are surely best dealt with by theology.

By contrast today Italy is rapidly becoming the most successful European absorber of American influences. She has profited much, but has also given richly in return to this latest of an endless chain of invaders. If Italians wear American ways with a difference, this is perhaps traceable to a familiarity with invasions dating back to the wars of Napoleon. Modern Italian literature, like modern Italian history, might be said to have been jerked into movement by the French Revolution, though preliminary reverberations had already been felt from the Encyclopedists by groups such as the Milanese *Società del Caffè*. Napoleonic invasions, Beauharnais' viceroyalty of northern Italy, Murat's reforms in the south, French laws and administrators, Neapolitan troops in the Russian campaign of 1812, were all part of a process of change leading up to Garibaldi's popular movements that stirred the whole torpid south into movement a hundred years ago. Links between history and literature are easy to forge, but it is obviously true that the beginnings of modern Italian fiction are closely tied to the Risorgimento. Without it there might have been no stories for the present anthology.

Till then the literary forms most favoured, since the *novelle* of Boccaccio and his school, had been chivalrous verse in the late Renaissance, followed by librettos and plays throughout the Baroque periods and even during and before the French Revolution, culminating in the tragedies of Alfieri, Monti and finally of Manzoni. Now, unexpectedly, borne on the nordic breezes of the Romantic movement, in came Sir Walter Scott, whose historical novel form helped, with many subtle and potent factors, to produce

Manzoni's *I Promessi Sposi*, the major work of creative imagination in Italian writing since Dante. Though one immediate result was to make fiction in Italy a respected art-form, Manzoni's combination of depth, lyrical balance, psychological penetration and all-pervading Christianity was personal to a genius and of little help for a school. And in fact the so-called 'Manzoniani' who tried to follow him turned his convictions into rhetoric and his humble piety into brash propaganda.

Later a less obvious side of Manzoni was to have an abiding influence: his realism, rejection of cant, and clarity of observation. These quantities had no echo at all until, at the end of the century, Verga and the Sicilian *veristi* took over some of that impalpable quality, his tone. The form they used was the narrative *novella* or short story, dormant since its great period in the early Renaissance, and now to become one of the major forms of modern Italian writing. Adapted to contemporary use, it is still to be found flourishing in the hands of such masters as Moravia, Soldati and Calvino today. What D. H. Lawrence admired most in Verga was dryness, compactness and sobriety. These apparently un-Italian qualities, called by pundits the 'pessimistic humanism' of the *veristi*, can certainly be partly linked to the dissillusion general all over Italy, and particularly in Sicily, after the Unification. *Verismo* concentrated on 'the unknown millions whom history ignores', as Manzoni called them: the labourers, petty farmers, artisans, whose hopes had been aroused and dashed. A parallel disillusion can be found in contemporary musicians such as Puccini and Mascagni. Modern equivalents, perhaps, are the famous 'neo-realist' films which came just after the recent war.

Until his return to regional origins, Verga, like Pirandello, had been writing for years about upper-class problems and complicated *états d'âme* in cities of the north. And this cosmopolitan phase may account partly for the paradox that, though their master was Manzoni, the main influence on these new regionalist writers, came from the new realist writers in France. Just as the upsets of half a century before had blown varied pollen from the north, now, throughout the peninsula, there was a sudden spate of books by Zola, Flaubert and Maupassant, some by Russians, and even by an American, Stephen Crane. But we have all seen how influences from abroad, and invaders too, have a way of being transmuted by contact with the Italian spirit. And in Italian hands the French writers' theories about the detached and self-effacing observation of daily life, which had been inclined to bridle their authors, now helped to produce lively and direct narratives, of which characters, atmosphere and background, in spite of treatments and situations taken from abroad, were more Italian than almost anything written since.

The chief problem in choosing our tales has been *embarras de richesses*. We hope that we have included nothing that is not the best of its kind, for our omissions, where so much had to be omitted, we feel that we can hardly be blamed. If it has happened that most of our stories touch sombre corners of life this may be partly due to the background of sombre realism behind the literature of the period. But in Italy the smile and the tear are seldom far apart and perhaps a later, companion volume might be devised with a preponderance of tales as humourously lively as *The Monument*. Various factors have further restricted our choice. Some of the chief writers of the period such as De Roberto or De Marchi, for instance, were novelists and did not give their best in short stories, and we decided against the artificial expedient of representing them by extracts. Here, on the other hand, are Boito's self-destroying fascinator, direct descendant of La Pisana in Nievo's *Le confessioni di un ottuagenario*, the next major work with a local setting after Manzoni's, and, at the

other end, D'Annunzio's earliest short stories, written under *veristi* influence but already foreshadowing a new di-
vergence into rhetoric; their insistence on the material and
voluptuous combined with the dramatic and external in re-
ligion, is expressed with a poetic power bringing a whiff,
some might think, of 'demoniac' forces from a region, the
Abruzzi, which is still one of the most primitive in Italy.

In between are to be found expressions of Manzoni's
'movement towards the humble': in Serao's compassion for
Checchina, which D'Annunzio would never have allowed
himself, in the elemental simplicity of Deledda, the vein
of mystical phantasy in Tarchetti, the light, unsentimental,
brushwork of Scarfoglio, De Amicis's Manzonian warmth,
Sacchetti's sincere nobility, and the avoidance of cant that is
common to them all.   In their modest way the regional
writers of the last half of the nineteenth century in Italy,
including even the minor ones, did contribute to the renewal
of Italian life and letters that was to flourish after the
second Risorgimento.

February 1961

ARCHIBALDO COLQUHOUN
NEVILLE ROGERS

The notes on each author are based mainly on the most informative
work of Luigi Russo, *I narratori* (Messina, Principato, 1951), and on the
notes in the pioneering anthology by Pietro Pancrazi, *Racconti e novelle
dell'Ottocento* (Florence, Sansoni, 1939), a book, like its late author, full
of charm and erudition.

All translations, except Constance Hutton's, have been made specially
for this collection.

2 T.

IGINIO UGO TARCHETTI

I. U. Tarchetti was born at San Salvatore Monferrato in 1841 and died in Milan in 1869. Most of his adult years he spent in the army commissariat, which he left a convinced and active anti-militarist.

The paradox was typical of his short, disordered life. He was the wildest and most tortured of the group of romantic writers in the north called 'Scapigliati' (bohemians), and his chief influences were Poe and Baudelaire, Hoffman, and Gerard de Nerval. He added Ugo to his name from admiration for Foscolo; even his appearance was romantic, for he was described by a friend as 'tall, pale gloomy, enclosed in his officer's uniform as in a golden tomb'. Both his life and writings showed a macabre fantasy, and he was the nearest Italy produced to the *poètes maudits*. His characters are usually sick in mind and body, haunt cemeteries, converse with sextons, and sense the skull behind every kiss. This determination to be demoniac went together with a certain freshness and candour, an engaging combination found in the tale given here. He might, in a way, be considered a precursor of modern writers influenced by the discovery of the subconscious.

His last novel, *Fosca*, tells of the love of a deformed epileptic girl for the author; the book was autobiographical, and he died before it was finished.

The story translated here was taken from an early book of stories, *Racconti fantastici* (1860). None of his work has been translated before.

Other books: *Amore nell'Arte, Racconti umoristici, Una nobile follia, Fosca*.

A. C.

THE GHOST IN THE RASPBERRY BUSH

IGINIO UGO TARCHETTI

Translated by Bernard Wall

In 1854 the entire population of a simple Calabrian village was filled with fear and amazement by a strange and awe-inspiring event.

I shall try to tell my astounding tale as accurately as possible, though the extreme difficulty of reconstructing it in all its true and significant detail should be appreciated.

The young Baron B. (unfortunately I am forbidden by oath to divulge his name) had, a few years before my story opens, inherited his paternal grandfather's large and prosperous estates situated in one of the most attractive parts of Calabria. The young heir had never ventured far beyond these mountains, covered with orchards and rich in game. In the old family manor, once a fortified feudal castle, the family tutor had taught him the rudiments of writing and the names of three or four Latin classics from which he could quote a few well-known lines when appropriate. Like all southern Italians, he had three passions: shooting, horses and love — passions that seem to run as naturally side by side as a trio of carriage horses. These he could appease to his heart's content, and indeed he had never really thought about anything else; it had never occurred to him that beyond the jagged crests of the Appenines there were other places and other men and other passions.

For the rest, as wisdom is not one of the indispensable requisites of happiness — rather the contrary, in fact — the young Baron B. was perfectly happy with his simple provision of quotations; and equally happy were his servants, his women, his labourers, and his twelve green-clad flunk-eys whose job it was to precede or follow his best carriage on ceremonial occasions.

There had been only one distressing event, one which, a few months before the events related in my story, had brought desolation to a family attached to the service of the establishment, and upset the castle's peaceful train of life. One of the Baron's maids, a girl who was known to have had amorous intrigues with several of the man-servants, had suddenly disappeared from the village. All efforts to trace her had been vain, and though suspicion had fallen on one of the foresters — a violent young man who had at one time had an unrequited passion for her — his calm and assured demeanour had been more than enough to dispel such vague and improbable suggestions.

This mysterious disappearance, however, which seemed to involve the possibility of crime, had deeply grieved the good Baron B., until he had gradually forgotten about it, distracting himself with shooting and love. Joy and tran-quillity had found their way back to the castle, the green-clad flunkeys were back at their good times in the antecham-bers, and before two months were out, neither the Baron nor his servants remembered the girl's disappearance.

Then came the month of November.

One morning Baron B. woke up a little upset by a bad dream. He jumped out of bed, threw open the window and, seeing that the sky was clear and that his hounds were pacing to and fro moodily in the courtyard and pawing at the gate to get out, he said to himself: 'I shall go shooting — alone. Over there some flocks of wild pigeons seem to have made themselves at home in my plantations; I shall make them pay for it with their feathers.' So he finished dressing, pulled on his top boots, shouldered his gun, waved dismissal to the two green-clad flunkeys who normally accompanied him on such enterprises, and issued forth, surrounded by all his hounds who tossed their heads and pricked up their large ears and jumped up between his legs, caressing his boots with their long tails.

Baron B. made straight for the place where he had seen the wild pigeons settle. It was sowing time and no tuft or blade of grass could be seen in the freshly-ploughed fields. The autumn rains had so softened the soil that he sank into the furrows up to his knees at every step and felt in danger of losing his boots. Moreover the dogs, who were unused to this kind of sport, behaved in such a way as to nullify his huntsman's strategy, while the wild pigeons themselves had placed sentinels on outpost duty, exactly like a worthy regiment of the old Imperial Guard.

Though annoyed by the pigeons' precautions, Baron B. continued to follow them with undaunted zeal, but never came within range of a single shot. Soon he became thoroughly tired and thirsty, and just at that moment noticed a flourishing little raspberry bush, covered with ripe fruit, growing in a nearby furrow.

'How very odd,' said the Baron to himself, 'a raspberry bush, here of all places, and covered with berries. How lovely and ripe they look!'

And he uncocked his gun, placed it beside him, sat down, and proceeded to pick the raspberries, their purple granules prettily silvered with dew. Thus he quenched the thirst that had begun to beset him.

He remained in this position for half an hour or so, at the end of which time he noticed that strange things were happening to him.

The sky, the horizon, indeed the whole landscape, no longer seemed quite the same; that is to say they didn't appear different in themselves, but he no longer felt the same sensation when looking at them as he had felt an hour before; to use a familiar expression, he no longer saw them with the same eyes.

On looking at his dogs, he felt that there were some
that he had never seen before, and yet, on reflection, he
recognized them; or was it that he was eyeing them and
patting them with more respect and diffidence than usual?
Indeed it almost seemed to him that he was no longer
their master. To put this to the test he started calling
them: ' Azor, Fido, Aloff. ' The dogs thus summoned
promptly came towards him wagging their tails.

' Well, that's all right at any rate, ' said the Baron,
' my dogs still seem to be mine. But what a curious sensation I have in my head, a weight... And what are these
strange desires I seem to have, these wants I have never
had before, this kind of confusion and doubleness I feel in
all my senses? Could I be going mad? Let's see, let's set
our ideas in order... *our* ideas — yes, that's exactly it, because they don't all seem to belong to me. Easier said than
done, to set them in order, because my brain is so disor-
ganized, or... to put it better... differently organized. There
seems to be something growing there, something extra,
something trying to find room for itself in my head. It
doesn't hurt exactly, but it is pushing and knocking against
the walls of my skull in a rather uncomfortable way... I
feel as though I were a double man. A double man! How
peculiar. And yet... yes, I now see beyond all doubt that
it is possible to be a double man. I would like to know
why these rain-soaked anemones, which I have never looked
at in my life before, now strike me as so charming and
lovely... Look at their bright colours, their simplicity and
grace! Let's make a bunch of them. '

And the Baron, still without getting up, stretched out
his hand and picked three or four flowers which, strange to
say, he put at his breast like a woman. And then he had an
even stranger sensation: he wanted to stretch out his hand
again and yet at the same time he wanted to hold it back;
so that his arm, impelled as if by two hostile yet equally

powerful wills, remained in its original position as if paralysed.

'My God!' exclaimed the Baron and, having with a violent effort got out his state of rigidity, immediately started examining his hand to see if it was broken or damaged in some way.

And it was then that he noticed that his hands were short and well-shaped, that his fingers were rounded and tapering, and that his nails formed perfect ovals; and he noticed all this with unwonted satisfaction. Then he looked at his feet and perceived that they were small and slender within his great top boots, and again he felt a sensation of pleasure, and smiled.

At that moment a flock of wild pigeons rose up from the neighbouring field and began flying within gunshot. The Baron instinctively bent over, snatched up his gun, cocked the trigger; and then—fantastic as it seemed—he became aware that he was frightened of his gun, that the bang of the shot would scare him; so he refrained and let the gun fall from his hand, while an inner voice whispered: 'What pretty birds! How pretty their feathers are! They look to me like wild pigeons...'

'Hell!' the Baron exclaimed, pressing his hands to his head, 'I just don't understand a thing about myself any more. Am I myself, or am I someone else? Or am I myself and someone else at the same time? When have I ever been afraid of firing my gun? When have I ever felt sorry for the wretched birds that ravage my freshly-sown fields? My fields! But I almost feel as if my fields aren't mine any more... This must stop, it has gone on quite long enough. I must get back to the castle; all this may be the result of a fever; if I go straight to bed perhaps it will pass.'

And he made to get up. But simultaneously another

will that seemed to be within him held him down, almost
as if it had said: 'No, let's sit here a little longer.'

The Baron felt himself giving way to this will the more
readily as a group of young labourers appeared round the
bend of the road flanking the field on their way back to the
village. He watched them with an inexplicable sensation
of interest and desire; he noticed that some of them were
rather handsome; and when they passed near him and sa-
luted him, he returned their greetings with an embarrassed
nod and realized that he had blushed like a girl. Then,
sensing that getting up would no longer be difficult, he rose,
and, when erect, it seemed to him that he was lighter than
usual; his legs felt neither stiff, nor loose; his movements had
more grace than usual though in fact they were the same as
ever—indeed, he felt that his walk, his gait and his bearing
in general were just the same as they had always been.

He made to shoulder his gun, but felt the same fear of
it as before, and had to get used to the feel of it on his arm,
holding it a little away from his body as a frightened child
would have done.

When he reached the point where the road divided, he
found himself in two minds as to which fork to take to get
to the castle. Both forks led there, but in the normal way
he took one rather than the other. Now, he felt first like
taking one, then the other. He tried to advance but was
held back by the same phenomenon as before—by the two
wills that seemed to have possession of him, both working
with equal force within him, each paralysing the other and
nullifying its action. He remained at the fork of the road
as if turned to stone or stricken with catalepsy. Then, after
a moment or two, he became aware that the state of rigidity
had passed, that his hesitation had disappeared, and he took
the road he was in the habit of taking.

Hardly had he gone a hundred yards than he met the
wife of the magistrate, who greeted him courteously.

'Since when', wondered Baron B., 'has the magistrate's wife greeted me in this friendly way?' Then he remembered that he was Baron B. and that he knew this lady intimately, and he was amazed at having asked himself such a question.

A little further on he met an old woman rummaging for a handful of dry sticks along the hedge.

'Good morning, Caterina', he said, taking her in his arms and kissing her on both cheeks. 'How are you? And what's the news of your father-in-law?'

'Oh, your Excellency, what condescension...' the old woman began, frightened out of her wits by the Baron's unwonted familiarity, 'I will tell you...'

But the Baron cut her short: 'Take a good look at me for pity's sake', he implored, 'and tell me whether I'm still myself. Am I still Baron B.?'

'Oh Sir...' she said.

He didn't wait for any more, but continued his way along the road, his hands in his hair, exclaiming: 'I have gone mad; I have gone mad!'

And as he proceeded he often stopped to look at things or people that had never aroused his faintest interest before, for he saw them under a new light. The pretty peasant girls hoeing in the fields, their dresses tucked up above their knees, held no attraction for him but seemed uncouth, slovenly and graceless. And when by chance his eye fell on his dogs who were trotting ahead of him, their noses to the ground and their tails dangling, he said: 'What an odd thing! Vizir, who was only two months old, now seems at least eight, and has insinuated himself into the band of special favourites'.

He was still a little way from the castle when he met some of his servants walking along the road and chatting; and, extraordinary to relate, he saw them double; he experienced the optic phenomenon that one gets by converging both pupils towards one centre so as to cross one's vision; only he realised that the cause of the phenomenon in this case was of quite a different order, for, though he saw them double, the doubles were not exactly alike; he saw them as if he had two people inside him both looking through the same eyes.

And from that moment this curious duality began spreading to all his senses; he saw double, he heard double, he touched double; and, stranger still, he thought double. That is to say, one and the same sensation produced two reactions within him and these two reactions were examined by two different reasoning forces and judged by two different consciousnesses. In other words he felt two lives within his single life, but two lives that were opposed, separate, and with divergent natures; two lives that could never commingle, but warred against each other for dominion over his senses. Hence the duality of his sensations.

And that was why, when he saw his servants, he knew very well that they were his servants; and yet, driven by a stronger impulse, he could not resist approaching one of them, kissing him delightedly, and saying: *'Dear* Francesco, I'm so happy to see you again. How are you? And how is our Baron?'—while knowing perfectly well that he was the Baron. 'Tell him that he will be seeing me soon at the castle'.

The servants drew back in dismay, and the one who had been kissed said to himself: 'I would give my eyes to know whether that was really the Baron who spoke to me. I feel I have heard those words before... I don't know... and that expression, that look, that kiss... I'm sure it isn't the first time I've been kissed like that. And then... my good master has never honoured me with such familiarity before'.

A few steps further on Baron B. saw a pergola that backed on to a corner of a garden fence so that when it was

covered with leaves it was quite impenetrable by inquisitive
eyes. He could not resist the desire to go inside, though
at the same time another will was urging him to press on
towards the castle. He yielded to the first impulse, and
as soon as he had taken a seat under the pergola he experienced an even more curious psychological phenomenon.

A new consciousness took shape within him; the whole
web of a past he had never known spread out before his
eyes; pure, sweet memories, which his own life could never
have produced, rose up and gently disturbed his soul. They
were memories of a first love and a first fall, but a more
sensitive and delicate love than any he had ever felt, and
a sweeter and more generous fall than any he had ever
undergone. His mind unfolded in a world of affections
he did not himself acknowledge; it coursed through regions
he had never seen, and called up sweetnesses he had never
known.

And yet neither these memories nor the new life that
had added itself to his, were able to obscure his recollection
of his own life. The two streams of consciousness were
separated by an imperceptible thread.

After a few minutes under the pergola, Baron B. felt
a desire to press on in the direction of the village. And
this time the two wills acted on him in harmony so that
the impulse he felt was too strong for him to proceed at
his ordinary pace; he had to break into a run.

From that moment the two wills began to dominate each
other and dominate him with equal force. If they acted
in unison then his body's movements were headlong, con-
vulsed and violent; if one fell silent his movements were
regular; if they acted in opposition his movements stopped
altogether and paralysis set in until the stronger will established supremacy.

While he was running in this peculiar way one of his
servants saw him and, fearing an accident, called after him

by name. The Baron wanted to stop but was unable to do so; he slowed down and even paused for a moment, but this led to such convulsive lurches and jerks that he seemed possessed, and he was forced to continue his headlong career towards the village.

The village seemed quite different, and he felt he had been away for many months; he saw that the church-tower had been recently repaired and, though he knew this perfectly well, he felt as if he did not know it.

As he sped along the street he bumped into numbers of people who looked at him in amazement. He raised his hat to everyone though knowing that he shouldn't, and they reciprocated by taking off their caps, marvelling at such courtesy. But what seemed odder was that all these people looked on his running and his greetings as almost natural; they felt that they had glimpsed, intuited or understood something in these actions of his, though they didn't know quite what. Yet none the less they were frightened and thoughtful.

When he reached the castle he finally stopped. He entered the antechambers and kissed each of the maids in turn. He shook hands with his green flunkeys, and even threw his arms round the neck of one of them, fondling him tenderly and addressing him in the most loving terms.

At the sight of which the maids and the other green flunkeys dashed off screaming and locked themselves in their rooms.

Then Baron B. went up to the other storeys and visited all the rooms in the castle. When he reached his own quarters he threw himself on his bed and said: 'I have come to sleep with you, your Lordship'. In the following moments of repose his ideas fell into place once more—he recalled everything that had happened in the last two hours, and felt prostrated; but this lasted for a split second only, after

which he fell back under the sway of the will that was di-
recting him instead of himself.

He began repeating the words he had just uttered: 'I
have come to sleep with you, your Lordship'. Fresh memories stirred in his soul; they were double memories, that
is, memories of impressions that one and the same fact
leaves in two different souls, and he was receiving both
impressions in himself. But these memories were not like
the ones he had had when under the pergola, for those had
been simple whereas these were complex; those had left one
part of his sould empty, neutral, in the position of judge,
whereas these invaded the whole of it; and as they were
memories of love, he realized in that moment in what lay
the great unity and enormous complexity of love—an emotion which, by the inexorable laws of life, was shared
between two people and hence only half understood by
each. What he felt was the full and complete fusion of
two spirits, a fusion compared with which love is only an
aspiration and the sweets of love only a shadow, an echo,
a dream. It would be useless for me to try to express
more exactly the singular state in which he found himself.

In this way he passed about an hour, and when it was
over he began to notice that his sensual delight was dimi-
nishing and that the two lives that seemed to animate him
were separating. He got off the bed, passed his hands
over his face as if to brush aside something light—a veil, a
shadow, a feather—and felt that his touch was no longer
the same; he felt that his features had changed and he
experienced the sensation he would have felt if he had
touched someone else's face.

Nearby was a mirror and he ran to look at himself in
it. Strange. He was no longer himself; or at least though
he saw his reflection he saw it as if it were the reflection
of someone else, he saw two images in one. Beneath the
transparent skin of his own face there floated a second face

with airy, evanescent and yet known features. And that seemed to him the most natural thing in the world, for he knew that there were two people enclosed within his unity, that he was one and at the same time two.

When he turned his eyes away from the mirror it was to let them fall on an old full-length portrait of himself on the opposite wall. 'Ah, that is his Lordship, Baron B. How he has aged!' he said; and he went back to look at himself in the mirror.

But the sight of the portrait had brought to his mind that in one of the corridors of the castle there was a portrait of a face similar to the one that had shown itself evanescently beneath his own in the mirror, and he felt a craving to look at it. He hastened in the direction of the corridor.

Several of his maids who passed him as he went were seized by an even worse panic than before, and they ran off to call the green flunkeys who were assembled in the antechamber trying to decide what to do.

Meanwhile a large number of people had collected in the courtyard. The news of the Baron's follies had spread like lightning through the village and brought the doctor, the magistrate and other important people hurrying to the castle.

When they finally made their way into the corridor they found the unfortunate Baron standing in front of the portrait of a girl—the very girl who had disappeared from the castle some months before. He was in a state of indescribable nervous excitement, as if in the grip of an epileptic fit. Every atom of his vitality was concentrated on the portrait; it was as if there were something inside him that wanted to escape from his body and enter the figure in the picture. He was staring at it wildly and making leaps towards it as if drawn by an irresistible force.

But, more fantastic still, as he fixed the picture with his gaze, his outline seemed to suffer a transformation; it took on another aspect. Of course all the spectators recognized Baron B. in him, but at the same time they were aware of a strange resemblance to the figure in the picture. Crowded together in the corridor, they were seized by a great awe. What did they see? They were not quite sure, but they felt they were witnessing something supernatural.

No one dared draw near; no-one moved; panic had seized them all, and a shudder of terror raced through their every fibre.

Meanwhile the Baron continued to cast himself towards the picture; his state of exaltation increased and his face reproduced more and more exactly the face of the girl. Some of the onlookers seemed about to shriek, and yet a mysterious fear rendered them speechless and immobile. Then a voice suddenly rose from the crowd, crying: 'Clara! Clara!'

The spell was broken. 'Yes, Clara, Clara!' everyone cried, gripped by even greater terror; that was the name of the girl who had disappeared from the castle, and whose portrait was painted in the picture.

On hearing that cry the Baron leapt away from the picture and hurled himself into the crowd shouting: 'My murderer, my murderer!' The crowd scattered in all directions, leaving on the ground a man in a faint. This was the man who had cried out—the young forester who had been under suspicion in connexion with Clara's mysterious disappearance.

Baron B. was forcibly held back by his green-clad flunkeys. The forester, on recovering from his faint, asked for the magistrate and confessed to him of his own free will that he had killed the girl in an access of jealousy and buried her in a field, in the very place where he had seen the unfortunate Baron a few hours previously sitting on the ground and eating raspberries from the bush.

Baron B. was given a strong emetic which made him

bring up the undigested berries, and thus he was freed from the spirit of the dead girl.

Her body, from which the roots of the raspberry bush sprang, was dug up and given Christian burial in a cemetery.

The forester was brought to trial and condemned to twelve years' hard labour.

I saw him in his prison at Cosenza when I was visiting it in 1865. He had two more years to go. And it was from him that I heard this miraculous story.

CAMILLO BOITO

Camillo Boito who was born in Milan in 1836 and died in Rome in 1914, was one of the most important figures in architecture, art criticism, and Italian cultural life generally during the last part of the nineteenth century and the first years of this. He belonged to a talented family; his brother Arrigo Boito, chiefly known as a musician and lyric poet, also achieved fame as an occasional writer of fiction. Their mother was Polish and their father from the Veneto.

The few imaginative writings of Camillo Boito show an unusual combination of qualities: dramatic intensity, sense of atmosphere, a delicate touch with sensation, and a clarity that must owe something to the French. The same qualities can be found in his travel-diaries, which have the elegance and taste of an aesthete of the period.

A Thing Apart is a tale (never translated before) of the Venetian provinces, with their fierce hidden life, harking back in part to Nievo's *Le confessioni di un ottuagenario*. Under its original title, *Senso*, it has inspired one of the most distinguished films to come from post-war Italy, by Luchino Visconti.

Other books: *Storielle vane* (Milan 1876), *Senso (Nuove storielle vane,* Milan 1883), *Gite di un artista* (1884).

A. C.

A THING APART*
CONFESSIONS FROM A SECRET SCRAP-BOOK

CAMILLO BOITO

Translated by Archibald Colquhoun

Yesterday in my yellow boudoir Gino the little attorney was whispering at me in a voice hoarse with repressed passion: 'Contessa, take pity on me! Order me out, tell your servants never to admit me again; but in God's name rid me of this ghastly uncertainty, tell me if I may or may not hope.' As the wretched young man flung himself at my feet, I stood looking at myself impassively in a mirror.

My forehead with its tumbled ringlets is still smooth and clear as a child's. Not a wrinkle shows beside my wide-set nostrils, above my rather full red lips. Never yet have I found a thread of white in the long hair which, when loose, falls in lovely gleaming ink-black waves over my white shoulders.

Thirty-nine! Even to write those ghastly numerals makes me tremble.

I gave a light tap of my cool fingers on the little attorney's hot hand as it groped towards me, and moved to the door; then, on some sudden impulse (a praiseworthy one,

---

* See Byron, *Don Juan*, Canto I. cxciv:

> 'Man's love is of man's life a thing apart,
> 'Tis woman's whole existence.'

Byron's meaning is implicit in the application to the story of Boito's title, *Senso*, an untranslatable word which covers meanings involving sentiment, sentimentality, and sensuality, and refers here, more especially, to the contingent extravagances of behaviour patterns.

Edd.

I'm sure, of friendship or pity) I turned on the threshold and murmured—as far as I can remember—just one word: 'Hope!'.

My vanity really needs curbing. This disquiet, which gnaws away at my mind and leaves my body almost intact, is apt to alternate, I find, with over-confidence in my own looks; my only solace then is the mirror.

I am hoping, though, for solace of another kind in writing down what happened to me sixteen years ago, a time I find myself thinking over with acrid pleasure. These notes, kept under three keys in my secret private safe, can never be seen by any other human eye; when they're finished I'll throw the pages on the fire and scatter the ashes. But putting old memories on paper should help reduce their clinging bitterness. Every action, every word, and particularly every shame of mine in that agitated period of my past, is stamped on my mind; I am always trying to touch the marks of the scars, never quite sure if what I feel now is pain or a tingle of pleasure.

Oh, the joy of confiding in oneself alone! Free of scruples, hypocrisy or reticence, respecting the truth of memory even in what our silly social conventions make most difficult to proclaim aloud, our own baseness! I've read of saintly anchorites living amid worms and refuse and putrefaction, who considered themselves to be rising higher the more they wallowed in the mud. Self-humiliation exalts my spirit in the same way. I'm proud of feeling different from other women; nothing I lay eyes on seems to frighten me; there's bold force in my weakness; I'm like those women of ancient Rome who turned down their thumbs, like the women of whom Parini sings in one of his odes—I don't remember which—but when I read it I felt he might have been alluding to me...

If it weren't for fever of memory on one hand, and terror of old age on the other, I ought to be a happy woman. My husband, old and ailing, trusts me completely, lets me spend and do what I like; I am one of the first ladies of Trento, have no lack of admirers; and the envy of my women friends, instead of waning, seems to grow.

I was lovelier at twenty, of course. Not that my features have changed at all, or my body looks any less slim and lissom; but there was a flame in my eyes then which, now, alas, is there no longer. Even the black of my pupils seems, if I look at it carefully, a little less intense. They say that the very height of philosophy is to know oneself; I've been studying myself so eagerly and for so long, year by year, hour by hour, minute by minute, that I feel I really know myself through and through and can be proclaimed a true philosopher.

The peak of my beauty, I should say,—and a woman's looks always have one period of supreme flowering—was just after my twenty-second birthday, in Venice. The date was July 1865. I had been married only a few days and was on my honeymoon. For my husband, who could have been my grandfather, I felt a mixture of pity and contempt; he bore his sixty-two years and ample paunch with a show of energy, and dyed his few remaining hairs and thick moustaches with some smelly unguent which left yellowish blotches on the pillows. In other ways he was a good enough man, full in his own way of attentions for his young wife, inclined to guzzle and sozzle, haughty, with the timid and timid with the rough, indefatigable teller of dirty stories, not mean and not extravagant. He used to walk about with me on his arm looking proud as a peacock, yet still leer meaningly at easy women strolling near us in Piazza San Marco; in a way I enjoyed this as I would have been only too glad to fling him into their arms so as to rid myself of his attentions, and in another way felt rather put out.

I had taken him of my own free will, in fact chosen him myself. My family were opposed to such an ill-assorted match; nor, to tell the truth, was the poor man particularly ardent about asking for my hand. But I was bored with being single; I wanted my own carriages, jewels, velvets, and above all my freedom. To inflame the heart in that great paunch had taken some ogling; but once roused, he would not rest until he got me, and never gave a thought to the smallness of my dowry or to the future. Before the priest I pronounced a firm resounding 'Yes'. I was pleased with what I'd done, and don't regret it even today, after all these years. I felt no reason for regretting it even when my heart suddenly burst into flower and I found myself plunged into the blind transports of first passion.

Till after my twenty-second birthday my heart had been tight shut. My women friends, all susceptible to sentimental flattery, had envied and respected me; my coldness, my contempt for tender phrases and languid glances they considered as signs of a level head and a strong character. I had first got that reputation at sixteen, by flirting with a good-looking boy near home and then turning him down; the poor boy tried to kill himself, then when he recovered ran away from Trento to Piedmont, enlisted as a volunteer, and was finally killed in one of the battles of '59, I forget which. I was too young at the time to feel any remorse; and apart from that my parents, relatives and friends, all devoted to the Austrian government which they had served faithfully as soldiers and administrators, had found no better epitaph for the poor enthusiast than: 'A good riddance!'

In Venice I was born again. My beauty flowered to full bloom. Men's eyes when they looked at me shone with a gleam of desire; almost without seeing them I could feel their hot eyes on my body. Even women stared me in the face, then looked me up and down in admiration. And I would smile like a queen, like a goddess. In my satisfied vanity I became kindly, cosy, gay, witty; so complete was my triumph that it almost made me seem modest.

My husband, who had been one of the representatives of the Tyrolese nobility at the Diet of Innsbruck, was invited with me to dinners and receptions at the Imperial Deputy's. When I entered the drawing-room, with bare arms and neck and showing a good deal of bosom in a gauze-net dress with a long train, and a big tiara with ruby flowers and emerald leaves, I felt a quiver go round. My cheeks flushed with pleasure; I took a few slow, solemn, simple paces, looking at no one; and as the hostess came towards me and invited me to sit down beside her, I waved my fan before my face as if hiding myself modestly from the eyes of the astounded throng.

Parades in the cool of the evening, and open-air concerts I never missed. At the Café Quadri in St. Mark's I was surrounded by a cloud of satellites; I felt I was the sun to a new planetary system; I would laugh, joke, tease those who courted me by sighs and poems, and gave the impression of being an unconquered fortress, though I did not try to appear *quite* unconquerable in case anyone got discouraged. My court consisted mainly of young officers and Tyrolese officials, rather pompous and self-satisfied, so that the most fun were the ones who had kicked over the traces and acquired at least a wayward boldness from their follies. Among these I met one who stood out from the others for two reasons. To his carefree debauchery, so his friends told me, he brought such cynically immoral principles that he found nothing in this world worth respecting, except the penal code and the manual of military law. Apart from that he was very handsome and unusually strong; a mixture of Adonis and Alcides. He had a pink and white face, curly fair hair, beardless chin, tiny ears

like a girl's, and big restless sky-blue eyes; his expression
was gentle at one moment and violent the next, but both
gentleness and violence tempered by constant, almost cruel
irony. His head was set superbly on his strong neck; his
shoulders were not too square or heavy, but sloped gracefully; his muscular form showed clearly in the tight white
Austrian uniform, and recalled the statues of Roman glad-
iators.

This lieutenant in a line regiment, aged only twenty-
four, two years older than me, had already managed to
squander his considerable patrimony, and still went on
gambling, paying women, courting ladies, no one knew
quite how; but at swimming, gymnastics, feats of strength
he was invincible. He had never been in battle yet; but
he had no liking for duels, and in fact one evening two
young officers told me how he had once swallowed the
most appalling insults rather than fight. Strong, handsome,
corrupt, cowardly, he attracted me. But I did not let him
see this, for I enjoyed the riling and teasing of this Hercules.

Venice, which I had never seen and always longed to
see, spoke more to my senses than to my soul; her buildings, whose story I did not know or beauty understand,
meant less to me than the green water, the starry sky, the
silvery moon, the golden sunsets, and above all the black
gondola in which I would lie and let my thoughts meander
over voluptuous fancies. In the heavy July heat, after a
fiery day, my forehead would be caressed by a cool breeze
as I went by boat from the Piazzetta to the Island of Sant'
Elena, or further still towards Santa Elisabetta and San
Nicolò on the Lido; that breeze, impregnated with the
acrid smell of salt, enlivened my body and spirit, and seemed to be whispering in my ear the fervid mysteries of
true love. I would plunge my bare arm in water to the
wrist, wetting the lace on the short sleeve; and then watch

the drops falling one by one from my nails, like the purest
diamonds. One evening I took from my finger a ring given me by my husband, with a great diamond glittering
in it, and flung it far from the boat into the lagoon; I felt
I had married the sea.

One day the wife of the Imperial Deputy suggested
taking me to see the picture gallery at the Accademia; but
I understood almost nothing. Since then, by travelling and
mixing with painters (one of them, a man as handsome
as Raphael, was quite set on teaching me to paint) I have
picked up a certain amount of knowledge; but then, although I knew nothing, those gay colours—palpitating reds,
yellows, greens, blues and whites, all painted with such
warm sensual love, seemed to me not so much art as part
of Venetian nature itself; and songs which I had heard
sung by the wanton populace came back to my mind as I
stood before Titian's golden *Assumption*, or Veronese's
Last Supper, or fleshy, carnal, gleaming faces by Boni-
facio.

My husband smoked, coughed, snored, cursed Piedmont, bought cosmetics; I needed love.

Now for how it began, that terrible passion of mine
for the Alcides, the Adonis in a white tunic with a name
I didn't much care for—Remigio. I had got into the habit
of going every day to the Rima floating baths, on the lagoon between the garden of the Royal Palace and the end
of the Dogana. I used to hire, for an hour a day, seven
till eight in the morning, one of the two women's baths
called a *Sirena*, big enough to swim in. My maid used to
come and help me dress and undress; but as no one else
could get in I did not bother to put on a bathing suit. The
bath, enclosed by wooden walls and covered with an awn-
ing with big red stripes, had a plank floor set at the right
level under water for ladies of short stature to keep their

heads in the air. My whole shoulders would be out of the water.

Oh how lovely it was in that green but clear water, through which I could see my body wavering, right down to my slim feet!...with a few tiny silvery minnows splashing round me. I would swim the length of the *Sirena* or beat the water with open palms till white foam covered the diaphanous green, or stretch out supine, letting my long hair get soaked and trying to keep motionless on the surface for an instant; I splashed my maid, who ran off; and laughed like a child. Through a number of wide openings just under the surface the water could come and go freely, and cracks in the roughly made walls gave me glimpses of the outside world if I put my eye to them—the red campanile of San Giorgio, a line of lagoon with boats flitting swiftly by, and, floating very near my *Sirena,* a slice of the Military Baths.

I knew that every morning at seven Lieutenant Remigio went swimming. In water, he was a hero diving from a high board, fishing up bottles from the bottom, swimming out under the cabins of the enclosure. I yearned to see him, I would have given anything to lay eyes on him, so attractive did I find that agility and strength of his.

One morning, as I was examining a livid mark on my right thigh, perhaps from some slight bruise, which was marring the rosy pink of my skin, I heard a sound outside as of a person swimming very fast. The water ruffled, fresh wavelets made a shiver run all over my body, and by one of the wide gaps between the bottom and the walls a man suddenly swam into the *Sirena.* I did not shout, or feel afraid. He might have been a marble statue, he was so gleaming and superb; but his broad chest was heaving with deep breaths, his sky-blue eyes were shining, and his fair hair running with drops of water like a shower of glinting pearls. He straightened up, half-veiled still

by the quivering water, and raised smooth muscular
arms; he seemed to be thanking the gods and saying:
'At last!'

So our love-affair began; and from then on I saw him
every day either at the parade, or the café, or a restaurant
where my husband, who had taken a fancy to him, often
invited him. I saw him in secret too, in fact soon these
hidden meetings of ours became almost daily. Often we
would spend one or two whole hours alone together, while
the Count slept between lunch and dinner or wandered
round the city, then have another two or three hours together in public, occasionally giving each other a passing
squeeze of the hand. Sometimes he would press his foot
on mine and hurt me so much that I flushed scarlet; but
I even enjoyed the pain. Never had I seemed so beautiful
to others and to myself, never so healthy and gay and pleased with myself and with life and with everything and
everyone. The wicker-chair on which I sat in St. Mark's
Square became a throne to me; the military band, playing
Strauss waltzes and Meyerbeer melodies in front of the Pro-
curatie Vecchie, seemed to be addressing their music only
to me, and even the blue sky and old buildings to be
enjoying my happiness.

Our meeting places were not always the same. Sometimes Remigio would await me in a closed gondola by some
dirty quay on a long dark alley issuing in a narrow canal,
overlooked by twisted tumble-down houses with rags of
all colours hanging from the windows; sometimes, throwing prudence aside, we would take a boat at some frequented part of the city, even on the Mole in front of the
Piazetta. Or, with a thick black veil over my face, I would
go to him in a house by the San Sepolcro barracks, passing
in the soupy darkness of the stairs officers and soldiers who
never failed to offer me some sign of their gallantry. In

that house, which the sun never entered, a musty smell of damp mingled with a nauseating stink of tobacco in unventilated rooms.

* * *

This little attorney Gino is a bore. He fixes me with such staring eyes that often make me laugh, but freeze me too at times; he says he can't live without my giving him some word of affection; he begs, cries, sobs, and keeps repeating: 'Contessa, d'you remember that day when on the threshold of this very room you turned and said in the voice if an angel, "Hope!"?'...and on and on he goes, begging me to take pity on him, sobbing and weeping. I can stand it no longer. Some days ago I let him hold my hand; he kept kissing it so violently that for days my skin had blotches on it. Yes, I've really had enough. Yesterday I lost patience and shouted at him to leave me in peace and never to try and get into my house again; if he dared appear I'd have him thrown out by the servants and tell the Count the whole story. The little man went so pale that his eyes looked like holes in a plaster face; he got up from the sofa and swayed out without looking at me. But he'll be back, he'll be back, I know. It's rather dreadful, though, to find that the only way I can be really stirred is by raking up the memory of a man of whose vileness, in spite of my passion, I was completely aware.

Every now and again Remigio used to ask me for money. At first he was careful to give some explanation; it was for a gambling debt, or a dinner he had to give his brother-officers; he would be returning the money in a few days. Later on he asked for a hundred or two hundred florins without any excuse at all; once he asked me for a thousand lire. I gave it, and enjoyed giving it. I had some

money of my own put aside, and my husband was very
generous to me and liked me asking him for things; but
a moment came when he said I was spending too much.
I was offended, and reacted violently; he, usually so mild
and easy-going, held out for an entire day.

That was a day when Remigio needed, urgently and
immediately, two hundred and fifty florins; he was very
caressing, said all sorts of sweet things to me, and his tone
was so throbbing with love that I was only too pleased to
be able to give him a diamond brooch which had cost, if
I remember well, forty gold napoleons.

Next day Remigio did not turn up for our appointment.
After walking up and down some of those little alleys
beyond the Rialto bridge for a good hour, with people
glancing at me slyly and making jokes at my expense,
finally, with cheeks aflame and eyes full of tears I despaired
of meeting my lover and, almost out of my senses, imagi-
ning all sorts of disasters, rushed off to his rooms. His
servant, who was polishing his sabre, told me that the
lieutenant had not been seen since the day before.

'Out all night?' I asked, not quite understanding.

The soldier, whistling, gave a nod.

'In God's name, quick, go and get news of him; something dreadful might have happened to him; he may be
wounded, killed...'

The soldier shrugged his shoulders with a grin.

'Answer, can't you, where is your master?' I cried and
seized the soldier by an arm and shook him hard as he
went on laughing. He brought his moustache right up to
my face, and pushed me back, as I went on crying 'Do
reply, please!'

Finally he grunted: 'Out supping with Gigia, or Cate,
or Nana, or all three together. Nothing dreadful at all!'

At that moment I realized Lieutenant Remigio meant
everything to me. My blood froze, I fell senseless on a

bed in the dark room, and if he had not appeared in the doorway at that very second, my heart might have burst with a paroxysm of suspicion and rage. I was jealous to the point of madness; if the occasion arose, I could have become jealous to the point of crime.

The very vileness of the man attracted me. When he exclaimed: 'I swear to you, Livia, that I'll never love or embrace any other woman but you', I believed him; and I would gaze at him adoringly kneeling before me, as if he were a god. Had he asked me: 'Would you like your Remigio to be a hero?' I'd have answered 'No'. What did I care about heroism? Compared to his vice the most perfect heroism would have seemed insipid; his lack of faith, honesty, delicacy or reserve seemed to me signs of pristine and potent vigour before which I was glad, nay proud, to bow as slave. The fouler seemed his heart, the more superb his body.

Only twice would I have liked him any different, and then only for a second or two. One day we were passing along a quayside running under the Arsenal wall. It was a gay sunny morning; in the lilac air, on the left, shone tall chimney stacks with reversed hoods, and white cornices, and red rooves, while to the right ran the long Arsenal wall, severe, enclosed. One's dazzled eyes rested gratefully on the dark shadow of an alley or arcade; the water gleamed every shade of green, reflected every colour, merged suddenly into blobs and streaks of dense black. On the quayside, which had no balustrade on the water, ten or twelve urchins were running and leaping, yelling at the tops of their voices. They were of all ages. One of the smaller ones, a sturdy child with fair curls crowning a chubby pink face, was making a fiendish din, shoving and pinching his comrades, then running away.

I stopped to look at the scene, while Remigio described

its grandeurs in the past. Suddenly that little devil of a child, unable to stop its impetus on the edge of the quay, went flying into the canal. There was a scream and a splash, then yells from all the children and all the women chatting in the street or looking out of windows; but through the hubbub came a sharp, piercing, desperate cry from the young mother, who flung herself at the feet of Remigio, the only man there, and cried: 'Save him for me! Please save him for me!' Remigio's reply was an icy 'I can't swim!' Meanwhile one of the older boys had jumped into the water, seized the child by his blond curls, and pulled him on to the side. It all took a second. The screams turned to frantic applause, women and children wept with joy; people came rushing up from all directions to look, and the blond cupid glanced around with his blue eyes, amazed at all the fuss. Remigio gave me a violent jerk and pulled me out of the crowd.

The other time my lover disappointed me was this. Once in the Café Quadri he had been heard talking loudly in German with Tyrolese bureaucrats against the Venetians. A gentleman sitting in a corner all of a sudden jumped to his feet, squared up to Remigio, who was in uniform, and cried: 'Filthy army!', then flung some visiting cards in his face. There was a scuffle. Next day seconds were to arrange the duel; Remigio, who had noticed his adversary to be gaunt, small and very slim, refused either pistol or rapier and insisted on sabres, being sure of the strength of his own arm, though the choice of weapons lay with the challenger. The Venetian let himself be overruled; but before the duel could take place he was arrested and Remigio ordered to transfer at once to a new post in Croatia.

At hearing this news I was in despair; it seemed impossible to live without him. And I worked so much on the wife of the Imperial Deputy, while my husband also

4 T.

lobbied the Governor and the generals at my request, that Remigio was eventually posted to Trento, where the count and I were returning just about that time. Till now all had favoured my blind passion.

* * *

It is three months since I've seen this scrap-book of mine. I did not dare take it with me travelling, and was sad, I must confess, to leave it behind at Trento. Going over those memories of so many years ago makes my heart beat faster, and I feel a warm air of youth round me again. The manuscript was shut away under triple locks in my secret safe behind the alcove in my bedroom; it was closed in a big envelope with five seals on it, and some words in big letters written on it before leaving: *I confide the secret of these papers to my husband's honour, that he may burn them, without unsealing, after my death*; I was sure that whatever suspicions the count had, he would carry out his wife's wishes most scrupulously.

A moment or two ago my maid gave me some news which rather put me out: Gino, the little attorney, is getting married.

There's man's constancy for you! There's undying passion! 'Contessa Livia, I'll kill myself; your image will be with me to the very last drop of my blood; treat me like a slave, but allow me to adore you like a goddess!...' phrases from melodrama. A few months, and it's all vanished! Love, thrills, vows, tears, sobs, all gone! How foul human nature is. Those black eyes in his sallow face seemed positively agleam with the deep sincerity of a passionate soul. How his lips used to stutter and his veins throb and his hands tremble and his whole body squirm humbly beneath my feet! The wretched little man really deserved the kick I gave him.

And who is he marrying? A chit of a girl of nineteen, whom her relations won't allow to come here because the Contessa Livia is known to be flighty; a dreary creature with a couple of swollen apples for cheeks, fat red hands, ostler's feet, and an impertinent little saint's air. And to think that the man who is marrying a little doll like that has dared to love me and to tell me so! It makes me put my head in my hands.

* * *

That officer of mine sixteen years ago may not have been a great man, but at least he was a real one. He used to squeeze my waist till he nearly suffocated me, and bite my shoulders till they bled.

Vague rumours of war were beginning to go round at the time, followed by the usual contradictory news and denials: they're arming, they're not, yes, no; soon feverish and mysterious movement began spreading from troops to civilians, trains became late, carried soldiers and horses and equipment and guns, while newspapers continually denied all suggestions of mobilization. I refused to believe the evidence of my own eyes, and in my terror at the thought of a war believed the newspapers. I was afraid for my lover's life; but I was even more afraid about the long, inevitable separation which would be bound to follow for us two. In fact, on the last day of March, Remigio was ordered to report to Verona. Before leaving he was granted two days leave, which we spent together in the squalid bedroom of an inn on the little lake of Cavedine, without leaving each other even for a minute; and he promised to come and see me soon, and I promised to go to Verona if he could not get away. As we embraced for the last time I slipped into his pocket a purse with fifty *marenghi*.

The Count, on his return from the country ten or twelve days after Remigio's departure, found me thin and pale. I was in fact suffering a great deal. Every now and again I felt my head going round and round, so that three or four times I swayed and had to lean against a wall or piece of furniture to avoid falling. The doctors, whom my worried and attentive husband insisted on consulting, kept on saying as they shrugged their shoulders: 'It's just nerves'; and they recommended exercise, food, sleep, and amusement.

We were now in the middle of April and troop movements were quite open; soldiers of all kinds cluttered the roads; regiments marched by to the sound of bands and drums; aides-de-camp galloped along; old generals trotted by, bent slightly over their saddles, followed by a glittering prancing staff. These preparations filled me with all sorts of terrors. Every single Austrian soldier would be killed off; Garibaldi's hordes of red demons would butcher all who fell into their hands; I foresaw a general massacre.

And inside I was raging; in six weeks only four letters had reached me from Verona. The postal system was practically non-existent now; letters had to be consigned, with much begging and bribing, to anyone willing to face the hazards and interminable delays of travelling, and who either had or dared to move from one place to another. Unable to endure any longer the anguish, day and night, of Remigio's silence, I decided to try the journey to him myself. But how could I manage it without my husband knowing? How could I, a young and lovely woman, move about among brutish troops made bolder by loosened discipline and anticipation of danger?

One morning at dawn, when I had fallen asleep after an endless night of fretting, I was suddenly woken by a sound; I opened my eyes and saw Remigio standing beside me. It was a dream, I thought.

The dawn was spreading a faint pink light throughout the room; I jumped out of bed to shut the curtains of the bed-alcove, and we began talking in whispers. I felt worried; the Count, who slept two rooms off, might hear; at that hour my lover could have been seen furtively entering by the servants. He reassured me in a few impatient words; as at other times he had tapped on the ground-floor window where my maid slept; she had opened the front door very quietly and he had got in without anyone suspecting a thing. My maid did not matter, as she knew all; but getting out would be worse; we'd have to hurry. I jumped out of bed again, and put an ear to the keyhole of my husband's room; he was snoring.

'You're stopping in Trento, aren't you?'

'Don't be silly.'

'A day or two at least?'

'Impossible.'

'One day then?'

'I leave in an hour.'

My heart, full of gay hopes a minute before, filled with fear and apprehension.

'And don't you try and keep me back. Things are serious in war.'

'Curse the war!'

'Curse it indeed. It must be ghastly, from what I hear.'

'Listen, why can't you run away and hide? I'll help you. I can't bear to think of your life in danger.'

'Silly idea. They'd find me, catch me, and shoot me as a deserter.'

'Shoot you!'

'I need your help.'

'My life, all of me.'

'No. Two thousand five hundred florins.'

'God, what can I do?'

'D'you want to save me?'

'At all costs.'

'Listen then. With two thousand five hundred florins two hospital doctors and two at brigade will make me out a genuine certificate of illness, and come and visit me now and again so as to confirm to headquarters that I've got some disease which makes me incapable of serving. I don't lose rank, I don't lose pay, I avoid all danger and stay quietly at home, hobbling a bit, maybe, from acute sciatica or a lesion of the leg-bone, but quiet and content. I'll find some little bureaucrat to play cards with; I'll drink, eat, sleep; staying at home all day will be a bore, but at night I can get out, hobbling prudently a bit. How d'you like the idea?'

'I'd like the idea, if you were in Trento. I'd come to you every day, twice a day. Once you're considered ill, isn't it the same if you're in Verona or Trento?'

'No, according to regulations a sick officer must be near his headquarters, under the constant and conscientious supervision of doctors. But as soon as the war's over, I'll come back here. It'll be a fierce war, but a short one.'

'Will you always love me, always be faithful, never look at another woman? Swear it?'

'Yes, yes, I swear it; but the hour is passing, and I need those two thousand five hundred florins.'

'At once?'

'Of course, I must take 'em with me.'

'But I doubt if there's fifty gold napoleons in my desk. I never keep much money by me.'

'Well, find it.'

'How can I find find it? Ask my husband at this hour, just like that? With what excuse, to give to whom?'

'Love shows by sacrifice. You don't love me.'

'I don't love you? I'd willingly give my whole blood for you.'

'Just words. If you haven't money, give me jewels.'

I did not answer, and felt myself go pale. Remigio, noticing the impression his last words had made on me, grasped me in those iron arms of his, and changed his tone, repeating:

'You know I love you infintely, Livia darling, and will love you till my last breath. But save that last breath for you, save me if you love me.'

He took my hands and kissed them.

I was conquered. Going to the desk I took out the three little keys of the safe; I was afraid of making a noise and walked on tip-toe, although my feet were bare. Remigio came with me into the cubby-hole behind the bed-alcove; I locked the door in case the Count heard, opened the safe with some difficulty in my agitation, and drew out a complete array of diamonds, murmuring:

'Here, take these. They cost nearly twelve thousand lire. Can you sell them?'

Remigio took the jewel-case from my hand; he looked at the jewels and said:

'There are always money-lenders.'

'It would be a pity to let them go for little. Try and find some way of being able to recuperate them.'

My heart was torn. The tiara, particularly, suited me so.

'Can I have the money too?' asked Remigio. 'It would come in useful.'

I searched about in the safe for the gold napoleons, which I had left in a little heap, uncounted, and handed them to him. He gave me a hurried kiss and made to go. I held him back. He made a gesture of impatience and pushed me away, saying:

'Let me go, if you value my life.'

'You'll be quiet, won't you? You know how your boots squeak. Wait just a second, I'll see if my maid is there; she'll have to go with you.'

The maid was in fact waiting in a room nearby.

'Write to me soon, won't you?'

'Yes.'

'Every two days?'

I wanted to give a last kiss to this lover of mine whom I so loved; but he had vanished.

Opening the shutters, I looked out into the street. The sun was gilding the high tops of the mountains. By the gate were standing the stable boy and the coachman. They raised their eyes and saw me; then they saw Remigio come out of the palace and walk hurriedly off, his hands deep in the pockets of his bulging clothes.

* * *

I went back to bed and wept for the entire day; all my natural vitality left me. The doctor next morning found me with a high fever. He ordered me quinine, which I did not take; I longed to die. A whole week after Remigio's visit the maid brought me, in her usual placid way, a letter which, as soon as I saw it, I tore frantically from her hands; I had guessed right, it was from him—the first since his departure—and I began reading it so eagerly that when I got to the end I had to start all over again; I had not understood a thing. But I remember every word of it still, so often did I reread it, and so often have the terrible events which followed come back to my mind.

Livia darling,

You've saved my life. I sold the set of jewels to an old Jew, for very little actually, but panic here is such that I couldn't get more—two thousand florins, enough to fill the doctors' aching bellies. Before my enforced illness I found myself a fine room near the river Adige in Via Santo Stefano, number 147 (write to me at that address); it is big, clean, with an anteroom to myself opening directly on to the stairs; I have laid in a supply of tobacco, rum, playing cards and complete sets of Paul de Kock and Alexandre Dumas. There's no lack of agreeable company (all male, don't worry), gamblers, and if it weren't for having to act lame and not being able to leave the place by day, I'd call myself the happiest man in the world. There's but one thing I lack, Livia, and that's you, my darling, whom I'd like to hold in my arms day and night. So don't worry. I'll read the war bulletins while smoking my cigar, and the more Italians and Austrians go to hell the better I'll be pleased. Love me always, as I love you; when the war's over, and these swines of doctors who are costing me the earth leave me in peace, I'll come rushing to seize you in my arms more ardently than ever.

Your Remigio

This letter left me disconcerted and rather revolted: it was so vulgar. Then, going over it, I gradually persuaded myself that the tone in which it was written was a pretence at lightness and gaiety, and that my lover had made a painful effort to restrain the impetus of his heart, avoid throwing more fuel on my passion, and so soothe my anguish. Again and again I studied the letter in every phrase, in every syllable. All his others I had burnt as soon as I received them; this, though, I put away in a pocket of my purse, and often took out when I was alone, after locking the doors of my room. In time I felt it all confirmed my rosy theory; those expressions of affection were all the more felt because they were so jotted; and those vulgar cynical phrases came to seem like sublime and generous sacrifices. I so needed to believe that my own frenzy could be excused by his; and his cowardice, as I thought myself its cause, seemed elating. But my racing brain did not stop there. Who knows, I thought to myself, who knows if this letter may not be all a generous deceit! Perhaps he has already left for the battlefield, is already at grips with the enemy; but, caring for me more than for himself, he was telling me these soothing lies to avoid my dying of distress. As soon as this thought came into my mind, it quite overcame me. My sleeplessness, my aversion to food, my physical ills brought on a state of real mental exhaltation.

I was leading an almost solitary life. Already our circle was narrowing, as the noble families of Trento were opposed to the Count's political opinions and had politely avoided us for some time; the young men, full of enthusiasm for Italy, made no bones about cutting and hating us; the officials of the town, not knowing how the war would turn out, no longer set foot in our house in case they compromised themselves in one way or another; the only people we saw, in fact, were a few pro-Austrian nobles, lost and parasitic, and an occasional high Tyrolese functionary, tough, stubborn, stinking of beer and bad tobacco. The military had neither the wish nor the chance to bother about me. My affair with Lieutenant Remigio, known to all except my husband, had increased my isolation, for which I was grateful, as I needed it in the state of mind in which I had been living for some time. Remigio had not written again after that awful letter. I would dream up dangers for him, the more horrifying for being uncertain. The definite risk of a battle I might have been able to bear; but I found it a maddening uncertainty not even to know if my lover was at the front or not. I wrote off to a general I knew in Verona, to two colonels, then to some of the young officers who had paid me such court in Venice; none of them replied. I wrote letter after letter to Remigio; nothing.

Meanwhile hostilities were beginning; civilian life was oppressed; railways and roads were used only for munitions, by ambulances, supply wagons, squads of cavalry passing amid clouds of dust, batteries of guns which made the houses shake, infantry regiments following each other interminably like a great sinuous snake trying to embrace the whole earth in its huge coils.

One hot breathless morning, the 26th of June, came news of a deadful battle: the Austrians defeated, ten thousand dead, twenty thousand wounded, standards lost, Verona still ours but about to fall, like the other fortresses, to the infernal impetus of the Italians.

My husband was away on his country estate, and would be there a week. I rang violently at my bell: my maid did not come; I rang again; a manservant appeared.

'Are you all asleep? Cursed slackers! Send the coachman here at once, d'you hear?'

A few minutes later Giacomo came in, looking flustered, and still buttoning up his livery.

'How many miles from here to Verona?'

He thought a little.

'Well?' I said sharply.

Giacomo was making his calculations:

'From here to Roveredo about fourteen; from Roveredo to Verona must be...I'm not sure...with two good horses it might take ten hours, more or less, not counting stops.'

'Have you ever driven from Trento to Verona?'

'No, signora contessa; I have from Roveredo to Verona.'

'That's just as good. From here to Roveredo takes two hours, I know.'

'Two and a half, signora contessa.'

'Well then, two and ten make twelve altogether.'

'Let's say thirteen, signora contessa, at a good trot.'

'How many horses has the count taken with him?'

'His usual black mare.'

'Then there are still four in the stables.'

'Yes, signora contessa; Fanny, Candida, Lampo, and the stallion.'

'Can you harness the lot?'

'All together?'

Giacomo gave a smile of benevolent pity.

'Excuse me, signora contessa, that can't be done. The stallion...'

'All right then, harness the other three.'

'Lampo's gone lame; poor Lampo, he can't even drag himself along at walking pace.'

'Then harness Fanny and Candida as usual, in God's name!' I shouted, stamping my foot, and added: 'To-morrow morning at four.'

'Certainly, signora contessa; and excuse me, just to know what to take, where are we going?'

'To Verona.'

'To Verona, mercy on us! In how many days?'

'One.'

'Excuse me, signora contessa, but that just isn't possible.'

'I wish it, d'you understand?' replied I in a tone so imperious that the poor man scarcely summoned up courage to stutter:

'Take pity on me. If we couple the two mares, the master will throw me out in the street.'

'I take the responsibility. Just obey and don't worry about any thing else', and I gave him four *marenghi*. 'I'll double that when we get back, on one condition though, that you don't say a word to anyone.'

'There's no danger of that; but what about the clutter on the roads, the wagons, the guns, the rough troops, the gendarmes' interfering?'

'They're my worry.'

Giacomo bowed his head, resigned but not persuaded.

'What time shall we reach Verona?'

'When Heaven wills, signora contessa; and it will be a miracle if we reach there alive, you, signora contessa, me and the two poor nags. I don't matter, but think of you and the horses!'

'All right then. At four, and keep your mouth shut. If you do I'll give you what I promised; if not, I'll dismiss you on the spot without wages. D'you understand? Now remember that everyone, including my maid, must think we're going to the Marchesa Giulia's at San Michele.'

Giacomo frowned again, then bowed and left the room.

At dawn we were in the carriage, and off. I had shut the door-curtains, and peered out through a slit at dusty troops slogging along who, thinking the carriage had some grandee in it' had lined up along the ditches; some even gave a military salute.

Every now and again we had to slow up, to my annoyance, or even stop a few minutes and wait for great swaying wagons to get out of our way; things seemed to be going much better than Giacomo had thought. A patrol of horsed gendarmes did stop the carriage once, but on seeing a lady inside, just called out gallantly: 'A good journey to you!' A little beyond Roveredo, at Pieve, we stopped to give the horses a breather; then at Borghetto they were unharnessed as they seemed at the end of their tether, and we spent three hours, which to me seemed like three years crouched as I was in the carriage, listening to groans and curses from the soldiers dropping off their mounts for a few seconds by the inn, under the shade of scraggy trees, to munch a hunk of bread and gulp down some water. I must have called out at least ten times to Giacomo, who came to the carriage window with a frown, forcing himself to be respectful, taking off his hat, and repeating: 'Signora contessa, another ten minutes.' Eventually we got on our way again. The Adige, beside which we were driving, was almost dry, the fields parched, the road blinding white; there was not a fleck in the blue sky, the sides of the carriage were burning hot, and in that heavy air and thick dust I felt suffocating. My forehead was pouring with sweat, I was stamping with impatience. I took no notice of the

Chiusa, listening for the crack of Giacomo's whip. At Pescantina we stopped for another rest; the poor beasts could only just walk, and it was still another ten long miles to Verona. The sun had vanished in a fiery ball. More troops, carts, police patrols, dust, and occasionally a terrific clatter and sharp squeaking of brakes, or a confused terrifying buzz in which I could make out groans and curses and snatches of obscene songs sung by voices hoarse with exhaustion. Till then we had been moving with the flow of men and vehicles, now we were beginning to meet ambulance wagons, groups of lightly wounded soldiers on foot with arms round each others' shoulders, bandages round their heads, green-faced, bent, hobbling, ragged. Remigio, my Remigio! And I called out to Giacomo to thrash up the horses with his whip handle. Night was coming on. Towards nine we reached the walls of Verona; and such was the panic and excitement that no one took any notice of the carriage and we reached the hotel *La Torre di Londra* without any trouble. Not a room was to be had, not a corner in which to sleep, either in that hotel or, I was assured, in any hotel in town; they had been requisitioned by officers. The horses, utterly exhausted, were tethered in the courtyard; Giacomo was attending to them; and I could finally jump out.

I found a little urchin to lead me on foot to number 147 Via Santo Stefano.

We had to walk up and down the street a number of times, looking above the doors, before making out the number of the house by the faint gleam of a rare street lamp. If Remigio was there, I wanted to give him a surprise; I was trembling all over with impatience, but he might be in bed, or have company, and although I longed to see him at once, I thought it best to send the boy ahead of me as scout. He was a sharp-witted lad and understood at once; what he had to do was ring, ask for the lieutenant on urgent business, insist on the door being opened, go in and tell any story that came into his head, such as that there was a gentleman lodging at the hotel who wanted news of his health as soon as possible. As the urchin came out he was to leave open the front door and the one to the apartment. I hid nearby, in an alley between the street and the river. The boy rang. From the first floor came an angry voice.

'Who is it?'

'Is Lieutenant Remigio Ruz here?'

'The other bell, the middle one; curse you.'

The boy rang the other bell. A minute passed, like eternity to me, and no one appeared; the boy rang again; then from the second floor came a woman's voice:

'Who's that?'

'Is Lieutenant Remigio Ruz here?'

'Yes, but he's seeing no visitors.'

'I've got to talk to him.'

'Tomorrow morning, after nine.'

'No, tonight. Is he afraid of thieves?'

Another minute went by and finally the front door opened.

Remigio was there! My heart felt bursting with joy, my head swam and unable to keep on my feet, I leant against the wall. Shortly afterwards the boy came back; he had been well cursed, but been able to leave the front and street doors on the latch. My strength returned. I gave the sharp little lad some money, and sidled into the house. I had foreseen a need for matches; on the second floor landing were two doors, above one of which was tacked Remigio's visiting card; I pushed the handle, it gave, and without a sound I entered an almost dark room. I was near the very peak of all my hopes, could already feel the arms of my lover, for whom without a moment's hesitation I'd have given all I had and my life too, crushing me impetuously to his broad chest; I could feel his teeth on my skin, and was tasting in anticipation a whole world of frenzied delights.

Joy made me weak; I had to sink on to a chair, set next to the door. I heard and saw as if in a dream, lost to reality. But near me someone was roaring with laughter; a woman's laugh, shrill' coarse, uncontrolled, which gradually brought me to. I listened, got to my feet, and, holding my breath, made towards an open door through which I could see a big brightly lit room. I was in shadow, and invisible. Oh why did God not blind me at that moment! There was a table with remains of supper; and behind the table, lounging on a wide green sofa was Remigio, tickling the armpits of a girl who was whimpering and twisting about to free herself, while he kissed her on arms, neck, shoulders, whatever turned up.

I could not move now; I was nailed there to my post, my eyes fixed, my ears stretched, my throat sore.

The man, tired of playing, seized the girl by the waist and sat her on his knee. Then they began talking to each other, amid many an interruption for slaps and kisses. I could hear the words, but the meaning escaped me. Suddenly the girl pronounced my name.

'Show me the pictures of the Contessa Livia.'

'You've seen them often enough.'

'Show them to me, please.'

The man, still lying full length on the sofa, raised a corner of the table cloth, opened a little drawer and drew out some papers. The girl put on a serious look and searched about among them for the photographs, stared at these a long time, then said:

'Is she beautiful, the Contessa Livia?'

'You can see for yourself.'

'You don't get it; I want to know if you find her more beautiful than me.'

'No woman's more beautiful than you.'

'D'you see how, in this photograph, the ball dress leaves

her whole bust and arms bare...' The girl arranged her blouse and compared herself to the portrait.

'Look, d'you think I'm more beautiful?'

The man kissed her between the breasts and exclaimed: 'Millions more!'

The girl, by the lamp, stared into the man's smiling eyes, took the four photographs one by one, and very slowly tore each of them into four pieces; then she let fall the bits on the table amid the plates and glasses. The man went on smiling.

'But you, naughty, tell her you love her too.'

'You know I tell her as little as I can; but I need her, and we wouldn't be here together, my dear, if she hadn't given me that money. Those cursed doctors made me pay through the nose for my life.'

'How much did you have over?'

'Five hundred florins which have already partly gone. I'll have to write to my banker at Trento; a *marengho* for every sweet word.'

'And yet...' said the woman with eyes full of tears, 'and yet it worries me...'

He pulled her down close to him on to the green sofa, murmuring: 'No tears, now'.

At this point my heart turned inside out; love became hate. I found myself in the street, wandering without knowing where I was going; in the dark groups of soldiers lurched by me, hand-carts from which came long-drawn groans or screams of pain, a hurrying citizen or so, a terrified peasant; no one took any notice of me, sidling along the sides of the houses dressed in black with a thick veil on my head. Then I came out into a wide avenue planted with dark trees, with the river on the right refreshing the heavy air a little. The water was scarcely visible in the dark; but I had no temptation to suicide even for a second. Already, without my realizing it, an idea, still fitful and vague, was beginning to take control of my whole mind and soul, the thought of revenge. I had offered all of myself to that man, lived for him, felt I would die without him, risen to heaven with him; and he was giving his heart and kisses to another! The scene at which I had been present came before me clearly again; again I saw that love-play before my eyes. I had rushed to him, overcome all obstacles, flouted all dangers, dragged my name in the mud; I had rushed to help him, to comfort him: and found him perfectly healthy, handsomer than ever, and in a woman's arms! And both he who owed all to me, and that woman, were jeering at my dignity and affection, abusing me! And I was paying for their orgies! And that blond woman was boasting of being more beautiful than me when naked; and he, he himself (supreme insult!) was proclaiming her more beautiful!

All this emotion quite overcame me; the rage boiling in me had brought on a violent fever, and I was trembling all over. I had no idea where I was; I did not want, and would have been unable to find, a passer-by to take me back to the hotel so that I could shut myself up in the carriage again. I sat down on the river bank and fixed my eyes on the black sky. No relief there; so back I went on to the streets, feeling I was going mad. I was utterly exhausted; it was eighteen hours since I'd eaten. By chance I found myself near a modest café and, after passing the window a number of times and finding it looked empty, I went in, settled into the farthest and darkest corner, and gave some order. In the opposite corner, lounging on a narrow red sofa surrounding the big, low, damp, half-lit room, were two officers, smoking and yawning.

Shortly after two more officers came in: a young one who might have been about eighteen, tall, thin, with little moustaches, and a man of about forty, thickset, with a purplish blotched face, warts, big black eyebrows and great bushy moustaches under his thick nose; in his mouth he had a Bohemian pipe with a short stem and a huge bowl, from which issued great clouds of smoke that went up one after the other to blacken the ceiling. The young man went straight over to the officers in the corner. I heard him saying: 'I've seen forty die in two hours under the surgeons' knives in the operating theatre; they were throwing aside arms and legs as if playing football with them, and trepanning and patching up heads...'

'They ought to trepan our generals', snorted the Bohemian with a frown.

No one took any notice of me.

Then a girl came in, alone; she looked like a street-girl, and went and sat down next to the thin young officer. She asked in a loud voice:

'Buy me a coffee, will you?'

After an exchange of remarks to which I paid no attention, one of the two lounging officers said to the girl, without moving:

'You know, Costanza, I've seen your Lieutenant Remigio.'

'When!' asked the woman.

'Today. I went to visit him. He was with Giustina. D'you know Giustina?'

'Yes, that blond girl with three teeth missing.'

'I didn't notice that.'

'Take a careful look at her. And how was Remigio?'

'A bit of pain in the leg, which gives him twinges now and again, and he's hobbling, that's all: quite providential, his illness. Others risk their necks, toil and moil in hellish heat, hunger, suffer all the curses of this war, and there he is eating, drinking gaily, and with someone to keep him, what's more.'

'Who d'you think keeps that handsome piece?'

'A lady.'

'An old bag.'

'No, my dear, a lovely young lady, and a millionairess and Countess to boot, who is madly in love with him.'

'And she pays for the lieutenant's girls, does she?'

'She certainly gives him money, and a lot of it.'

'Poor fool!'

'Remigio calls her his Messalina. He didn't tell me her surname, but he confided to me that she's from Trento and is called Livia. Does anyone here know Trento?'

The slim young officer said:

'I'll ask round and let you know by tomorrow night, if we're still in Verona. Contessa Silvia, did you say?'

'Contessa Livia. Livia, remember,' shouted the lounging officer.

Costanza went on:

'Is Remigio really ill, though?'

'Oh yes, that he is. Or he wouldn't be paying four doctors: one from his regiment, another chosen by the general from another regiment, and two from the military hospital. They visit him every three days, pound and prod his leg and pull him about and make him yell. Once he fainted; now he's better.'

'Just see how his leg heals when the war ends.'

'Don't say such a thing, even in jest,' observed the second lounging officer, who had not said a word till then; 'you know that at the very suspicion of malingering the lieutenant and his doctors would all be shot within twenty-four hours, one as a deserter from the field of battle, the others as accomplices and for taking bribes.'

'And they'd deserve it, by God,' exclaimed the Bohemian, without taking his pipe out of his mouth.

The young officer added:

'General Haupmann wouldn't wait twenty-four hours.'

At these words an idea, already vaguely in my mind, all of a sudden took clear sudden shape; I'd got it, I'd made up my mind in a flash; 'General Haupmann' I repeated to myself.

The fumes going to my head made me push back my veil from my face; I felt burning hot, and called for some water. The officers now noticed me and came round at once. 'Aha, what a beauty!' 'Is there anything you want?' 'Would you care for a glass of Marsala?' 'Can we keep you company?' 'Waiting for anyone?' 'What eyes!' 'What kissable lips!' The slim young officer had thrown himself down beside me on the sofa; being the youngest, he wanted to show himself the keenest. I tore myself away from his hands and tried to get to my feet to escape, but the two others held me back; the dirty Bohemian was looking on and smoking.

I turned to him with a cry of: 'Sir, I am a lady; help me, take me home to the *Torre di Londra*.' The Bohemian came forward, pushing the others aside and almost sending the young officer recruit head over heels; then, hard-faced, serious, he put his pipe in his pocket and offered me his arm.

I went out with him. On the way, which was not far, he addressed only a few respectful words to me. I asked him who General Haupmann was, where his headquarters would be, and other information which I had my own good reasons for wanting to know. I learned that the general was Fortress Commander with his headquarters in Castel San Pietro.

The doors of the hotel were still wide open, though midnight had sounded some time before; there was much coming and going of military and civilians. I thanked the officer stinking of tobacco, and settled down as best I could on the cushions of my carriage in a corner of the yard. Exhausted as I was, I soon dozed off; but I was suddenly woken by a loud knocking on the carriage door. The raucous, vulgar voice of the Bohemian was repeating:

'It's me, signora contessa. May I have a word with you, with all due respect?'

I lowered the glass, and the officer handed me some-thing; it was my purse which I had forgotten on the café table as I was about to pay and there had been that scuffle. The other officers had found it and handed it to this one, who now said solemnly:

'There is not a piece of paper, not a coin missing.'

'But were the papers in it read?' And I thought of Remigio's letter, the only one I had kept, and which I didn't want to leave my hands for anything in the world.

'No, signora contessa. Your visiting cards and Lieut-enant Remigio's miniature were seen; nothing else, I declare on my honour.'

Next morning, before nine, I had the carriage driven to Fortress Headquarters. The wait had seemed inter-minable. I shouted at Giacomo to whip up the horses. A crowd of soldiers of all kinds, wounded men, and townsfolk were crowding in the square in front of the castle; I had no difficulty in reaching the general's ante-chamber, where a wounded veteran took my visiting card. He returned a few minutes later and told me that General Haupmann wished me to pass into his private apartments, where he would come and pay his respects as soon as he had dispatched some urgent business.

I was led through loggias, corridors, and terraces to a drawing-room overlooking the entire town from three big windows. The Adige, punctuated by bridges, twisted in an S shape, with the first of its coils at the feet of the hillock on which rises Castel San Pietro, and the second below another brown fretted castle; from amid the houses of the town rose the pinnacles and towers of old basilicas; and in a large open space lay the huge oval of the ancient arena. The morning sun livened the town and hills, gilded the mountains on one side and on the other threw a placid light on the vast green plain dotted with white villages, houses, churches and spires.

Into the room, with a great noise of laughter and fun, burst two little girls with clear pink and white faces and straw-blond hair. On seeing me they looked embarrassed at first, then soon gathered courage and came up to me. The bigger one said:

'Signora, do sit down. Would you like me to call mummy?'

'No, little girl, I'm waiting for your daddy.'

'We haven't seen daddy this morning. He's so busy.'

'I want to see daddy, too,' cried the younger one. 'I do love daddy.'

At that moment in came the general, and the children ran to meet him, clung round his legs, and tried to jump on to his shoulders; he took each up in turn and gave them a kiss, and the two little girls laughed excitedly while two tears of happiness sprang into the general's eyes.

'Do excuse me, signora; if you have children you will feel with me.' He sat down opposite me and added: 'I know the Count's name, and would be happy to do any service you may desire.'

I signed to the general to get the children away, and he said in a voice full of sweetness: 'Now, girls, you must go; I have to talk to this lady.'

The children gave a step towards me as if to give me a kiss; I turned my head; and they went off eventually, looking a little flustered.

'General', I murmured, 'I am here to do my duty as a faithful subject.'

'The contessa is German?'

'No, I am from Trento.'

'Ah!' he exclaimed, looking at me with some surprise and a touch of impatience.

'Read that,' and with a resolute gesture I handed him Remigio's letter, which I had found again in a pocket of my purse.

The general read it, then said:

'I don't understand; is this letter addressed to you?'

'Yes, general.'

'Then the man who wrote it is your lover?'

I did not reply. The general took a cigar from his pocket and lit it, rose from his chair and began walking up and down the room; suddenly he came and stood in front of me, stared me in the face, and said:

'Well, be quick. I'm in a hurry.'

'The letter is from Remigio Ruz, lieutenant in the Third Regiment of Grenadiers.'

'Well?'

'It makes things quite clear. He has feigned illness, and bribed four doctors.' And I added in the quick tones of hatred: 'He is a deserter from the field of battle.'

'I see. The lieutenant was your lover and has thrown you over. You are taking your revenge by getting him shot, and his doctors with him. Is that right?'

'The doctors don't matter.'

The general stood there a little, thinking, with knit brows, then handed back the letter I had given him.

'Signora, think it over; secret denunciation is vile and what you are doing is murder.'

'General,' I exclaimed, raising my face and looking at him haughtily, 'do your duty.'

That evening, towards nine o'clock, an orderly brought a note to the hotel, where I had finally found a room. It went:

At exactly half-past four tomorrow morning, in the second courtyard of the castle, Lieutenant Remigio and the doctor of his regiment will be shot. This paper will give you entry to

the place of execution. The undersigned begs the signora
contessa to excuse him for not offering her, also, the spectacle
of the other doctors being shot; but for reasons which it is
pointless to go into here, they are being referred to another
Council of War.

GENERAL HAUPMANN

At half-past three, in pitch dark, I left the hotel on
foot, accompanied by Giacomo. At the bottom of the Castel
San Pietro hill I told him to leave me, and began the
ascent of the rough track alone; I felt hot, suffocating;
not wanting to take the veil from my face, I undid the
top buttons of my dress, and turned the corners of my
collar back; the air on my breast made me breathe better.

The stars were growing pale and a yellowish dawn
was spreading. I followed some soldiers who went round
a corner of the castle and entered a courtyard enclosed by
dark high walls. Two squads of Grenadiers were already
lined up there. No one took any notice of me amid the
silent soldiers in the half-light. Bells could already be
heard from down in the town, from which a myriad other
confused sounds came up. A low door in the castle squea-
ked, and two men came out with hands tied behind their
backs; one was thin, dark, and walking straight on, with
firm step and head high; the other, with a soldier on
either side supporting him with great difficulty by the
armpits, was dragging himself along, sobbing.

What happened next I don't know; someone was reading, I think; then I heard a crash, and I saw the dark
young man fall, and in the same second I realized that
Remigio was stripped to the waist, and those arms, those
shoulders, that neck, the limbs I had so much loved, suddenly dazzled me. Into my mind flicked a picture of my
lover, when at Venice, in the *Sirena*, he had squeezed me
for the first time in those steely arms of his, full of ardour

and joy. I was brought to my senses by a second crash; on that still heaving chest, whiter than any marble, a fair-haired woman had thrown herself as blood spurted.

At the sight of that woman all my scorn awoke again, and with scorn came dignity and strength. I felt conscious of my rights; and moved towards the entrance, proud at a difficult duty done.

By the gate I felt my veil being torn from my face; I turned and saw before me the frowning dirty face of the Bohemian officer. He pulled the stem of his pipe from his huge mouth, brought his moustache close up to my face, and spat on my cheek...

* * *

I'd said that little attorney Gino would be back. All it needed was a line from me: *Come, let's make it up*, for him to come rushing. He jilted that doll of a bride of his a week before the wedding day; and every now and again he repeats, as he hugs me almost with the vigour of Lieutenant Remigio: 'Livia, you're an angel!'

ROBERTO SACCHETTI

A Piedmontese, Sacchetti was born in Montechiaro near Asti in 1847 and died in Rome in 1881. He was a gentle, simple person, sincere, patriotic, hard-working, and poor all his life. For years he earned his living as a type-setter, writing in his spare-time—sometimes working until three o'clock in the morning. There is a sadness and resignation about all his work which somehow avoids gloom or bitterness. He possessed a rare ability to express goodness with sincerity.

None of his work has been translated.

His other books are *Cesare Mariani* (1876), in three small volumes; *Entusiasmi* (1881), a posthumous novel in two volumes; *Candaule* (1884), a volume of short stories.

A. C.

WEDDING EVE

ROBERTO SACCHETTI

Translated by Lovett F. Edwards

I

The political trials of 1833 at Genoa brought to the fore
the name of a certain Siro Xerega of Bisagno who, though
described by the investigating authorities as one of the most
dangerous ringleaders of the conspiracy, was unknown to
any of his supposed accomplices. Forty-six years later, the
case of Siro the leech is still a mystery in his own village.

The life of Siro Xerega had always been even and serene, like a sun-drenched summer day; a trifle monotonous,
perhaps, but even the shadows are filled with the warm
reflection of the sun which pervades everything. In all
his past there had been neither great affections nor great
misfortunes. There had not even been a great sorrow.
He had lost both his parents while still a baby; but, as he
himself put it, God had taken them from him so quickly
in order that he should not grieve overmuch. Nor did
anyone take their place. To be sure, a guardian was appointed for him, to whom the Sisters of Charity gave some
sort of stipend for his maintenance. But it was a guar-
dianship in little more than name.

Little Siro meanwhile lived by his wits, with a freedom
which, save for his natural good nature, was unfettered;
he wandered at his own free will from Bevio to Santa Zita,
to San Pietro, to San Francesco, to the Rubaldo, and along
the banks of the river from Foce to Incrociati; he found
his meals at the nearest board and slept wherever he found
a resting place. Almost all doors were open to him, as to

a bringer of good luck; and there was not a cock-sparrow gayer, more innocent, or a greater chatterbox than he.

Everyone greeted his coming, no one stayed his going; a real land of Cockaigne.

He paid them back with every kind of service. As the years passed, he learnt three or four trades and he practised them as need arose with the most complete impartiality. He pounded spices for the chemist, sorted threads for the weavers, worked the bellows for the blacksmith; but most often he worked as a tailor, a trade that he eventually adopted.

The priest taught him to read and write, the schoolmaster to play the violin and sing in the choir. One day the doctor, meeting him in the street, asked his help in 'operating' on a poor stonemason, and found him so steady and so careful that he offered to teach him bloodletting. Siro accepted without hesitation; why shouldn't he do bloodletting too? The arrangement suited both of them. The boy went up in social standing, and the doctor was relieved of three-quarters of his work. When they sent for him, he would send Siro on ahead with his lancets. The thing soon became a habit; the people first called for the leech and only later informed the doctor.

As to getting married, he had long said: 'My home is very small and very peaceful; perhaps afterwards I would find it cramped and wearisome. A wedding day is always a fine day, but the day after not always so. In any case, there's plenty of time.' So he did not commit himself always to stay a bachelor: there's always time. Sometimes, in jest, he would say that a man must be *called* to matrimony, and that so far he had never heard the call; 'Try to call me loudly,' he would say to the girls of his own age . But the fact remained that none of his mischievous childhood companions, with whom he used to play hide-and-seek and tag, none of those tomboys to whom he had given so many nuts and apples and later, when they were bigger, so many flowers, had ever taken it into her head to 'call' him. Playing the violin in the orchestra on feast days, or singing from the steps of the organ, he saw their idylls end in matrimony; he was at all their weddings, one after the other. The last of them was twenty-seven, and when he greeted her after the ceremony it seemed to him that he was saying good-bye to his own youth. That day, when he reached home, he looked at himself in the glass and did not like what he saw. His face was too lean, his nose twisted, his mouth too big.

But he soon got over it and became gay, carefree, and content once more. He no longer thought of such melancholy things till the day when the daughter of one of his contemporaries got married. This was a new generation, with all its arrogance. The bride was irreverent to the extent of not wanting to dance the old country-dances and told him there and then to strum a polka.

This warning was serious. Siro found his nose even more crooked, his mouth even bigger: a wrinkle or two more, a lock or two less. He was almost forty. No matter! He bought a new violin and studied polkas, mazurkas and waltzes.

But if the girls passed him by, the shrewder of the mothers began to court him. Siro was no longer a youth (indeed, had never been a youth), but he had become a catch, the best catch in the neighbourhood; through his needle, his lancets and, most of all, his thrift, he had got together a modest competence, and there was plenty of gossip about what he had and even more about what he had not. They began to talk about his pile, then to whisper about his rolls of *genove*, and then about his hoard—finally they said 'a hatful', and a 'hatful' it remained. No one can be rich with less; and no one can remain a bachelor with so much. All those apathetic girls had implacable mammas. Had Siro resisted, the blockade would perhaps have lasted half a century; but at the first assault he surrendered.   There could hardly have been a more formidable one; for Irene was the most charming, as her mother Tonia was the shrewdest, of all the people of Bisagno.

They both came on that fatal morning.

They lived close up against the city wall to the north, in the suburb of Incrociati, the birthplace of Siro's mother. From the top of the Gerbino bastion, their little plot in the midst of the clear grey of the stone-quarry seemed like a kerchief of green and white chequers, with here and there a clump of red flowers.   The two gardeners forded the river hand in hand.   Though it was a working day, they were both dressed as for a festa.   Their little patent-leather shoes with silver buckles shone as they jumped across the stepping-stones.   Siro was cleaning the windows when he saw them coming.   The sun did not dart its rays more brightly than Irene's eyes, and the little channels that wound beneath their feet were not more deceitful than Tonia's smiles.   They looked like two quails being drawn softly, softly towards the decoy; but with this difference, that this time it was the quails who were coming to ensnare the decoy.

They greeted Siro with curtsies and presented him with a pasty and a bouquet of wallflowers since, if he did not know, it was the day of the blessed San Siro, who should grant him a hundred years of peace, a sackful of happiness and joy for full measure.   And while the poor fellow was blushing with thanks, and only wanting to know how and why, Tonia insinuated that the idea had been all Irene's. Ever since the day when the Sor Phlebotomist had cured her of a sprained ankle, she had marked this day on her calendar with a big pin in order to show her gratitude. After the compliments had been washed down with two fingers of white wine and everyone was feeling cosy, the women rummaged about the house, which was big and airy and everything you like, but a 'church without saints'.

'Without madonnas,' corrected Siro, laughing.

Tonia noted all the cobwebs and drew with her finger on the dusty furniture: 'What a pity! What a pity!' How it cried out for a willing hand to put everything in order...! They went down into the garden with the leech: *Jesu Maria*, what a disaster! Tomatoes rotting on the ground, the lettuces covered with blight, the sage all gone to seed and what a lot of nettles in the chicory! She must certainly come here one Sunday and give it all a good going over.

'Do come! Come whenever you like!'

Tonia pointed out the front of the house to him... how much nicer it would look if there were curtains at the windows, a box of wallflowers on the windowsill, and above them, among the blooms, when he came back from work, some eager little face...eh! Irene had stayed at the window and was looking out at him, laughing. Siro was deep in thought.

'I don't want to pry into your affairs, but have you ever thought of tying the knot?'

Siro, from old habit, moved his head from right to left, but did not quite shake it. This time he could not say no. He had considered it, yes...but not very deeply...and, for some time past...

'Perhaps, after all, it's best; one has a more settled life, dines at home, doesn't stay out till the milk; one gives up old fads and fancies and one relishes the sweetness of life...especially when one has what is needed.'

Half way down the stairs Siro caught Tonia by the arm.

'Who would have me?'

'Oh, the fool, the old fool!'

'I'm forty, you know...'

'But that is...that is just in your *prime*.'

'Do you really mean it?'

'Eh, so...'

Half an hour later the two gardeners, holding hands, forded the Bisagno. Irene's eyes were shining and Tonia's smiles more cunning than ever; the little shoes shone in the sunlight and their striped skirts fluttered gaily.

Siro watched them from the window. The two quails had escaped the snare; they had cheated the decoy and had taken it with them. Siro had allowed them to rob him of his heart.

Siro did not see Irene again till the first Monday in August, a fortnight later. He met her by chance and asked her to come to his house to collect her platter. When he had closed the door, he took her two hands and firmly, in a few breathless words, asked her if she would have him as a husband. The girl, in no way dismayed, looked him straight in the face, tossed her head and laughed. That day she was not wearing her little striped dress but in her working clothes was even more attractive; a red kerchief, crossed over her white blouse, barely covered her shoulders and breast; her short skirt showed her slender and provocative ankles. Siro was still holding both her hands as if he wanted to dance a rigadoon; he stammered, trembling:

'Will you?'

And thrust out his nose like a question mark.

Suddenly Irene turned serious and said frankly and proudly:

'Of course I will.'

The poor fellow was almost ready to swoon with happiness. He drew back his hands and joined them in a gesture of adoration before this sixteen-year-old angel who had granted him, poor Siro, the outcast of two generations, the gift of her flowering youth, of her splendid dawn. So much generosity confounded him; how could he ever repay it?

Irene once more made a tour of the little house, but this time like a mistress visiting her own domain, examining here and rummaging there. Siro followed her humbly, eagerly, analysing his own sentiments, anxious that she should be pleased, fearing lest she should not find everything to her liking.

It was she who was so good to be content with so little!

He blindly accepted her proposals, her desires: let her do what she liked...let her have the say...let her command. The inventory was almost over when Siro went to his desk, an old desk, a gift from the doctor. He opened it; and in it was a druggist's mortar, filled to the brim with gold coins; *savoias, genovas,* gold *scudi,* and a pile of napoleons. The girl stood dazzled; then, seized by an indefinable caprice, thrust both her hands into the little hoard, scrabbling through it to relish to the full new and hitherto unknown delights.

II

On the eve of the great day, Siro went in the afternoon to get the necessary affidavits and documents from the Curia and then went on to do a few minor jobs in the town. As he passed by a goldsmith's shop in the Piazza Bianchi he saw in the shop-window a wonderful necklace, made of large gold medallions joined by exquisite filigree. In the centre was a heart and under it a tiny cross. He had already presented his wedding gifts to the bride; none the less he was overcome by the temptation to give her a surprise and bought the necklace, intending to put it around her neck as his only greeting when he went next day to take her from her house. But then he thought: why not go right away, this very moment, and take it to her? It was true that when he had said good-bye to the women he had said that he would not be back that evening and, since they had so many things to do, they had approved his thoughtfulness. He felt a little ashamed of going back to see them again, but when he thought it over, eagerness to show her his new purchase seemed reason enough. He left the town by the Pila Gate and, confused by his own uncertainties, mechanically took the road towards Bisagno.

In the end, his eagerness prevailed; next day, amid so many emotions, his gift might pass unnoticed. The kind thought would certainly please Irene and they would pass together some of those seemingly endless hours which he was already finding so hard to fill.

The bloodletter went straight to his goal, the modest cottage tucked away in a bend of the bastion. The door faced the road on the farther side. As he had arrived from the river side, Siro had to go around the garden, skirting the high elder hedge; he walked briskly yet carefully for the ground was broken and he could scarcely see... At the corner, where the elders were thick and leafy, there was a sort of arbour where the women had placed a bench to sit and rest in the noon-day heat; on the outside, the branches projected far out over the precipitous rocks. Siro stooped in order to make his way beneath them; then halted suddenly. He recognized Irene's voice. She was speaking in the garden only a couple of steps away; if the two women were there, he thought, he would surprise them. He held his breath and listened tensely.

But it was he who got the surprise. Irene was obviously not talking to her mother, since she said: 'It's a miracle

that we can get a few moments to talk to-night. Be good!
If you only knew all I had to do to spare you these few
moments! So listen; we mustn't see one another again
for a time. But whatever people may say, you know that
my every thought is for you, that I am yours, I am still
yours and always will be yours...' She repeated caressingly
'always...always...' in a stifled voice as if her lips were
not free. There was a pause.

Poor Siro was stupefied:

'She is his...and I?'

Irene went on:

'I will get word to you when you can come; you know,
the usual way. Now go! Mamma may be back at any
moment...' There was the sound of a loud kiss. 'And
remember what I told you. Good-bye.' Then more kisses,
hasty and passionate, from behind the hedge. The leaves
of the elders quivered as if a north-easter were blowing
and beat on Siro's head as if recoiling from those tender-
nesses. A man's voice replied: 'Good-bye!'

That was the only word spoken by the unknown.
There was a vigorous rustling in the hedge and an ava-
lanche of twigs and pebbles; and a scramble down the
slope...a light step in the garden. It was all over.

III

Siro too scrambled on to the path. It was dark; in
the shadows he could just make out a denser shadow
growing more distant, the shadow of Irene's unknown
lover. She had said to him: 'I am yours, yours for ever.'
So he had taken with him everything, all Siro's treasure,
all his life. Siro followed him, like a little boy runs after
someone who has taken a precious toy from him. He
followed, fainting, stunned, without thinking of anything,

without knowing why or where. His head was swimming
and his heart seemed rent in two. He felt very tired and
his legs gave under him, but he swayed and walked on.
He walked groaning, unaware that he was voicing the
lament of suffering nature, the lament that sick men make
when they are in delirium.

He could see his own village on the far side of the
Bisagno in the wan gleam of the half-light; here and
there a single window was alight. His little house stood
out, gloomy and earthy-grey, above the others. Behind
it, the golden aureole of an hour earlier had become a
great dark cloud, a black monster that seemed ready to
crush it. Down below him, the rocks in the river seemed
like heaps of bones in a cemetery. Behind them, towards
San Francesco, a line of lights shone like torches at a
funeral.

Siro went back again to the Pila Gate. The unknown
continued his way towards the Rubaldo, then suddenly
turned to the left, crossed the river by the Santa Zita
bridge and took the San Pietro road to the mouth of the
river, to Foce. He skirted the shipyard and passed the
Customs House. Siro knew the Customs Chief there;
at one time he had often passed an evening there over a
game of taroc, when they would exchange views at length
on women and marriage. He was on the point of giving
way to habit and stopping at the door, but then he saw
the other one ahead of him and forgot everything else.
They passed through the suburb. It was by now full
night. In the open doorways of the mean-looking houses
he could see the everyday preparations for supper. The
poorer fishermen were sitting on their doorsteps and every
now and then one of them, recognizing Siro, would greet
him and look to see whom the leech might be visiting
at that late hour.

Soon they were clear of the houses. The unknown

hastened his pace and plunged into the shadows. Finally, Siro could no longer see him and felt bewildered and lost.

The darkness about him grew denser, a darkness filled with fears, with invisible chimaeras, incomprehensible menace, images and voices of the void. It was like the times when he had been a boy. He would have followed that man for ever; he was a guide, a vague, uncertain aim that drew him onward. He no longer felt any desire for vengeance. Should that other one have turned and asked him: 'What do you want?', he would perhaps have thrown himself weeping at his feet...But instead he had vanished like a phantasm; it seemed like an atrocious and mysterious mockery, a jest of fate. Siro remained alone, lost, weighed down by an infinite and inexplicable anguish.

IV

Siro looked about him in dismay.

He was a few steps from the seashore. The waves, huge, grey, and leaden, beat upon the sands. The rain-showers galloped through the skies to assaults unknown. A sullen bellowing came to him from the void. In the faint gleams of light, black shapes whirled and rose, perched on the cruppers of the whitecaps, sank and reappeared. The harsh cry of a seamew three times pierced through the dark uproar. The black shapes, like great monsters, launched themselves onward; then, sliding on the waves, they came swiftly and silently to land. Out of the darkness they leapt on to the beach. It seemed like a trysting-place of ghosts. They came from everywhere. Siro was overcome by an instinctive dismay and ran, tottering. He fell flat on the steps of an archway, rose and took shelter under the arch. There he remained kneeling, his hands gripping the heavy bars of the grating, his forehead on the stone.

Little by little he began to recover his senses. He recognized the spot. In the happy days of his childhood, in one or other of his escapades, he had stopped here and, falling asleep, had been later awakened by just such a night as this.

A thread of reddish light pierced the darkness and remained high above on the opposite wall. He turned and saw light filtering through a crack behind him. He put his eye to it and looked down on a remarkable scene.

The crack opened high up under the roof of a fisherman's storehouse, against which the archway backed. A rough mat of plaited reeds from one doorpost to the other sheltered it from the seaward side. Trawls and drag-nets covered the three walls. Ten or twelve persons were grouped there, chatting, men of different ages and classes, some in everyday clothes, others in sailors' jerseys or mountaineers' coats. They formed a circle around one of them who, kneeling at a bench in the middle of the shed, was reading in a low voice. He was holding some sheets of thin paper up to the weak light of a lantern. With his right hand he was stroking the butt of a pistol lying in front of him. At intervals he would stop in his reading and lift his head, and a low murmur rose from the men around him. Only occasional words reached Siro's ears. They seemed to refer to the failure of some business or other. It might have been a smugglers' hide-out. 'Dates from Palermo damaged in transit...work on the Neapolitan *pasta* begun again...the straw from Florence delayed...rye from Piedmont destroyed by storms...it is hoped to forward goods by the end of the season...supplies will be by the mountain route...' One phrase struck him: 'Withhold delivery of coke from Marseilles...sales postponed...'

A few months earlier, Siro had run an errand for his benefactor, Doctor Vaccarezza, to a coastwise skipper in Sampierdarena about some business matter and the man had replied in those very words. The doctor had then sent him round by the east coast road as far as Portofino to repeat the news to various persons, with so many recommendations to secrecy that he had guessed that some political intrigue was afoot.

At other times he had carried out similar missions. One day, coming to Genoa to look for some samples of sweetmeats, he had been given a parcel containing books. The doctor, Siro knew, had no dealings of this sort; as they say, he was up to the neck in politics. Without confiding in him in any way, he had often talked to Siro of the ancient Republic of St. George, of the fallen greatness of Liguria, of Italy, and of the heroic strivings, the unlucky essays, the still living hopes of the patriots... When Siro expressed himself grateful for all the doctor had done for him, the doctor would cut him short, saying: 'It's nothing; one day, perhaps, I will ask you for something much greater in exchange.' Last June, at the time of the sad story of poor Ruffini who had cut his own throat in despair, believing himself to have been betrayed, the old doctor had seemed to him in a very excited state and had spoken freely to him about mysterious vengeances and imminent revolts.

The reader kept repeating every few moments: 'Sales postponed, postponed sales,' and at these words which seemed to end every sheet, the faces of the company became sadder and gloomier. At last he stopped reading and asked: 'Anything else?' 'No!' a little old man replied. 'Has everyone understood?' All present bent their heads in silence. Then the reader opened the little lantern and put the sheets into the flame till they caught light. He placed them on the bench and turned them over and over again with close attention until the last and tiniest piece was reduced to ash.

Then they all gathered around the white-haired old man, for whom it seemed they all had the greatest respect. They asked him for explanations and he replied and took decisions with vigorous firmness. All nodded respectfully.

Then he called:

'Liberio.'

A young man dressed as a sailor, tall, slim, and of finely cut features, came forward:

'You understand,' the old man rebuked him severely, 'that your imprudence may cost dear. Who told you to announce the sales?'

'I thought...' said the other humbly.

'You are not here to think, but to ask, to carry out, and above all to obey...'

There was a pause, and then the old man went on:

'What did you think?'

'I thought it would anticipate, would hurry on, the effects of "the wind".'

'And the wind has nearly blown us all out to sea; for three days it has been blowing from Piedmont and all the chaff is in the air; at this very moment we are all of us under the flail.'

They looked around uneasily.

'You will answer for everything; it is your affair now. Why did you call us?'

'To report on my mission to the company.'

'And I have come to take it up again in its name. Now hear its orders. When is the market fixed for?'

'Tomorrow night.'

'You must cancel it before mid-day. Don't send other agents, do it yourself. When you have ended your round, give back the sack to the wire-drawer of Santa Zita and leave for Marseilles immediately, without delay. You will find credentials there. Are we agreed? Give me your hand for the sign.'

The young man humbly bent his proud head and stretched out his right hand. The old man placed his own hand over it and, bending his middle finger, traced some invisible lines on it, and added 'Go!' Then, after the sailor had left, he summoned the others around him.

'Ausonio, the wire-drawer of Santa Zita must be warned before the day is out.'

Siro listened with the greatest anxiety; that name meant Doctor Vaccarezza.

'Then go to him and tell him...'

The cry of a falcon interrupted him.

'Silence! Two, three, four, five, six...from the landward side.'

The harsh cry of a seamew, such as Siro had already heard, replied.

'The seaward side is clear. Turn out the light.'

The quick tread of men walking in the darkness, and then silence. Siro, almost without knowing why, found himself outside the archway. He walked with great strides; everything seemed to him a bad dream and he started rubbing his eyes to waken himself. He went up the beach again. A strong sou'wester was blowing; the sky was cloud-filled and the sea turbulent. Siro forged ahead as best he could, stumbling and wavering. Suddenly he felt himself seized by the collar from behind. A voice said: 'That's two of them!' Siro turned and made out the figure of a heavily-built man. Still holding Siro fast by the collar, the man opened the slide of a dark-lantern which he was holding and thrust it into his face. 'Let's see what sort of Jacobin faces you'll make at me...' Then, suddenly letting go, he stepped back and exclaimed in wonder: 'Why, it's the leech!' and burst into laughter. It

was the brigadier at the customs post, his friend. 'I'm
sorry,' he said, 'but I took you for one of the conspira-
tors,' and laughed more delightedly than before.

'Have you patients at Foce?' he asked, taking Siro by
the arm and dragging him along with him.

A few steps farther on they met two of the customs men.

The commandant stepped aside for a moment and gave
some orders in a low voice. The guards moved quickly
away, making down the coast. He took Siro's arm again.
'To be sure, I took you for a *carbonaro* but after all I'm
not sorry to have nabbed you. You have accounts to settle
with me. Do you know, you old devil, that we haven't
met for a month? It is a month, isn't it?' 'It is,' replied Siro absentmindedly. 'And you owe me a revenge.'
They had arrived at the door of the guardhouse. 'Come
in,' said the commandant, 'we'll probably need you in
any case.' And before Siro could think of protesting, he
dragged him into a huge barrack of a room which was
used, as was shown by a rifle-rack on one side and a wri-
ting-table and a steelyard balance on the other, both as
an office for denunciations and as a guardroom.

A customs man and a *carabiniere* were on duty.

The commandant asked the latter:

'Where is your sergeant?'

'He went out with the patrol.'

'You look after the prisoner. Is he hurt?'

'My bayonet must have pierced his hide in the scuffle.
His jacket is bloodstained, but he won't say a word.'

'Well, devil take him!' exclaimed the brigadier shrug-
ging his shoulders. 'Siro, have you got your lancets with
you?'

At a sign, the customs man took the lantern, unhooked
a huge hey from a nail, and opened a door at the end of
the room. They went into another room, as large as the

first, a warehouse for sequestrated contraband, converted into a temporary prison for the occasion. The sight of the prisoner shook Siro out of his stupor; he recognized the Liberio of the mysterious tryst on the beach. He was lying on a mattress in a corner, between a barrel and a mass of packets, boxes and rifles thrown down higgledy-piggledy.

'Up,' said the sergeant, 'and show the Signor Phlebo-tomist your scratches.'

The prisoner did not move; leaning his head on his hand, he gave the brigadier a glance of supreme indif-ference.

'Up!' repeated the brigadier impatiently.

Siro broke in to say that it was not necessary; he could very well look after him where he was. He knelt down by the mattress. He opened the man's jacket, cut away the woollen waistcoat and the shirt with his surgical scis-sors, and examined the wound. It was really only a scratch. He dressed it quickly, covered it with gauze, and bandaged it. The prisoner let him do what he would, as though he were not concerned. He did not open his mouth.

The fineness and nobility of the lines of his beardless face, his very white skin, and the quality of his shirt show-ed that he belonged to a class that the sailor's coarse clothes could scarcely disguise.

Then the brigadier took Siro into a little room which served him both as an office and a dining-room.

'Surely you're not thinking of going out in this wea-ther?'

It was raining hard. The brigadier made Siro sit at an old leather-covered desk, on which violet-stained circles showed that it was more used to glasses than to inkpots.

'Now I've got to act as turnkey too. Stay and keep me company. A bottle will do us both good.'

'What has he done?' asked Siro.

'Who? That fellow? A *carbonaro*, a Jacobin, stupidity and rubbish of all kinds and God knows what else...
Pah! they take their brains on lease from the French.
A fine harvest they've got from those weeds that have
drawn the marrow out of them; when we were after them
they kept as quiet as mice, and when we try to treat them
properly they start their little games again. There's only
one way...'

'How was he arrested?'

'The patrol of *carabinieri* came on him near the shipyard and recognized him from his description.'

'Do they know where he comes from?'

'It seems so. There is only one way...to my way
of thinking, he must go with the sixty down there at
San Giorgio and then...down the rathole. There's only
one way...'

Siro broke in again:

'What will he get?'

'Eh...unless he's a person of standing, it'll be the gal-
leys if he squeals; otherwise, a noose and good riddance...
But forget these gaolbird woes and let's talk about us.
I heard a good one about you, that you're getting married...is it true?'

Siro darted a glance at him; then he nodded.

'I meant to say...look out for yourself, Siro, if you
don't want to get into my bad books,' said the brigadier,
with palm outstretched over Siro's head, threatening him
in jest. 'But, seriously, what about finishing that nice
wine from Michelaccio...'

Then he added, pompously twisting his dyed mousta-
chios: 'Marriage is a fine thing...for bachelors, eh?'

Siro managed to force a smile, bewildered and desolate. Then he bent his head.

The brigadier, once off on his favourite theme, went

on to preach and to argue from examples and anecdotes re-cooked so many times that even he himself had begun to swallow them as true.

Once again Siro interrupted him:

'When will they come and take him?'

'Who? Who? That fellow again? In an hour or two, perhaps now, as soon as the patrol gets back; but, I must say you're becoming a bit of a bore...'

This time the brigadier seemed really hurt by Siro's inattention. 'I'm beginning to believe in that marriage,' he muttered crossly.

Then he fell silent, leant his elbow crossly on the desk and began meticulously to wipe every last drop off the carafe in order to calm his bad temper. This task did not take long; in half an hour he began to snore and to sway about. At last he got up to look for a more comfortable place for his slumbers.

'I'll wait', said Siro, 'and have another look at that wound before he goes.'

'As you like,' grumbled the brigadier and went through a little door into his own room.

Siro slipped into the guardroom; the customs man was asleep, stretched out flat on a bench. The *carabiniere*, with arms crossed over his musket and hat over his eyes, was leaning against the window in so prudent and discreet an attitude as to make hazardous any judgement on the concessions that his mind may have made to the vulgar exigencies of sleep. A huge white cat, crouched on the steelyard, slept heavily. The hanging lantern flickered and sputtered.

Siro, with the involuntary movement of a sleepwalker, crossed the room, took the service lantern from the bench, unhooked the key from the wall, went straight to the door of the storeroom, opened it, entered, and closed it after him.

The *carabiniere* moved and looked indifferently at what

the leech was doing. Then he set himself to pace slowly up and down. The cat remained silent, solemnly licking its whiskers; the customs man alone did not move.

V

Siro halted in the doorway. Behind the guardroom door the soldier's steps, like the oscillations of a pendulum that is slowing down, passed, passed again, became slower, and then died away. The purring of the cat began again. The squall was over.

The leech approached the mattress.

The prisoner was awake and darted at him a cutting glance of desperation that did not ask for sympathy. Siro put down the lantern and leant over him.

'Signore,' he said in a hoarse voice, 'you do not know me; but I can perhaps be of service to you. I could pass on to any person the warnings that you promised to give him.'

He waited in vain for a reply. Outside could be heard a slow and measured dripping from the eaves.

'I know', he went on, 'that the fate of many depends on you. A serious mission has been entrusted to you; if you would like to confide it to me, I will carry it out faithfully according to your intentions.'

The young man did not move or open his lips, but merely looked at him with a proud and infinite disdain.

'Don't you think me capable? Well, I can tell you that Doctor Vaccarezza of Santa Zita—you know him—has many times given me similar tasks and I have always carried them out. He would be able to tell you. So give me a line, a word, for him; I will warn him and he will see to the rest. Would that be all right?'

But the other remained silent. Siro bent his head sadly.

'You reject my services? Yet I offer them with all my heart; why reject them? Your silence may cost the lives of many good men. I could save them, and I would do it so willingly.'

He spoke humbly and entreatingly.

'At least,' he went on, 'tell me the danger that threatens Doctor Giulio. That good signore has been a father to me; I owe him so much, I owe him everything, I would be so happy to help him...so happy. I can't let him be lost. Tell me, tell me how I may save him...he has a large family...'

He wrung his hands and sobbed as he spoke. The young man watched him writhe and shiver, looking at him coldly and impassively. Then he said:

'Friend, you seem to be a good fellow, but the job you are doing is not so good,' and he curled his lip in a smile of profound disgust.

Siro did not understand. The young man went on, raising his voice:

'You've played your part well and I offer you my sincerest compliments. You have real gifts and will certainly get on. You're as slippery as a snake and will crawl far. But you are wasting your time on me; now that your masters, who are certainly listening behind that door, know that you have done your duty zealously and faithfully, what more do you want? You annoy me with your filthy presence. Go, and leave me in peace.'

Siro with clasped hands implored him:

'Be quiet. Speak softly or all is lost. Signor Liberio, I entreat you...'

At the name, the other pursed his lips contemptuously.

'You are well informed. Do you intend to deny that I owe this night's good fortune to you?'

7 T.

He sneered and turned his back. Siro went on, stammering, entreating. He had understood hazily Liberio's suspicions, but was so wrapped up in his own troubles that he had not the spirit to take offence. He was only deeply grieved, and tried to find new and more effective ways of persuasion, but did not find them. He looked around him in dismay. The storm had begun again and in the midst of the gusts of wind a distant clock struck the first morning hours. He knelt down beside the mattress.

'Listen, time is passing; they may come at any moment to take you. Do you want to have the misery of Doctor Giulio's poor little ones on your conscience?'

Then he murmured despairingly:

'It is true you do not know me and are suspicious of me; but put me to the test, signore. Find some other way.'

Useless. A creak was heard from the room next door; the customs man turned over in his sleep and sighed. Siro put his hand on the young man's shoulder.

'Listen, there is a way. You don't want me to carry out your mission; very well, do it yourself. Dress in my clothes. They won't recognize you. Go out. I will remain in your place; it's better so, and safer. Why didn't I think of that before?'

He murmured to himself: 'I might be mad in an hour or so, who knows?'

Liberio turned quickly. In the light of the frequent lightning flashes he gazed intently at the wan, desolate face of the leech.

'Quickly, quickly. Time is passing, I tell you.'

'Do you really mean', asked the youth, getting up and sitting on the mattress, 'that you would sacrifice your life for me?'

'Oh, my life,' muttered Siro gloomily. 'Once it was dear to me, it was beautiful, good, peaceful; but I staked everything on one card, on one person who should have given me paradise, but instead has given me despair ... you see, I ... fate has played a cruel joke on me; my misfortune is a woman, a beautiful girl. If you could only see her, like a little Madonna. I am no longer young, but I believed in her. I offer you my life, if you can make any use of it; in any case, tomorrow I shall not know what to do with it.'

The young man said:

'Very well. I accept your sacrifice, in the name of the holy cause to which I belong.'

Siro took off his clothes hurriedly and threw them over.

But Liberio was beset by a fresh doubt.

'What are you doing? There's not a moment to lose; hurry up,' Siro said to him. 'Get dressed. Oh God, are you still doubtful?'

The young man looked fixedly at him and gripped him by the hand.

'Are you sure', he asked in a low voice, 'that nobody will follow me in the round that I must make?'

'God alone knows,' said Siro, deeply hurt. 'If your suspicions are unjust, He will enlighten you. I have nothing more to say.'

He was silent; the storm broke out with fresh fury. Crashes and whistlings that sounded like cries and lamentations filled the air. Liberio looked out of the narrow window at the heavens furrowed by the lightning flashes. He was no longer calm. He trembled. The clock struck again. Siro leapt up:

'Liberio,' he said, 'do one thing, take ...'

He drew one of his knives out of the bag and handed it to Liberio.

'Kill me; at least you will be sure then. Kill me, and you will take a great weight from me ...'

The young man was moved; he pushed Siro's hand away and said:

'I believe you...I believe you...you are a good man.'

'Yes...Then quickly, quickly, get dressed...'

Siro helped him on with the short trousers, the wide waistcoat and black tail-coat, and put the round beaver hat on his head. Then he ran to the door, peered through the keyhole, and turned.

'Go. It's almost dark. Walk openly; the door to the street is on the right; it is only closed. Don't turn around but open it without hesitation. They will think it is I... Go, and may the Lord be with you.'

Siro pushed him to the threshold. Liberio turned:

'Have you any message to give me?'

'No.'

'No one I should greet? The doctor?'

'Oh, yes...'

'No one else?'

'Else? No, no one else. I wanted to give all my love to her...but it doesn't matter any more.'

He shook his head, and a sob cut short his words.

'Go...go out,' he said. Liberio embraced him and for a moment those two noble hearts rested upon one another. Then the young man broke away and murmured with great tenderness:

'Good-bye.'

Siro reeled and fell fainting, murmuring:

'It was he.'

Once before he had heard that word; he recognized the voice. Something rose within him; he dragged himself to the mattress and stifled in it the cry that burst from his breast. Then he said to himself: 'Ah well, what does it matter?'

The storm died away in the distance. A quiet half-light filtered through the little window. A great chiming of bells broke out, from Foce to Staglieno, from the distant hamlets of the mountains and the river. But the bell of All Souls broke in with its harsh silvery clang of sad augury, seeming to say that in the midst of so much joy on earth and in heaven, there was one who was suffering.

VI

At Incrociati, everything was in commotion for Irene's wedding.

The ceremony was to be held early, before mass. Everything was in readiness at the church and in Tonia's house.

Even the band from Santa Zita had arrived. Only the bridegroom was missing. The musicians had gone to fetch him and accompany him in triumph to the bride; but they found his house shut. They had all waited for him on the bank of the river.

Meanwhile, day began to dawn. The wind that came swirling down from the mountains drove far seaward the squalls that had raged throughout the night, and the sun rose above Sestri in a perfectly clear sky.

Siro's delay began to be incomprehensible. But at last the well-known beaver hat and the even better-known black tail-coat of the leech could be seen in the midst of the gardens on the far side of the Bisagno. One of the girls remarked that the skinflint had not even bothered to put on his best clothes. Irene noticed that the leech was walking more briskly than usual and seemed to have grown a good twenty years younger. When he was about a gunshot away the musicians gave a blast on their instruments, the boys clapped their hands and shouted long life to the bridegroom. The figure stopped, seemingly surprised and embarrassed by this welcome. 'He's running away,' someone shouted. The tail-coat disappeared amid the shrubs in the gardens. Everyone laughed, thinking it a joke of some sort. Irene turned pale and faint, as if thunderstruck. The bridegroom was not coming.

Half an hour later, a youth forded the Bisagno and went to look for him. In a thicket he found the leech's clothes, torn and disordered; the waistcoat had traces of blood on it. The documents from the Curia were still in the coat pocket.

A few hours later a huge crowd milled around the Customs guardhouse at Foce. A prisoner who had been arrested during the night had opened his veins, they said, with a surgeon's lancet. And, an incredible thing, they whispered that the dead man was the leech of Santa Zita. The attorney-general and the judge had come from Genoa to examine the evidence. When the formalities were ended, the corpse was brought out on a bier and put under the portico to wait for the sextons. A young peasant, whom no one recognized, pushed through the crowd, took one of the hands which was hanging from the bier, and murmured: 'My saviour.'

During the day, the strange news spread through the whole Bisagno valley, and by the next day the rumours born of the evening gossip had become gloomy and fearful legends. At Incrociati, once they were sure that Siro had been arrested during the night, they believed that what they had seen in the morning had been some phantasm of hell. As for Irene, she was never able to find a husband daring enough to face the phantom of whom she was believed to have been the victim.

The one who could find no peace was the brigadier. He took good care not to compromise his own reputation by dispelling the cloud that blackened Siro's good name; but he remained convinced that 'that brigand of a Jacobin

had murdered him with his own hands'. However, the
local authorities, notwithstanding the obscurity of the evidence, conferred by their sentence on the humble name
of Siro Xerega the glory of martyrdom; and certainly,
whatever may have happened, his sacrifice was not un-
worthy.

GIOVANNI VERGA

Verga was born in Catania in 1840 and died there in 1922. He is now generally acknowledged to be the greatest Italian writer of fiction after Manzoni, as well as the founder of the school of *verismo* and 'naturalism.' Until the age of forty or so he wrote novels about upper-class life in which the characters were tortured by psychological problems. He then returned to his Sicilian origins and began writing about peasants' lives, conditioned by what seemed to him inexorable circumstances. His work varies greatly. In his later stories and novels Providence becomes a kind of fatal power which can only be answered by passivity and patience. The author reports and exhibits, seeming to make no comment. He strips his language down to essentials. The quality that emerges is his own bare, harsh poetry.

All Verga's Sicilian novels and most of his short stories have been translated into English, with varying success. D. H. Lawrence's versions, uneven and sometimes inaccurate, give a truly Laurentian view of the originals. There is a fine rendering of the second of Verga's major novels, *I Malavoglia*, by Eric Mosbacher. *Cavalleria Rusticana* is one of the most famous of Verga's tales, partly because it is the origin of Mascagni's opera, first performed in 1890. Earlier, in 1884, a dramatized version had been given in Milan with Eleanora Duse as Santuzza. The story has been translated many times, and is given here only as a glimpse of a writer whose works should long ago have been in a collected edit-ion in English. Verga's pungent style, with its combination of tautness, lilt, and sometimes untranslatable Sicilian dialect, makes a new effort at presentation well worth a try.

Among his short novels *Jeli il pastore* and *La Lupa* are usually considered the finest. His collections of Sicilian tales are *Vita dei Campi* (1880) and *Novelle Rusticane* (1883). Verga's bibliography is extensive but, apart from the short stories, his fame rests on two great novels: *I Malavoglia* (1881) and *Maestro Don Gesualdo* (1888), part of a vast scheme of connected novels on the " defeated by life " (*i vinti*) of which only these two and a chapter and a half of *La Duchesse de Leyra* ever got written.

A. C.

CAVALLERIA RUSTICANA

GIOVANNI VERGA

Translated by Archibald Colquhoun

When Turiddù Macca, old Nunzia's son, got back from soldiering, he'd strut round the village square every Sunday in his Bersagliere uniform with its red cap, like a fortune-teller setting up stall and canary-cage. The girls, on their way to Mass, eyed him longingly with their heads in their shawls, and urchins buzzed around him like flies. He had also brought back a pipe with a life-like carving of a king on horse-back, and would strike sulphur-matches on the seat of his pants, raising a leg as if for a kick. But in spite of all this Lola, *Massaro* Angelo's daughter, had not shown herself either at Mass or on her balcony, as she had just got engaged to a man from Li-codia, a carter with four Sutini mules in his stable. On Turiddù's first hearing this, why, heaven and hell! he was going to tear the guts, yes the very guts, out of that fellow from Licodia! But he did nothing of the sort and vented his rage by singing all the disparaging songs he knew under the girl's window.

'Has he nothing better to do, Nunzia's Turiddù, than spend his nights singing like a lone sparrow?' asked the neighbours.

Eventually he ran into Lola on her way back from doing the pilgrimage to Our Lady of Peril; she did not turn a hair on seeing him, as if he'd never meant a thing to her.

'Nice to see you,' he said.

'Oh, Turiddù, they told me you were back the first of the month.'

'They told me other things too!' replied he. 'Is it true you're marrying Alfio the carter?'

'God willing!' answered Lola, drawing the two corners of her kerchief over her chin.

'God's willing to do whatever suits you! And God was willing for me to come all this way back only to find this bit of news!'

The poor lad was still trying to put a brave face on it, but his voice had gone hoarse; and he began following the girl, swaying so that his cap-tassel danced on his shoulders. As for her, she was really sorry to see him so glum, but hadn't the heart to encourage him by saying something pleasant.

'Listen, Turiddù,' she said at last, 'do let me get back to the other girls. What would people in the village say if they saw me with you?'

'Of course,' replied Turiddù, 'now you're marrying Alfio, who has four mules in his stable, you mustn't cause gossip. But my mother, poor thing, had to sell off our bay mule and our patch of vineyard on the highway, while I was away on service. The old days are over now and you don't give a thought to the time when we talked at the window in the yard, and you gave me that kerchief before I left; God knows the tears I sobbed in it as I went off so far that no one even knew the name of our village. Well, goodbye now, Lola, and like the proverb, "let's say it's rained and cleared, and friendship's over".'

Lola married the carter, and on Sundays she would sit out on her balcony, with her hands on her stomach to show off all the big gold rings given by her husband. And Turiddù would still stroll to and fro in the alley, pipe in mouth and hands in pockets, acting careless and eyeing the girls; but inside he was gnawed with bile at

Lola's husband having all that gold, and at her pretending not to notice him when he passed.

'I'll get my own back, and under her very eyes, the bitch!' muttered he.

Opposite Alfio lived *Massaro* Cola the vintner, rich as a pig they said, and with a daughter at home. Turiddù managed to get himself a job as *Massaro* Cola's watchman, and began hanging round the house and paying compliments to the girl.

'Why don't you go and say these pretty things to Lola?'

'Lola's a great lady now! She's married a crowned king, she has.'

'Crowned kings aren't for the likes of me!'

'You're worth a hundred Lolas, and I know someone who wouldn't give Lola a glance, or her patron saint either, when you're around; for Lola, why she's not worthy of wearing your shoes, Lola's not.'

'When the fox couldn't reach the grapes . . .'

'It said: how lovely you are, you dear little bunch of . . .'

'Hey! Down with those hands, Turiddù.'

'Are you afraid I'll eat you?'

'I'm not afraid of you or of your God either.'

'Eh! Your mother's from Licodia, we know! Hot blood you've got! Uh! I could just eat you up with my eyes!'

'Eat me up with your eyes, then, as that won't leave any crumbs; but meanwhile just help me up with this bundle, will you?'

'I'd help you up with the whole house, I would.' To stop herself blushing she threw at him a piece of wood she had by her, and missed him by a miracle.

'Hurry up now, as talk won't get us anywhere.'

'If I were rich I'd try for a wife like you, Santa.'

'I won't be marrying a crowned king like Lola, but

I've got a bit of dowry too, when the Lord sends the right man along!'

'We know you're rich, we know that!'

'If you know that then get a move on, as father'll be here at any moment and I don't want him to find me out in the yard.'

Her father began to get suspicious, but the girl pretended not to notice, as that tassel on the Bersagliere's cap was tickling her heart and forever dancing before her eyes. When the father ordered Turiddù out of the house, the daughter opened her window to him and chattered away with him every night, so that the neighbours talked of nothing else.

'I'm mad for you,' Turiddù would say, 'I can't sleep, can't eat.'

'Nonsense!'

'If only I were Victor Emanuel's son, so's to marry you!'

'Nonsense!'

'By the Madonna, I'd eat you up like bread!'

Lola, who listened every night hidden behind a pot of basil going flushed and pale by turns, called out to Turiddù one day:

'So you don't greet old friends any more, Turiddù!'

'Well,' sighed the young man, 'it's a lucky man who can greet you!'

'If you want to greet me, you know where I live!' replied Lola.

Turiddù, after that, went to greet her so often that Santa noticed, and slammed her window in his face. The neighbours showed by a smile or a nod when the Bersagliere passed. Lola's husband was away going round fairs with his mules.

'On Sunday I'm going to confession, as last night I had a dream about black grapes*!' said Lola.

* ill-omened in Sicily. (Tr.)

'Don't, don't!' begged Turiddù.

'No? Now Easter's nearly here my husband'll be asking why I've not been to confession.'

'Ah!' muttered old Cola's daughter Santa, as she waited on her knees for her turn at the confessional where Lola was being washed clean of her sins, 'I've no wish to be sent off to Rome for my penance!'

Alfio returned with his mules, full of money, and brought a fine new gala dress as a present for his wife.

'High time you did bring her a present,' his neighbour Santa said to him, 'as while you're away your wife's been dishonouring your house.'

Alfio was one of those carters with a grudge against the world, and on hearing such a thing said of his wife, he changed colour as if he'd been knifed.

'Heaven and Hell!' exclaimed he. 'If you're fooling, I'll leave you no eyes to cry with, you and yours!'

'I don't cry!' replied Santa. 'I didn't even cry when with my own eyes I saw Turiddù, Nunzia's son, go into your wife's house at night!'

'Right,' answered Alfio. 'Many thanks.'

Turiddù, now the cat was back, no longer hung round the alley by day, and drowned his sorrows at the tavern with friends. On Easter Eve they were having a plate of sausages. As soon as Alfio came in, Turiddù realized what he'd come about just from the way he stared, and laid his fork on the plate.

'Anything I can do for you, Alfio?' he said.

'Not a thing, Turiddù; I'd not seen you for a time and wanted to talk to you—about you know what.'

At first Turiddù offered him a glass, but Alfio brushed it aside. Then Turiddù got up and said:

'Here I am, Alfio.'

The carter flung both arms round his neck.

'If you come to the Canziria cactuses tomorrow morning we'll talk about that business, man.'

'Wait for me on the highroad at sunrise, and we'll
go up there together.'

By these words they exchanged the kiss of challenge.
Turiddù bit the carter's ear, and so made a solemn promise to be there.

His friends left the sausages and accompanied Turiddù
home, in silence. Nunzia, poor old thing, waited up for
him every night.

'Mamma,' Turiddù said to her, 'd'you remember when
I went off to be a soldier, you thought I'd never come
home? Give me a nice kiss like then, as tomorrow I'm
going afar'.

Before dawn he fetched the clasp-knife which he had
hidden under the hay on being conscripted, and set off
for the Canziria cactuses.

'Oh, Jesus and Mary! Where are you going to in such
a rush?' wailed Lola in dismay as her husband left.

'Nearby,' replied Alfio, 'but it'd be better for you if I
never came back.'

Lola, in her night-dress, prayed at the foot of the bed,
pressing to her lips the rosary which Fra. Bernardino
had brought her from the Holy Land, saying as many
Aves as there were beads.

'Alfio,' began Turiddù, after walking along for a while
beside his companion, who was silent with cap over his
eyes, 'I know as sure as God's true that I'm in the wrong
and should let you kill me. But before coming here I
saw my old mother, who'd got up to see me go on pretence of feeding the hens as if her heart had told her;
and as God's true I'll kill you like a dog so the poor old
woman don't cry.'

'Fine,' replied Alfio, taking off his jacket, 'then we'll
fight it out.'

Both were expert with the knife; Turiddù had blood drawn first and was fast enough to take the thrust on his arm; and back he struck, good and hard, at the groin.

'Ah, Turiddù! So you really are trying to kill me!'

'Yes, I told you so; now I've seen that old woman of mine in the hen-coop, she seems never out of my eyes.'

'Open them up then, those eyes!' yelled Alfio at him. 'Here comes a good one.'

As he crouched on guard, bent double to keep his left hand over his wound which was hurting and almost trailing his elbow on the ground, he snatched a handful of dust and flung it into his opponent's eyes.

'Ah!' yelled Turiddu, blinded. 'I'm done!'

He tried to save himself, gave desperate leaps backwards; but Alfio caught him another stab in the belly and a third in the throat.

'Three! That's for dishonouring my house. Now your mother will let the hens alone.'

For awhile Turiddù staggered here and there amid the cactuses, then fell like a log. Blood gurgled and foamed up in his throat. He could not even gasp: *Ah, mamma mia!*

EDMONDO DE AMICIS

De Amicis, who died at Santa Margherita in 1908 at the age of 62, was the most popular novelist of his day, a warm-hearted, sometimes sentimental, diffuser of morals for the new middle-classes. His stock is at present low in Italian literary fashion, and his sympathetic touch little appreciated.

In later life his style became more diffuse and influenced by journalistic rhetoric. But this early story, apart from offering an interesting contrast to Verga's treatment of a Sicilian theme, does show some of the positive qualities which made him into a major literary spokesman of his time.

His works run into many volumes. The most famous at one time was *Cuore* ('Heart'), which sold hundreds of thousands of copies in Italian and was translated into 25 languages.

The present tale comes from one of his earliest volumes, *La vita militare* (1868). It is set in one of the islands off the Sicilian and southern Italian coasts which have been used as prisons of various kinds since pre-Roman times.

A. C.

CARMELA

EDMONDO DE AMICIS

Translated by Isabel Quigly

I

The story I am going to tell took place on a small island seventy miles off Sicily. There is just a single little town on it, with only 2000 inhabitants, and at the time of my story, there were three of four hundred prisoners too; as well as a troop of forty soldiers to mind them, commanded by a junior officer, and changed every three months. The soldiers led a very pleasant life there, for two reasons above all: first because, apart from guard duty at the barracks and the prisons, occasional reconnoitres into the interior of the island, and some exercise now and then, they had nothing to do, and secondly because wine cost fourpence a bottle and was excellent. As for the officer, he enjoyed enormous freedom, and was able to say: 'I am the comman-der-in-chief of all the military forces in the place.' He had two men to act as clerks in his office in the main square; he had handsome lodgings, free, in the middle of the town; his mornings were spent hunting in the hills, his afternoons closeted with the town's chief citizens, and his evenings in a boat at sea, smoking fine two-cent cigars, dressed how he liked, without worries, without superiors, as unmolested and as happy as you could wish. The only trouble was the thought of such a charmed life lasting only three months.

The town stands on the seashore, and has a small har-bour, where in those days the mail-boat, plying between Tunis and Trapani, stopped every fortnight. Other ships rarely anchored there; so rarely, in fact, that when one was seen making for the port, the bells rang to announce the fact and most of the townsfolk ran down to the shore as if to see a holiday side-show.

The small town looks a pleasant and modest place, but a smiling one too; especially because of its large square in the centre, which, as always happens in a small town, serves the same purpose as the courtyard in a city tenement house. Between this square and the beach runs the main street, which is straight, narrow, and very short. The shops and public buildings are all in the square. There are, or at least there were in those days, two cafés; one patronized by the mayor, the gentry and others in authority; the other by the rest. The house where the troop commander stayed was on the side of the square that faced the sea; and, as the ground rose fairly steeply from the shore to the middle of town, from the windows of his rooms (he had two) he could see the port, a long stretch of beach, the sea, and the distant mountains of Sicily.

The island consists of volcanic mountains and great thick woods.

Three years ago, one fine April morning, the post boat coming from Tunis stopped at the harbour mouth of this little town. Since it first appeared the bell had been ring-ing continuously, and the whole population was gathered there, including the troop commander, the soldiers, the mayor, the judge, the parish priest, the chief of public security, the tax-collector, the harbour master, the chief of police, and a young army doctor attached to the troop to care for the prisoners' health. Two boats approached the ship and brought ashore thirty-two infantrymen and an officer, a handsome, blond, pleasant-looking young man (that's the way you put it), who, having shaken hands with his colleague, and politely replied to the authorities' cordial welcome, entered the town at the head of his troop, between two rows of curious townsfolk. When he had seen his men to their quarters, he went straight back to the group waiting for him in the square, and the mayor introduced people in turn, half gay and half serious, full of friendliness tempered with harmless pomposity. When the ceremony was over the group broke up, and the officer, left alone with his colleague, was taken to the house he was to use. Here the orderly that belonged to the officer who was leaving was packing up the trunks, and the orderly that belonged to the new officer was hastening the moment he could start unpacking by helping the other man. An hour later everything was in order.

The departing troop left that same evening about eight o'clock, seen off at the harbour by the new troop, and our lieutenant, as soon as he had said good-bye to his friend, went home to bed, because he was tired after the journey and his busy day, and wanted to sleep. And sleep he did, soundly.

II

The following morning, as soon as the sun rose, he left the house. He had not taken ten steps across the square when he felt someone tugging gently at the lappet of his tunic. He turned, and two steps away from him saw, standing stiff and motionless like a soldier saluting, a wild-haired girl, untidily dressed, tall, slim, and beautiful, with big, lively black eyes that stared straight into his face, smiling.

'What do you want?' asked the lieutenant, looking at her surprised and curious.

The girl gave no answer, but continued to smile and hold her hand up to her forehead in a military salute.

The lieutenant shrugged his shoulders and went on; but when he had taken another ten steps, he felt another gentle pull at his tunic, and had to turn again. There she was, still stiff and straight as a soldier on parade. He looked round and saw some people nearby, watching the scene and laughing.

'What do you want?' he asked again.

The girl held out her hand, pointing the first finger at him, and said smiling:

'I want you.'

'I see,' he thought. 'She wants money,' and, having searched in his pocket for some, he held it out to her and made ready to move on. But the girl, folding an arm across her breast, as if to protect herself with her elbow against the hand that held out the money, exclaimed again:

'I want you.'

And she began to stamp her feet hard, and ruffle up her hair with both hands, crying dully and monotonously as children do when they pretend to weep. And the people round about laughed. The lieutenant looked at the people, then at the girl, then at the people again, and then went on his way. He crossed most of the square quite freely; but when he reached the street that led down to the harbour, he heard a quick light step behind him, as if someone was running on tiptoe, and just as he was going to turn round, a soft voice murmured with a strange tone in his ear: 'My darling!'

He felt a shiver run through him from head to foot, and walked on faster, without turning. And again the voice said: 'My darling!'

'Oh, look here!' he cried, annoyed, and turning to face the girl, who drew back timidly. 'Leave me alone. Mind your own business. D'you understand?'

The girl looked very remorseful, then smiled, and stretching out her hand as if to caress the lieutenant, who moved away at once, she murmured: 'Don't be cross, my love.'

'Get away, I tell you!'

'...You're my darling.'

'Go away, or I'll call the soldiers and have you put in gaol'. And he pointed to some soldiers standing at the corner. Then the girl went slowly away, walking sidelong and looking back at the lieutenant as she did so, from time to time jutting out her chin and repeating softly: 'My darling!'

'What a shame!' the lieutenant said to himself as he took the road down to the harbour. 'She's so pretty.'

She really was lovely, a superb example of that proud, glowing Sicilian beauty that seems, not just to inspire love, but to impose it, and generally with just a single long, intent look that seems to gaze into the soul and arouse in the man looked at as much ardour as it expresses. She had very dark eyes and hair, a wide, thoughtful brow, and her lips and eyebrows moved quickly and jerkily, full of strength and life. Her voice sounded slightly tired and hoarse, and her laughter hysterical. After she had laughed she kept her mouth open a while, and her eyes wide.

III

'Why don't they keep her shut up?' the lieutenant asked the doctor that same evening as they went into the smarter of the two cafés together, when he had told him what had happened that morning.

'But where could they keep her?' said the doctor. 'She was in hospital in Sicily for more than a year and the town council paid for her; but then, as it was time and money wasted, they had her brought home again. There was little or no hope; the doctors there were the first to say so. Here at least she's as free as air, poor girl; and we can allow her that at least because, apart from the soldiers, she bothers no one.'

The officer asked why she bothered only the soldiers.

'Ah well! It's rather a mixed-up tale, you see. Everyone tells it his own way, especially the villagers, who are never satisfied with the plain unvarnished truth, and have to add their own to it. But the most likely fact, confirmed by the few educated people here, is this. Three years ago, the officer commanding the troop, as you are now, a very handsome youth, who played the guitar superbly and sang like an angel, fell in love with this girl, who was then and still is the most beautiful in the place...'

'She certainly is lovely,' interrupted the lieutenant.

'And the girl, of course, partly because of his beautiful voice, as they're mad about singing and music here, and partly because of his prestige as supreme commander of all the military forces on the island, but most of all because he was handsome, fell in love with him. But how! It was one of those passions you find here, if you know what I mean, burning passions fiercer than volcanoes—jealousy. agonies, rages, the whole tragic lot. All the family she had left was her mother, a poor woman whose only interest in life was her daughter, and who let herself be ordered about; so you can imagine what freedom she had... And people gossiped; but the facts seemed to have proved false the suspicions, the really quite excusable suspicions, that the girl's behaviour aroused; so much so that now everyone believes and says there was nothing wrong in it... It's strange, really; in fact hardly credible, because people say they spent half the day together. But, you know, there are people like that, especially in places like this; girls who are very ardent, very free, and spend all day with the man they love, and who look as if they have no idea of modesty, yet all the same are austere and firm, and as unapproachable as vestals. Well, the fact certainly is that the officer had promised to marry her, and that she had believed him and was nearly out of her mind with joy. She really was, you know; they say there were days when people really feared for her mind. And I can well believe it. Who can tell the pitch that women of that sort can get to? One day she became jealous of a girl—I don't know why—and if they hadn't got her away from her, would have killed her or injured her badly. And she wasn't the only one: no woman could now pass the officer's house and glance up at the windows, or turn to look at him when they met in the road, without her threatening some mischief. Well, the day came when the troop changed over; the officer promised he would be back in a couple of months, the girl believed him, and he left and was never seen again. The poor girl grew ill. Perhaps, if as she grew better she had gradually lost her last ray of hope, she might have managed to forget; but before she had time to get over her illness, she heard, I don't know how, that her lover had married. The blow was unexpected and terrible. She went mad. That's the story.'

'And then?'

'Then, as I told you, she was sent to hospital in Sicily; then she came back, and she has been here now for more than a year.'

At that moment a soldier appeared at the door of the café looking for the doctor.

'I'll tell you the rest later; good-bye,' said the doctor, and disappeared. The lieutenant, rising to say good-bye, banged hard on the table with his sword; a moment later he heard a voice crying in the square: 'I heard him! I heard him! He's in there!' And, as she said this, the mad girl appeared at the door.

'Send her away!' cried the lieutenant, jumping to his feet, as if he had shot up on a spring; and the girl was sent away.

'I'll go and wait for you at home!' they heard her saying as she left. 'I'll go and wait for you at home, my love!'

IV

Carmela's mother lived in a hovel at one end of the town, together with two or three peasant families, and earned a hard living by doing fine sewing. When her daughter was first mad she used to get occasional financial help from the better-off families in the town; but for some time now they had stopped giving it, seeing it was useless because the girl refused to sleep or eat at home, and there was no way of making her keep a new dress in one piece, even for a week. Her mother suffered indescribably, and with obstinate perseverance kept trying to make her daughter respond; but it was all in vain. Sometimes, after much begging, the poor girl let her persuade her into a new dress, and then all at once she would pluck and tear at it till it was reduced to rags. At other times, as soon as she had left her mother's hands, combed and neat in every detail, she would run her hands through her hair and in a moment ruffle it up like a fury.

Most of the day Carmela spent wandering about the steepest and loneliest hills, waving, talking, and laughing loudly to herself. Very often the police, passing by, would see her from a distance busily building little towers of stones, or sitting motionless on top of a terrace gazing out to sea, or lying on the ground asleep. If she saw them, she would gaze after them until they disappeared, and no speech or gesture or smile of hers would answer the signs they made her. In fact sometimes when they were at a distance she would make a movement with both hands, pretending to fire a rifle at them; but always quite seriously. This was how she behaved with soldiers; no one had ever seen her stop, or speak, or laugh with any of them. She passed them or went among them without answering a word to the witticisms they flung at her, without turning her head, without looking straight at anyone. And no one attempted to lay a finger on her or to pull her dress or anything of the kind, because it was said that she could slap a man's face hard enough to leave the marks of her fingers on it.

Wherever she was, as soon as she heard the sound of a drum she ran there. The soldiers would leave the town to go on an exercise by the sea, and she would follow them. While the sergeant gave orders and the lieutenant, from a distance, kept an eye on them, she would stand aside and with the greatest seriousness copy the soldiers' behaviour and with a stick imitate the movements of their rifles, while she repeated the commands in a low voice. Then suddenly she would throw away the stick and go and hover round the lieutenant, looking at him and smiling lovingly at him, calling him by the tenderest names, but softly, and covering her mouth with one hand, so that the soldiers would not hear.

When she was in the town she would nearly always stay in the square in front of the lieutenant's house, in a ring of boys she amused with every sort of joke. Sometimes she would make a wide-brimmed cylindrical hat out of paper and put it on the side of her head, and, leaning on a big stick and muttering in a nasal voice, she would imitate the way the mayor walked. Sometimes, with wisps of paper in her hair, with lowered eyes and pursed lips, moving one hand as if to flutter a fan on her breast, and swaying softly, she would caricature the few ladies in town when they went to church on feast days. Or again, picking up and old cap thrown out at the barracks by one of the soldiers, she would put it on and pull it down to her eyes, stuffing all her hair inside it, and with her arms straight and stiff at her sides she would make two or three turns round the square, walking slowly and solemnly, imitating the sound of the drum, serious, unbending, all in one piece like the toughest of conscripts. But whatever she did or said, no one noticed it any longer. The boys, especially the small urchins, were now her only audience. But the mothers were careful to keep them at a distance, because one day, unlike the way she usually behaved and for some quite unaccountable whim, she seized one, a boy of about eight, the handsomest of her audience, and kissed him so often and so furiously on his face and neck that he began to cry and scream, afraid that she was trying to suffocate him.

Very occasionally she went to church and knelt down, joining her hands like the rest and muttering something; but after a few minutes she would start to laugh and strike attitudes and make odd, irreverent gestures, so that the sacristan ended by coming out, taking her by the arm and putting her outside.

She had a beautiful voice, and when she was herself she had sung well; but since her brain had turned, she sang nothing and just hummed inarticulately and monotonously, as a rule when she was sitting on the doorstep of her home or outside the lieutenant's house, chewing Indian figs, which were, to all intents and purposes, her only food.

She had her hours of melancholy, too, when she neither spoke nor laughed, not even with the children, and then she would sit hunched like a dog outside the door of her house, her head wrapped up in her apron or her face covered with a handkerchief, not stirring whatever the noise around her or however often she was called, even by her mother. But this happened rather rarely; she was almost always gay.

She took no notice of the soldiers, as I said, and never even looked at them; all her tenderness was reserved for the officers. But these she did not treat all in the same way. Since she returned from hospital, the troop had

changed six or eight times, and the officers had been all ages,
had had all sorts of appearances and characters.   People
noticed that she showed a marked preference for the young
ones—even a few years made a difference—and that she
could very well distinguish the handsome from the ugly,
although they were all equally her 'love' and her 'darling'.
A certain lieutenant who was one of the first, a man of
about forty, all nose and belly, with a great roaring voice
and basilisk eyes, had never really found favour with her.
She had spoken softly to him the first time they met; but,
irritated, he had answered her rudely, accompanying his
words with a threatening movement of his hand, to make
her see that it would be best for her to stop once and for
all. And she had stopped, but had never ceased to follow
him whenever she met him in the road, or to spend many
evening hours at the foot of the steps leading up to his
house. When he came in or went out, she never said a
word; but she never moved from there. And she behaved
in the same way to two or three other officers who came
after him, whose character, appearance, and manners were
not very different from his. But some very young ones
came too, handsome men and kind, and over these you
might say she went mad, if she had not been mad already.
One of them got it into his head to cure her truly; but, having taken it lightly at first, he grew bored after two or three
days, and stopped. Another, less well-intentioned and more
materialistic, wondered: 'Must a pretty girl always be right
in the head?' And having answered 'no', he tried to persuade Carmela that, when it came to making love, reason
was not very important; but, strange as it may seem, he
met an unexpectedly obstinate resistance. She never said
'no' to him outright, perhaps because she failed to understand crearly what he wanted; bu, as if by instinct, whenever his attitude and behaviour—how can I put it?—
whenever his behaviour seemed decisive, she freed her

hands, one after the other, withdrew her arms and crossed them over her breast, and curled herself up, laughing oddly, like children when they think you are trying to tease them, but cannot quite see how, and by laughing try to show they have understood, just to make you tell them. But in those moments, with her face alight and her eyes shining, she never seemed mad, and looked very beautiful, and the reserve and reluctance that gave all her movements a certain tranquillity and grace greatly in creased her already splendid beauty. In fact, the few men who tried to get her were convinced it was hopeless. I was told that one of them, telling the doctor about his vain efforts, exclaimed once: 'I've seen plenty of women with virtue in their brains, in their conscience, in their heart, in whatever you like to think of; but women like this, with virtue in their blood—in their blood, mind you!—I must confess I've never seen.' People said that in every officer she liked she thought she saw the other, the man who had loved and abandoned her. This may not have been true, because if it had been she would have said something about what had followed, but she never said a word. Someone would often question her or refer to it; but she never gave a sign that she understood or remembered anything, she just listened very very carefully and then laughed. When a troop left, she went to see it off at the port, and when the boat drew away, waved her handkerchief; but she never cried, or gave any other sign of grief, but right away made her protests of love to the new officer. She seemed to like the newest officer rather better than all the others.

V

After a while the doctor returned and told this to the lieutenant, who, as he took his leave, exclaimed a second time: 'What a shame! She's so pretty!'

'She is,' said the doctor. 'And what a proud, noble character she must have had!' The lieutenant left. It was late at night, and there was not a soul in the square. His house stood at the opposite side to the café, and he walked across slowly, as if unwillingly. 'She'll be there,' he said to himself, and peered about, stretching forward and bending down to right and left to see if anyone was at the doors; but it was useless, for it was very dark. On, on, ever slower and slower, pausing, circling, looking suspiciously about... 'If I knew a criminal was waiting for me with a knife in his hand,' he thought at one point, 'I think I'd go ahead faster and more boldly;' and he took another ten or twelve resolute steps. 'Ah! There she is.' He could make her out; she was sitting on a step outside the door; it was so dark that he could not see her face. 'What are you doing here?' he asked, going up to her. She did not reply at once, but rose, went close to him, and, laying her hands on his shoulder, said softly, in a tone that sounded as if she were talking as sensibly as possible: 'I was waiting for you... I was asleep.'

'And why were you waiting for me?' the lieutenant asked, lifting her hands off his shoulders; they glided promptly down to embrace his arms. 'Because I want to be with you,' she answered. What a tone! he thought; it really sounded as if she made sense. And, taking a match out of his pocket at once, he struck it and raised it to Carmela's face to see clearly into her eyes. Tiredness—because she had been wandering about all day—and then the short sleep from which she was now waking, had taken

from her face some of its usual excessive, convulsive live-
liness, and had given it a shade of langour and melancholy
instead, so that just then it was truly enchanting, and
seemed anything but mad.

'Oh my dear, my dear!' Carmela burst out as soon as
she saw the lieutenant's face lit up, and putting out an arm
she tried to squeeze his chin between her thumb and first
finger. He took her by the arm; she seized the arm with
which he had pulled her with her free hand, and fastened
her mouth on his hand, kissing and biting it. The lieutenant broke away; ran into the house and shut the door.

'Darling!' Carmela cried again, and then, without
speaking, she sat down on the steps again with her arms
crossed on her knees and her head bent sideways. A little
later she fell asleep.

As soon as he got upstairs and lit the lamp, the lieutenant looked at the back of his right hand and saw faint
traces of eight small teeth, round which still gleamed the
wetness of Carmela's convulsive mouth.

'What sort of love is this!' he said loudly to himself,
and, having lit a cigar, he began to pace about the room
thinking out the timetable for his little troop.

'I'll think about that tomorrow,' he said suddenly, and
thought of something else. He sat down, opened a book,
read a few pages, and then started pacing again; then began reading again, and at last decided to go to bed. He
had already finished undressing when an idea struck him;
he sat thinking a moment, ran to the window, put out
a hand to open it...then he drew it back, shrugged his
shoulders, and went to sleep.

Next morning his orderly, tiptoeing into his room to
wake him when it was time, was surprised to find him
already awake, as he was not in the habit of waking on
his own. Smiling the man said: 'That mad girl's here,
at the door...'

'What's she doing?'

'Nothing; she says she's waiting for the lieutenant.'

The lieutenant made an effort to laugh, and then, watching the man brushing his clothes, he said to himself: 'This fellow's working hard this morning.' When he was dressed he said: 'Look and see if she's still there.' The man opened the window, looked down, and said yes.

'What's she doing?'

'She's playing with some stones.'

'Is she looking up?'

'No.'

'Is she right in front of the door or at the side?'

'At the side.'

'Then I can escape her.' And the lieutenant went down. But the noise his sword made gave him away.

'Good morning, good morning!' the girl cried, running up to him on the stairs; and when she reached him, she knelt down before him, took out a handkerchief, and, grabbing one of his legs just above the arch of the foot with her other hand, she began to dust his spur furiously, murmuring: 'Wait, wait, just a moment, be patient, darling, just a moment—there now, that's it, now it's all right...'

'Carmela!' the lieutenant burst out, and violently jerking his leg free of her small hand he almost ran away, upset and bewildered.

VI

Within a month the doctor and the lieutenant were close friends. The fact that they got on well, that they were the same age, and most of all that they were together from morning till night in a place where there were no other young men of their kind, meant that they grew to know each other intimately in a very short time and were as fond of each other as old friends. But during the month one of them, the lieutenant, had strangely altered his habits. When he was first there he sent to Naples for several large books, and for a couple of weeks did nothing in the evening but read and take notes and have long abstruse discussions with the doctor, which always ended with the words: 'That's enough; I think doctors can't do a thing about it, or anyway precious little.'

'Let's see how you manage it,' the doctor would reply, and then they would separate, to take the discussion up again the following day.

One day, after asking the mayor some questions, the lieutenant sent for the only tailor in the place, then went to the only hat-shop, and then to the only draper, and four days later he walked along the seaside dressed in a suit of Russian cloth, with a large straw hat and a blue tie. That evening when he met him the doctor said:

'Well?'

'Nothing.'

'Not even a sign?'

'Nothing, nothing.'

'It doesn't matter. Keep at it.'

And the lieutenant answered firmly: 'You needn't doubt that.'

The local tax-collector had for years been a singer and could play several instruments. One day the lieutenant went to see him and without preliminaries said: 'Would you be so good as to teach me to play the guitar?' And the tax-collector, starting that day, gave him guitar lessons morning and evening, and he learnt wonderfully well, and soon accompanied his teacher when he sang.

'You must have a fine voice yourself,' the tax-collector said one day. And the lieutenant had in fact an attractive voice. So he began to have singing lessons too, and in a month was singing Sicilian songs to the guitar so gracefully and sweetly that it was a pleasure to hear him. 'We had another officer who played really well too,' the tax-collector would say occasionally. 'There was a song,' he added one day, 'which he was always singing...a song... wait...oh, how well he sang it! It began—he wrote it himself, you know; it began:

> Carmela, at your knee,
> Quietly sitting,
> Gazing into your eyes,
> Kissing your lips,
> I'll spend my days.
> And when my last day comes,
> I'll hide my pale face on your breast,
> And calmly, like a child that's soothed,
> Die there with you.'

'Do say it again.' The tax-collector repeated it. 'Now sing it.' And he sang it.

Another day, after talking at length to the tobacconist near his house, the lieutenant went to the chief of police and said:

'They tell me you're a fine fencer.'

'Me? Oh heavens, it's two years since I even held a sword.'

'Would you like us to have a game occasionally?' 'I should say so!' 'Then let's fix a time.' And they settled one. And from that day on, every morning, everyone crossing the square could hear a great clashing of swords, and thudding of feet, and blows and cries in the lieutenant's house; and it was he and the chief of police fencing.

'You could spare yourself this experiment,' the doctor told the lieutenant one day. 'Has she given no sign?' 'None at all; but it was worth trying. They told me he played with the police chief every morning, and that exactly at that hour, as she didn't enjoy watching, she'd go down to the square...'

'Oh yes,' answered the doctor, 'this was all you needed!'

VII

A month and a half had passed since the new troop arrived. One night the lieutenant sat at table in his house, opposite the doctor, poking the candle flame before him with the point of his pen. 'How is this all going to end?' he said. 'I'll go mad myself, that's what will happen. I'm ashamed of myself, you see; there are times when I feel that everyone's laughing behind my back.'

'Laughing at what?' asked the doctor.

'At what?' the lieutenant repeated, to gain time before answering. 'Laughing at this...this zeal of mine, this pity of mine for that poor wretched girl, and at my useless experiments.'

'Zeal! Pity! People don't laugh at such things,' the doctor said, looking into his friend's eyes. And then: 'Tell me the truth: you're in love with Carmela,' he said.

'I am?' the lieutenant exclaimed heartily, and sat still and questioning, blushing to the roots of his hair.

'Yes, you,' answered the doctor. 'Tell me the truth. Be frank with me; aren't I your only friend here?'

'Yes, you're my friend; but just because I want to be frank with you I don't want to say what's untrue,' said the lieutenant. He was silent a moment, then began to talk fast, sometimes pale, sometimes burning red, stammering, becoming confused and contradicting himself, like a child caught in the act and made to confess its naughtiness.

'In love? Me? With Carmela? With a madwoman? Really, what can you be thinking? How can you have got such an extraordinary thing into your head? The day this happens...you can tell my colonel I've taken leave of my senses and they must shut me up in the madhouse. In love!...you make me laugh. I feel pity for that poor creature, yes; great pity; I don't know what I wouldn't give to see her cured; I'd gladly make any sacrifice for her health; if she were cured I'd be as happy as if she were a member of my own family. This is all true; but it's a very long way from being in love! I'm fond of her, that's true as well, as I think you're fond of her too, because pity always goes with fondness...And then I'm fond of her because they say she's always been a good affectionate girl, and that she really loved her first lover, honestly, with the idea of becoming his wife, and not wanting to hand over her honour before she bore his name. This is virtue, you know, and what is rightly called virtue, and I admire it, you see; and I admire the poor creature all the more because she deserved to be happy instead of wretched. How could I fail to be sorry for her, fond of her? Isn't the very character of her madness an expression of her beautiful soul? I've never heard anything from her lips but sweet modest words, and when she puts her hands on me, when she caresses me, when she kisses my hands, it's certainly the action of a madwoman, but there's nothing in it that passes the limits of decency. Have you ever seen her do an improper action? It's for this reason, I repeat, that I'm so fond of her. Poor girl, abandoned by everyone, reduced to living like a dog. I tell you plainly, I love her from my soul. And this very beauty of hers...because she is beautiful, as beautiful as an angel, you can't deny it; look at her eyes, her mouth...her hands; have you ever looked at her hands? And her hair? All ruffled up as it is she looks like a savage; but it's beautiful hair. And then, dressed otherwise...Well anyway, her very beauty makes me feel the more pity. When I look at her I can't help saying

to myself: 'What a pity one can't love by the eye alone!'
But if she had her wits like everyone else she'd have a
face that would turn the head of any man, you know.
And even now there are moments when, if I didn't know
she was mad, I'd be ready to do something crazy; for
instance, when she looks straight into my eyes and says
'Darling', and in the evening, in the dark, when I don't
see her face, but only hear her talking and telling me she's
been waiting, that she wants to stay with me till morning,
and that I'm her angel...and things like that. At times
like those she doesn't seem to me mad. I look at her,
listen to hear as if she were really herself and really knowing what she was saying, and I assure you that, while
the illusion lasts, my heart pounds...really it does, it
pounds just as if I were in love. And when I call her
by name I feel something, I don't know why, something...
I have an idea that she must answer in a way that will
show me she's suddenly been cured. 'Carmela,' I say to
her. And she says: 'What is it?' 'You're not mad, are
you?' I say. 'Mad?' she answers, and looks at me with
such a surprised air that I'd swear she wasn't. 'Carmela!'
I cry then, suddenly exalted with hope, 'tell me again that
you aren't mad!' Then she looks at me astonished for a
moment and then bursts out laughing. Oh my friend,
believe me, when this happens I could knock my head
against a wall. You know how much I've done to try
and get her reason back; but you don't know all. Almost
every evening I've brought her home, I've talked to her
for hours at a time, I've played and sung the songs her
lover sang, I've tried telling her I was in love with her,
showering caresses on her, pretending to weep and to despair, I've let her do what she likes with me, kiss me,
embrace me, caress me like a child...I've tried doing the
same to her, and you can imagine what I felt in my heart
as I did so; I can't tell whether it was shuddering, or fear,

or shame, or remorse, or all of them together; all I can tell you is that when I kiss her I tremble and grow pale as if I were kissing a corpse. And sometimes I've felt I was making a generous sacrifice and felt almost proud of it, and at other times I've felt I was committing a crime and felt horrified at myself. I have suffered all I can suffer, and it has all been pointless. And the more my despair grows the more fiercely this wretched fever in my heart burns. I can't sleep at night because I know she's crouched outside my door, and, with this idea hammering at me continually, I keep feeling I can hear her tapping on the windows and see her troubled face appear above the window-sill, and her two still, sightless eyes staring at mine. At other times I think I hear her coming up the stairs and jump to sit up in bed, or I feel I hear her roar of laughter coming up from the square, and that laugh feels like an icy hand on my heart, and I haven't the courage to look out of the window at her. And I start reading, and writing, but always with my mind on her, always sad, uneasy, always afraid, I don't myself know why. And when I wonder when this anguished life will end, and how, and what traces of it will remain in my heart, I don't dare to answer myself, I'm afraid of my answer, and I run my hands through my hair like a desperate man. Oh my friend, tell me I'm not going mad myself because I feel my head spinning and I can't bear this life...I can't, I can't bear it.'

And he held his hand out to take the doctor's; the doctor drew his armchair nearer, and, too moved to speak, laid his hands on his friend's shoulders, looked at him a moment, and embraced him.

Suddenly the lieutenant looked up and stared at the doctor with the beginning of a smile on his face. 'Well?' asked the doctor.

'And suppose she becomes sane again?' exclaimed the

lieutenant, his face grown suddenly calm. 'If she went back to what she was, if she got back her reason and her heart was as it was before, if those eyes lost that strange light, that still frightening stare for ever, if that mouth no longer laughed horribly, and one day she said to me seriously: 'I thank you and bless you, you have given me back my life, I love you, I love you...' and if she wept! If I could see her weep, hear her reason, find her always neat and tidy like other girls, see her go back to church to pray, and blush as she used to, and feel one by one as if in a new childhood all the affections for which she has lost all feeling! And if I could say that it was I who had changed her like this, I who had made her live again, I who had given her all the hopes of youth again, I who had restored her to her family and to love...Oh my friend,' he exclaimed, clasping the doctor's hand and gazing at him with swimming eyes, 'I would feel like a god, having created something myself, with two souls and lives, my own and hers; that creature would seem mine, I would think that destiny had sent her to me, and I would take her to my mother as if she were an angel. Oh, I think I'd go mad with joy! Oh, if it were only true! If it were only true!'

And his head fell on his hands as he wept.

'Oh my love!' they heard a cry just then from the square. The lieutenant leapt to his feet and said resolutely to the doctor: 'Leave me.'

The doctor pressed his hand, said: 'Courage!' and left.

The lieutenant stood motionless in the middle of the room awhile, then went to the window, opened it, drew back a step, and stood there for a moment watching the beautiful view that opened out before him. It was a clear, fresh, windless night, an enchanted night. Immediately below lay the lower part of the town: the roofs, the deserted streets, the port, the beach, on which the white moonlight poured so brightly that anyone walking past would have been seen as clearly as in daylight, and then the sea, calm and smooth as oil, and far far away the mountains of Sicily standing out sharply as if they were there close by; and over all a deep silence. 'If I could only enjoy this sweet peace,' he thought, gazing out across the great stretch of sea; and he went tremblingly to the window, and looked down. Carmela was sitting outside the door.

'Carmela!' he called.

'My love?'

'What are you doing there?'

'What am I doing? Why, waiting; you know that. I'm waiting for you to take me upstairs. Don't you want me this evening?'

'I'll come down and open the door.'

Carmela, all happiness, began to clap her hands and jump about.

The door opened, and the lieutenant appeared with the lamp in his hand. Carmela went in, took the lamp from him, passed ahead of him, and began to hurry up the stairs as fast as she could, murmuring, 'Come, come, my poor love,' and then turning to hold out her hand to him. 'Give me your hand, my handsome darling,' she said, and drew him by the hand into the house.

Here the lieutenant sat her down opposite him and with the patience of a saint began to go through all the tests and efforts he had made the previous days, and thought up new ones, trying them out again and again, with more and more care and solicitude and ardour, simu-lating love, hatred, anger, pain, despair, but always in vain. She would look at him and listen carefully and when he had finished ask him, laughing loudly: 'What's the mat-ter?' or else say: 'Poor darling, you make me sad.' And she would take his hands and kiss them with what seemed like the deepest pity.

'Carmela!' he exclaimed at last, trying another test.

'What do you want?'

He made a sign to her to come nearer. She came up to him very slowly, looking lovingly into his eyes, and then all at once she fell on to his breast, put her arms round his neck, and pressed her mouth to his, saying in a stifled voice, 'Darling, darling, darling!' The poor youth, who now no longer knew what to think, put his arm round her waist and, holding her with it, leant over gradually, taking her with him, until, almost without her realizing it, she was lying on the sofa beside the table. Carmela jumped abruptly to her feet, looked grave, seemed to think of something, and then murmured, looking rather upset:

'What are you doing?'

The lieutenant glimpsed a ray of hope and was silent and anxious, watching her.

Carmela stayed serious, or so it seemed, another minute, and then, smiling in a strange way as she had never smiled in the past, she said: 'Are we already married, we two?'

The lieutenant gave a kind of cry, and with his eyes raised to heaven and one fingertip between his lips, pale and convulsive, considered a moment what he should answer. And at that moment Carmela looked up at the wall, saw a big cylindrical hat hanging on a nail, gave a great shout of laughter, took it, put it on her head, and, grinning and calling, began to leap about the room.

'Carmela!' the lieutenant cried sadly.

She grew worse.

'Carmela!' the lieutenant cried again and flung himself towards her. Terrified, Carmela ran down the stairs and was in the square in a moment, still jumping, shouting and roaring with laughter.

The lieutenant went to the window.

'Carmela!' he called once more, exhaustedly, then covered his face with his hands and fell into a chair.

VIII

The following morning, as soon as he got up, he went to the doctor's house. As soon as he saw his friend's red eyes and tortured face the doctor knew he had come to ask for comfort and advice, and, sitting him down to face him, he began to give it. The lieutenant was not listening, and seemed absorbed in his own thoughts. But suddenly he grew calm again and, beating his forehead with the palm of his hand, exclaimed: 'Oh ... and to think I never thought of it before!'

'What?' asked the doctor. The lieutenant didn't answer; he took a sheet of paper and a pen, and began to write furiously. When it was done, he read:

Dear Sir,

Without preambles, military-fashion, I will start by saying that I am commanding the troop at—which you commanded three years ago during July, August, and September. Here I have met a girl of between 18 and 20, called Carmela, who has been mad for two years, and went mad, they say, for love of you. What happened to her after you left the island you should know, and you must know, too, the particular traits of her madness because they tell me someone here wrote to you about it. The girl's unhappy state has aroused in me, since I first saw her, a deep feeling of pity, and I have done all I can to bring her back to reason. I dressed like you, learnt to play and sing like you, copied all the habits of yours I could learn about from people who knew you, I behaved as if I loved her, I talked of you, I pretended to be you myself; but all in vain. You cannot understand how sad it has made me to see my hopes dashed, one after the other. But there is still one thing to try, and it is in your hands; do not deny it to me;

hear what I ask and be generous. They say that one of the best ways of restoring the mad to health is to represent in the minutest detail and with the most scrupulous exactness some important event that preceded their illness, whether it was, or was not, the direct cause of it. I thought that the exact repetition of the scene of your departure might have some effect on Carmela. I have questioned a great many people on the island and have not been able to find out anything except that you left at night, and that before leaving you had supper in your house with the mayor, the chief of police, and several other people. The details of that supper and of your departure are not remembered at all or are remembered hazily. I beg you from my heart, as one who asks for charity that costs the giver little or nothing and may give life and happiness to the receiver—write me all you remember; tell me about the people, the talk, the behaviour, everything. And above all try to tell me the hours, the very minutes, in which the most important incidents followed one another, more or less, and describe things in a clear and orderly way. Do me this great favour I am asking you; do it, I beg you; I shall be grateful to you for the rest of my life. I will not add any more, but trust in the nobility of your heart; I shake your hand in good comradeship and say farewell.

'What d'you think?'

'Wonderful,' answered the doctor, who had been listening with the greatest attention: 'D'you know his name? His regiment? Where he is?'

'The mayor knows it all.'

'And d'you think he'll answer?'

'I think so.'

He answered; he answered with an eight-page letter that gave all the particulars asked for about the people and things concerned, about the conversation, the sequence of events, everything. But there was not a single comment on, or allusion to, his past love, not one word referring to anything but that supper and his departure; not a syllable outside the questions he had been asked; not even a word of pity for Carmela. But from that bare, crude letter it could be seen that, as he wrote, he must have felt remorse very strongly, otherwise he would have made at least a conventional expression of regret and repentance. At the end he would have said at least: 'I hope... etc.' But there was nothing: 'An hour after midnight the steamer left. Greetings.' And then the signature.

IX

'I see!' exclaimed the doctor as soon as his friend had finished reading the letter. 'Now I see why none of the many guests who were at the supper was in a position to tell us any details. I should think not, after drinking all those toasts!'

The same day they both began to get busy for the great test. They both went to see the mayor, the judge, the tax-collector, the chief of police, and all the others, with whom they were now on the friendliest terms; and, with the doctor arguing scientifically, and the lieutenant arguing from the heart, with reasoning, explaining and demonstrating, they managed to make them all understand what it was about, and drum into each one the part he was to play. 'Thank heaven!' exclaimed the lieutenant coming out of the tax-collector's house, the last one they visited, 'the worst is over.' And they sent for Carmela's mother, to whom it was much easier to explain the whole business than it had been to the mayor and the other important people, all of them good folk, undoubtedly, but not very bright when it came to understanding something of the kind.

For some days Carmela had not been feeling well and was almost always at home. The lieutenant and the doctor went to see her. She was sitting on the ground outside the door, leaning back against the wall. When she saw

them she got up, a little less hastily than usual, went up
to the lieutenant and tried, as always, to embrace him,
softly murmuring the usual words.

'Carmela,' he said, 'we have some news for you.'

'News, news, news,' Carmela repeated softly, running
the palm of her hand three times over his cheek.

'I'm leaving tomorrow.'

'You're leaving tomorrow?'

'Yes, Im leaving. I'm going away from here. I'm leaving this place. I'm going away with all my men. I'll get
on the ship, and the ship will take me far, far away.'

And he raised his arm as if to indicate a great distance.

'Far, far ...' murmured Carmela looking in the direction he had indicated. She seemed to think a moment,
then said airily, quite indifferently: 'The steamship ... that
smokes.'

And she tried to embrace him again, calling him by
the usual names.

No good, he thought, shaking his head.

'We must tell her often,' murmured the doctor. 'Wait
till later.'

And they went away, after telling Carmela sternly not
to follow them.

The supper was fixed for the next evening. That same
evening Carmela sat as usual outside the lieutenant's door.
As soon as he came home he brought her upstairs, where
the orderly, as he had told him to, had arranged everything to look as if he were really leaving. Table, chairs,
and sofa were loaded with linen, suits, books, and papers,
all jumbled together, and in the middle of the room were
two open trunks into which the soldier was beginning to
put things.

When she first saw all this disorder, Carmela seemed
slightly surprised, and looked straight at the lieutenant,
smiling.

'Get everything ready for me to leave,' he said.

Carmela looked round the room again, frowning—something she never did. The lieutenant watched her carefully.

'I'm going far away from here, I'm leaving on the steamship.'

'You're leaving on the steamship?'

'Yes... tomorrow evening I'm leaving.'

'Tomorrow evening,' Carmela said mechanically, and when she saw the guitar on a chair, she touched the strings with one finger and played them.

'Don't you mind my leaving? Aren't you sorry you'll never see me again?'

Carmela stared into his eyes, then looked down and hung her head, just as if she were thinking. The lieutenant said no more and began talking to the soldier in a low voice, helping him to fold the clothes.

The girl watched them without moving. After a while, the lieutenant went up to her and said:

'Now go away, Carmela; you've been here long enough; go home, get along now.'

And taking her by the arm he pushed her gently towards the door. She turned and held out her arms to put them round his neck.

'I don't want you to!' said the lieutenant.

Carmela stamped her foot two or three times, groaned, held her arms out again, clasped him round the neck, ran her lips over his cheek without kissing it, as if she were thinking of something else, and then very quietly went away, slowly, without laughing, without turning back, with a face that expressed nothing, like an absentminded man who thinks of a hundred things at once and of nothing.

'What does this mean?' thought the officer. 'Is it a good sign? I hope to God it is! I hope so!'

Next day he stayed indoors and refused even to see

Carmela, although he knew very well that she was sitting at the door as usual. The whole afternoon he spent getting ready for the test that evening. His flat consisted of two rooms and a kitchen. Between the bedroom and the front door was a larger room, whose windows, like those of the bedroom, looked out over the square. In this room he had the supper table laid. His neighbour, the innkeeper, lent him a big dining-room table, came himself to cook the few dishes needed, laid the table as luxuriously as he could manage, and then served the meal himself, as he had done three years ago for the other officer. Towards nine in the evening the doctor arrived, the first of the guests. 'She's here, down below,' he told his friend as he came in. 'She complained that she hadn't yet seen you. I asked her if she felt well, and staring straight into my eyes, she said: "Steamship," without laughing. Well! Who can tell what goes on in her head? Only God. Oh, let's have a look at this wonderful spread!'

And when they had both glanced at the table, they began working out between them the best way of performing this play—or rather this drama, for it was a drama, and a serious one. When they were agreed, the doctor said: 'Have they all learnt their parts?' And the lieutenant said he hoped so.

Shortly before ten o'clock they heard a clatter of footsteps and a confused sound of voices below af the door. 'Here they are!' said the doctor, looking out of the window. 'It's really them.'

The soldier went down to open the door. The doctor lit the four candles on their holders on the table.

'How my heart's pounding!' said the lieutenant.

'Courage,' said his friend, squeezing his arm.

Just then they heard Carmela exclaim: 'I'm going on the steamship too!' and clap her hands.

'Courage!' the doctor repeated hurriedly in his friend's

ear. 'Did you hear that? She's beginning to get the idea
into her head; it's a good sign. Cheer up, here are the
guests.'

The door opened and there appeared, smiling and bowing, the mayor, the judge, and all the others who met
in the café. While the lieutenant greeted and thanked first
one and then another, the doctor said a word in the ear of
the orderly who was standing motionless in a corner, and
the man disappeared. After a minute, without anyone noticing, he came back with Carmela, and both of them, gliding
along on the wall on tiptoe, slipped into the next room.

'Let's sit down,' said the lieutenant.

They all sat down. The noise of the chairs scraping and
the long, contented, gluttonous 'Ah' as they sat down at
the table, drowned the slight noise the orderly made holding back Carmela who, exclaiming 'I haven't seen him
for a whole day!', opened the door and tried to fling herself
on the lieutenant. The orderly stopped her, put a chair
near the door, and sat her down; then he opened the
shutters in the middle of the door just enough to leave
a small space open, where she put her face and remained
watching. None of the guests turned in her direction, no
one looked at her either then or later, and Carmela made
no other movement.

Gradually the confused noise grew louder—of cutlery
and glasses and plates, of laughter and discordant voices
all trying to talk more loudly than the rest. All of them,
including the doctor and the lieutenant, ate heartily and
drank toasts gaily. First they praised the discipline, good
behaviour, courage and courtesy of the troop; then they
gave exaggerated compliments to the food and wine; then
they talked of the weather, which was beautiful—it was
a magical night—and of the journey, which would be
delightful; then they talked politics, then about the soldiers again, then again about the journey, and so on, and

so on, talking ever louder, emptying their glasses ever faster, till their faces were red and their eyes sparkled, and the movement of their lips grew awkward and the words tumbled out confusedly. Almost without realizing, each one of them was taking his part seriously and playing it perfectly. But the more the others forgot the reason for their presence and grew wild with gaiety, the harder the lieutenant felt his heart beating, and the more clearly his face showed the fury of his soul. But no one noticed, apart from the doctor, who kept telling him softly to bear up, and kept an eye on Carmela. She sat still and intent all the time, her face peering between the shutters. The orderly, seizing his opportunity, had left.

At one point three soldiers came into the room, each picked up one of the three trunks that stood in a corner, and went away. Carmela watched all their movements until they disappeared, and then went back to looking at the table.

The doctor murmured a word in the mayor's ear.

'A toast!' the mayor exclaimed at once, rising to his feet with difficulty and holding out his glass. 'A toast to the health of this brave lieutenant commanding the fine troop that's leaving the island and bequeaths it for ever and perpetually a beautiful, imperishable, immortal memory of the fine troop commanded by this brave lieutenant...'

He thought a moment and then said resolutely:

'Hurrah for the lieutenant who's leaving!'

And all the others, clinking their glasses noisily and spilling wine on the table, cried: 'Hurrah!'

The mayor fell back heavily into his chair.

Others made toasts of a similar kind, and then they all began at the beginning again, talking at once about the soldiers, politics, wine, and the journey.

'Sing us a song!' the doctor cried to the tax-collector.

All the others joined in asking him. The tax-collector made a face, excused himself, made them beg a little longer, then smiled, coughed, picked up the guitar, and sang two or three verses. The other guests, starting to talk again, interrupted him. 'Now it's my turn,' said the lieutenant, and they were all silent. He took the guitar, tuned it, rose to his feet pretending to sway, and began... He was pale and his hands shook as if with fever; all the same he sang his song with a sweetness and tenderness that were really enchanting.

> 'Carmela, at your knee,
> Quietly sitting,
> Gazing into your eyes,
> Kissing your lips,
> I'll spend my days.'

Carmela was listening, growing more and more intent, frowning harder and harder like someone absorbed in thought.

'Fine! Beautiful! You sing like an angel!' all the guests cried together. The lieutenant went on:

> 'And when my last day comes,
> I'll hide my pale face on your breast
> And calmly, like a child that's soothed,
> Die there with you.'

The words, the music, everything was just as it had been that other night. 'Fine! Beautiful!' repeated the guests. The lieutenant fell into his chair as if exhausted; they all started shouting again; Carmela was as still as a statue and her eyes were dilated, staring at the lieutenant's face; the doctor looked at her out of the corner of his eye.

'Silence!' cried the lieutenant. They were all silent, and, as the window was open, they could hear below in

the square the gay music of flutes and violins and a murmur that sounded like a crowd. Ten or twelve musicians
from the town were there, surrounded by most of the
townsfolk who really believed the troop was leaving.

Carmela shook herself and looked towards the window.
Slowly her face began to grow alive, and her large eyes
moved restlessly from the window to the lieutenant, from
him to the guests, from them to the window, as if she
wanted to listen to the music properly but at the same
time not lose a single movement that all those people
were making.

When the music stopped, most of the people crowding
the square and clapped their hands as they had done on
the previous occasion three years before.

At that moment the orderly hurried up and announced
in a loud voice:

'The ship awaits you, sir.'

The lieutenant rose and said:

'We must go.'

Very slowly Carmela rose, still staring at him and
pushing her chair slowly away.

All the guests rose and gathered round the lieutenant.
At the same moment Carmela's mother appeared, slipped
unseen into the next room, embraced her daughter and
said lovingly: 'Be brave; he'll be back in two months.'

Carmela looked at her mother, slowly freed herself from
her embrace, and without a word, turning her head very
slowly, fixed her eyes on the lieutenant.

All the guests were shaking hands with him, murmuring confused thanks, good wishes, and farewells; he
put on his sword and his cap, and slung a bag for the
journey over his shoulder.

As he did all this, Carmela, without realizing, had opened the door and taken a step forward; she was looking
wild-eyed from the lieutenant to the guests, to the orderly,

to her mother beside her, rubbing her forehead with both hands and ruffling up her hair, sighing breathlessly and trembling convulsively all over.

The music broke out again in the square and there was another burst of applause...

'Come on!' the lieutenant said resolutely, and made ready to go.

A high, desperate, rending scream broke from Carmela's breast. At the same moment she leapt on to the lieutenant, clasped him with superhuman strength round the waist, and started to kiss him furiously on the face, neck, and chest, wherever she could, sobbing, crying, groaning, patting his shoulders, his arms, his head, as a mother would do to a child saved from the waves where a little earlier she had seen him hold out his arms and call for help. After a few minutes the poor girl fell senseless on the floor, her head at the lieutenant's feet.

She was saved.

The lieutenant flung himself in the doctor's arms, already open and waiting for him. Carmela's mother leant down to kiss her daughter and bathe her with tears. All the guests looked up to thank heaven. The music continued to play.

* * *

Four months later, on a beautiful September night, so light that it seemed like day, the ship which had left Tunis that evening and had stopped, as always, at the port of our little town, was rapidly approaching the coast of Sicily. The water was so calm that the ship seemed not to move. The passengers were all up on deck gazing in silence at the clear sky and moonlit sea.

At some distance from the others, and looking at the wake of the ship, were a young man and woman leaning against the rail, their arms tightly interlaced, their heads almost touching. Far away they could still dimly see the island they had left. They watched it for a long time, standing there motionless, until the woman, raising her head, murmured:

'And yet, you know, I'm sad to leave my poor town, where I suffered so much, where I saw you for the first time, where you gave me back my life.'

And she leant her head on the man's shoulder.

'We'll go back one day!' he said, making her turn her head slightly to look into her eyes.

'And will we go back to your house?' she asked gently.

'Yes.'

'And will we sit in the evening and talk at that window where you used to call me?'

'Yes.'

'And will you play your guitar again, and will you sing me that song again?'

'Yes, yes.'

'Sing it now!' Carmela exclaimed suddenly. 'Sing it softly.'

And the lieutenant put his mouth to her ear:

> 'Carmela, at your knee,
> Quietly sitting...'

Carmela flung her arms round her husband's neck and burst into tears.

'My poor, good child!' he said, holding her fast against his breast. 'Here, here, on my heart, always here.'

The poor girl shook herself suddenly, looked round, looked at the sea, at the island, at her husband, and exclaimed:

'Oh, it's a dream!'

The young man broke in:

'No, my angel, it's awakening!'

And the ship went on, seemingly borne by the wind,

SALVATORE DI GIACOMO

Di Giacomo was born in Naples in 1864 and died there in 1934. Most Italian critics acknowledge him to be the best dialect poet since Belli. One or two of his poems are still heard all over the world as they are the lyrics of some of the most famous Neapolitan songs, such a *A finistrella*. Both his poems and his short stories are about the lives of the poor of the Neapolitan slums and seaboard. But though his subjects were close to those of the *veristi*, he seems to have nothing to demonstrate or avenge; he sees with the lyric eye of a painter or poet. The visual element is always strong in his work, particularly in short stories such as *Assunta Spina* or the tale translated here.

Di Giacomo has been little translated. The plot of *Pasquino* bears strong similarities to that of *Cavalleria Rusticana*: nevertheless between them lies all the difference between the Neapolitan and the Sicilian character. Mrs Constance Hutton, who lived in Naples for over thirty years until her death there in 1940, was Di Giacomo's only close English friend, and translated some of his short stories and other works. Her version of his plays *Mese Mariano* was given in London in 1913. The present translation has been found among her papers and is printed for the first time.

A. C.

PASQUINO

(FROM 'SCENES OF NEAPOLITAN LIFE')

Ce n'est pas un conte.
Diderot.

SALVATORE DI GIACOMO
Translated by Constance Hutton

Opposite the little station of the Cumean railway on the Corso Vittorio Emanuele stands a low grey house in a garden. A long wide terrace runs the length of the house at the rear, beneath which lies the Bay in all its rapturous glory of colouring. A place of peace and of pause; yet here only a few years ago, at the sign of the 'Pasta Fina', was the rendez-vous of some of the most desperate and determined members of the Camorra[1]; here knife-thrusts have been given and shots have been fired; and in the garden, near the white rose tree, a man was done to death by order of one of the '*Camorristi*' convicted of the Cuocolo murder only last year.

Some assert that on summer nights, when the moon is high, a cry of anguish may be heard, a slim figure seen to stagger and fall...

* * *

Of all the celebrated *Camorristi* who frequented Gennarino's *bisca* or gambling den, Pasquino was the most renowned. Had Pasquino said 'Kill yourself', Gennarino the Calabrian would have died to please him. For this giant, who loved no friend and feared no foe, worshipped with sublime devotion that vagabond and audacious boy, that little Don Giovanni of fallen women, that slim delicate

[1] The *Camorra* is the equivalent, on the South Italian mainland, of the Sicilian *Mafia*.

stripling with the hand of steel and the heart of stone. Though a mere youth, Pasquino was already famous for his unrivalled courage and his daring deeds, deeds for which the authorities had prudently enrolled him amongst the specially supervised. Most times the eel slipped through the fingers of the police, disappearing for two or three weeks but reappearing again sometimes to undergo a short patient imprisonment, before starting all over again and then returning once more to the prison of S. Francisco or the Carmine. Scarcely anyone knew his real name, nor had his nick-name been earned by any such talent as that of the famous Roman Pasquino of the satires for, though witty and sharp-tongued, Pasquino was far from having any literary acquirements of even the most popular description. The name simply suited the graceful, agile youth with little fair moustaches and prettily curved lips, for nowhere as in Naples does a nick-name so accurately describe the person on whom it is bestowed. This Pasquino was a handsome lad with small, well-shaped features and aristocratic hands, on which he bestowed as much care as on his white regular teeth. While all the men who were *malamente*, i.e. of the *mala vita*, smoked the coarse cheroot known as a Napoletano, Pasquino only smoked cigarettes; he never sang *a figliola* or a *fronne, e limone,* the traditional songs of the Camorra, nor did he even wear his hat cocked at an impossible angle as is their wont. When a game of billiards began he would draw out his silver tobacco-case, roll a cigarette with the dainty skill of a Sevillian tobacco-girl, then spring with feline grace on the edge of the table and light it from the lamp swinging above while he sang in a sweet high tenor:

> *Noi ti mirammo insieme*
> *Nel dì dell'ultim'ora?*
> *Stella del nostro amore!*

And when he, the only one unmoved by his superior skill, had won a game, he would pocket his winnings indifferently and light another cigarette, still humming *Noi ti mirammo insieme*; while his silver tobacco-box, with the nude figure painted inside the lid, passed from hand to hand amongst his admirers, who gazed with wonder and envy on this bad edition of a Fortunio who could afford to have so artistic a reproduction of his *innamorata*.

* * *

Such was Pasquino of the *bisca*. There he was thought to have a good heart, a pretty mistress and money in his purse. But to know his true life which began at ten o'clock at night and end at day-break, would have meant following him in his nocturnal peregrinations, and belonging to the flying squadron of police, and entering the house of ill fame where he lorded it as the feared and adored master of the wretched beings who frequented it.

On winter nights when cold and rain have cleared the streets, on lovely summer evenings when the full moon lights the deserted squares and penetrates the lurid *vicoli*, in nocturnal hours when every honest Neapolitan sleeps, then the *others* wake! To realize some of the tragic romances, the sordid dramas enacted then, one would have to be Don Cleofa y Zambullo* astride limping Asmodeus and pass over the roofs of some of the houses in the of Pendino or Porto quarters. Occasionally the police appear

---

* In *El diablo Cojuelo*, by Luis Velez de Guevara, 1579-1644, Don Cleofa, fleeing over the rooftops from the police, finds himself in an astrologer's room where he releases from a retort the devil Cojuelo, who can lift roofs and show him what is going on below them. In *Le Diable boîteux*, the adaptation by Lesage, 1668-1747, the devil is named Asmodée.

Edd.

to surprise Love armed—armed, too, without a license; proud indeed are they if they catch some grandee of the Camorra, but mostly they are doomed to disappointment, for those women never betray their lovers, no Samson of the *mala vita* has ever known a Delilah. The sacrifices of any one of these women for her man are great indeed. She belongs to him body and soul, whether he be kind or cruel, handsome or plain, but on one condition: he must be *guapo*, ready to fight on the slightest provocation, nay, eager to pick a quarrel with or without a protest. And she loves the desperado devotedly, passionately, violently. Morally lost though she may be for him, she will deprive herself of all she possesses and values materially: of her rings and ear-rings and her crêpe shawl, of her household goods, and even of her little necklace of pearls vowed to the Madonna of the Carmine in gratitude for some favour conceded. With the price of her own dishonour she will buy him a revolver so that he may learn to avenge himself and *dichiararsi* (challenge to a duel), in the name of the Lord! And so deep, so sanguinary, are the obligations which bind him that they form a chain—a love chain!—the first link of which is welded on the fourth or fifth floor of some lurid house in a squalid street—a house in which maybe the rotten stairs have more than once run blood, blood which has flowed unheeded past the faded image of the patron saint and the wan Madonna fitfully illumined by the flickering lamp swaying before it; and the last link is forged by the iron bar of the prison of San Francesco or the Carmine, whence in the silence of night may often be heard the mournful sound of prisoners' lullabies.

With these chains are bound all the men who carry arms without a license, all the smooth-faced patrons of the lowest order of billiard-saloons and gambling-dens, all the frequentors of the fourth-rate theatres and of the criminal courts of Castel Capuano. And hopelessly bound with these chains are all the lost women, dragged by them to prison and hospital and death, these poor victims of Love, for whom Love itself becomes a persecution and a martyrdom. Pasquino's mistress was one of these. They called her Fasulella and she adored him.

* * *

Towards the close of a glorious summer evening Pasquino slouched into a bar in Via Toledo and called for a vermouth. He tossed it off and flung down three coins.

'Have you seen *O russo?*'* he asked the barman, whom he knew and who knew him.

'He's not been here.'

'Not been here?'

'No'

'Sure?'

'I tell you I've not seen him.'

'Right. I'll find him myself. If he comes in here, tell him I'm looking for him.' And he turned on his heel and went out. Half an hour later a cab rattled full speed down Corso Vittorio Emanuele. In it were Pasquino and Viscardi, *'O russo.* The former had found his friend and was taking him to a *dichiaramento* as though it were a banquet. The rendez-vous was at the 'Pasta Fina', famed for its *spaghetti* with shell-fish sauce and its roast capons. The night was serenely beautiful. Far below, Naples glittered as in a garland of light, and a murmur, the mysterious murmur of night, rose to the silent and deserted Corso. The cab had almost reached its destination where, just before it stopped at the 'Pasta Fina', Pasquino saw a motionless figure inside the gate and called out: 'Halt'.

* (Neapolitan dialect for red-i.e. red-haired man).

He and *'O russo* sprang out and approached some men awaiting them. A few brief words, then suddenly a shot rang out and Pasquino fell. The bullet had hit him full in the chest, passing straight through a lung. In a second his adversary was upon him, raised a loaded stick, and dealt him a ferocious blow on the head. Pasquino, the death rattle in his throat, shrieked '*Mamma mia*! Alfonso! Alfonso! Don't kill me for love of the Madonna!'

But Alfonso's companion urged menacingly:

'Let him have it! Let the girlish little thing have it!'

A second later three men fled and both cabs vanished. Pasquino lay there alone, motionless, supine in the middle of the path, blood forming a little pool as it flowed on and on from the ghastly wound from that blow. The handsome lad looked pitiful as he lay there in the soft beauty of the summer evening, his wide eyes staring sightless at the cold full moon. Yet, tragic and horrible as the sight was, there was something poetic about it too...

RENATO FUCINI

Fucini was Tuscan born and bred; he was born at Monte rotondo near Pisa in 1843 and died at Empoli in 1922. Almost unknown outside Italy he was one of the most evocative and mordant of writers on the Tuscan countryside. He is spontaneous, modest, and limited, and has an intimate quality reminiscent of the nineteenth century school of Tuscan painters—the *Macchiaioli*. His world of Tuscan peasantry is varied and lively; it can be lonely, but is usually friendly and seldom sad. He avoids the savage or the tragic, and his tales are still widely read in Italy, particularly by children.

His prose presents some difficulties to the translator, as its effect is partly due to scattered scraps of Tuscan dialect which give the originals added spontaneity.

Books by Fucini about Tuscany and the Maremma are: *Le veglie di Neri* (1884); *All'aria aperta* (1887) from which the present stories are taken; *Nella campagna toscana* (1908); and also reminiscences and travels.

A. C.

THE WITCH

RENATO FUCINI

Translated by Neville Rogers

The air was chilly, there was a fine steady drizzle, and, at every gust of wind, the trees along the road sent a shower of heavy raindrops and yellow leaves cascading down upon its muddy surface.

An old woman of seventy years or more came trudging along, accompanied by her little grandson, aged about nine. They huddled close together under the shelter of the green oilskin umbrella they were sharing, and with their already filthy shoes, went stumbling into every miry puddle, she because she was unable to see the puddles, and he because he revelled in them.

'Nice day for a stroll, Granny Pelagia!'

'I meant to get over to the Capannacce,* with God's help. I'm afraid I shan't make it, though. But who might you be?'

'Toh! Don't you know me? It's Maria del Tognetti!'

'Yes, yes! Of course. I can tell you now, by your voice,—Maria del Tognetti! Sorry, Maria! I really did'nt recognize you. I'm pretty near half blind. Then, with my apron over my head like this, if you hadn't come up and spoken to me I honestly wouldn't have spotted you. I'm going to the Capannacce, to poor Veronica's. Her baby's ill, and nearly dying, so they tell me. The other people who've been caught in this awful weather today are all thinking about getting home—and I go and take

---

* A group of farm-buildings, divided into the accommodation variously required by peasants, live stock, produce, and equipment.

it into my head to go plodding right up there! But I'm afraid I simply shan't last out. You've no news, I suppose, Maria? Could it be true, what they're saying,—that the little boy's had a spell put on him?'

'So they *say*. But then...'

'Lord, Lord, what evil folks there are around in the world! Oh dear, oh deary me! Honestly, Maria, I can't budge another inch! However, seeing as I started out I do want to try and see if I can't get there *somehow*. And you, Maria,—all of you all right?'

'Mustn't grumble. But, oh, Pelagia dear, if you only knew just what I have to put up with from that wretched lad of mine. Smoking and boozing seem to be just about all he's good for!'

'But why don't you just tell him, straight out...?'

'Pelagia, dear...!'

The two women stopped in the middle of the road and, though the rain was now falling more heavily than ever, they launched into a most heated discussion. Cecchetto, taking advantage of the brief halt, darted away from under the umbrella and applied himself to the construction of mud dams across the little streamlets that were running down the cart-tracks along the road.

Maria particularly wanted to get home early, so she hurried off, after gently rebuking the foolhardy old woman, and wishing her God's reward for her charitable act. Cecchetto, like a half-drowned chick, returned to the shelter of the umbrella and on they went, his granny leaning on his shoulder.

On the covered veranda of one of the four buildings of the Capannacce a group of peasants were standing around a young woman who was sitting there with a baby on her knee as frail and as white as a corpse. It writhed with pain and its thin moaning was so faint as to be hardly heard.

With rough tenderness the mother tried to soothe it. Every now and then she turned to glare ferociously at the two roads which had their junction at the threshing-floor. The men around her, grim and silent, were glaring likewise across the fields, and in their eyes too was evil.

Underlying a calm resignation that half-masked the sorrow in their faces gleamed a savage fury that was horrifying to look upon.

What kind of storm was about to burst in their poor minds?

For some time now the baby, which, to start with, had seemed the very picture of health and beauty, had begun to wither before their eyes. For form's sake the parish doctor was called in, but after three of four visits he realized that they thought him a lunatic because he had spoken of 'iron tonics' and 'sea air.' So he thought he might as well spare his horse the journey, and they had seen no more of him.

Meanwhile the baby went from bad to worse. All the gossips of the neighbourhood had been consulted without the slightest result; then they had had him blessed by the priest and his worms exorcized, but all to no effect, and by now there wasn't a soul in the family who knew a saint to turn to.

Among the peasants in that block of cottages who enjoyed the highest reputation for wisdom and experience a kind of council meeting was held, and it was resolved to call in the witch Doctor.

'Ooh! Now I *am* glad!' exclaimed a wrinkled old dame, grandmother of the poor child, when the men returned home and gave her the cheering news. 'Now I *am* glad! And may God and the Most Blessed Virgin be with us, now we've done something for the poor bairn at last!' And, conceiving him to be as good as cured, she rushed over to kiss her little grandson, who tried to avoid her caresses by peevishly twisting away and hiding his face.

The witch Doctor duly came. At long last he appeared, to be greeted and caressed like a minister of Providence,— Professor Baronto, cattle-dealer, retired carter and, in his spare time, benefactor of suffering humanity.

Bidding them show him the baby he peered at it closely for a few minutes, while his lips made incomprehensible mumbling motions; then, with huge hands, black and gnarled, he carved out some sort of cabbalistic signs in the air, and, with a cheerful wave to the peasants, whose eyes, now big with wonderment, were all fixed intently upon his own little foxy ones, he announced that a moment or two of hard thinking would be required. He asked for an olive twig that had been blessed by the priest, lit his pipe, and ensconced himself with his meditations in a corner of the kitchen.

In the imagination of the men of the household the child was already cured and fit for work: already they could see him as a fine upstanding youth, driving the May furrows and singing away under the August sun. They passed him from arm to arm, while their broad smiling mouths planted kisses on the tired eyelids.

The women bustled nervously about and, having laid the babe in its cradle, lit a roaring fire and began to dry Baronto's muddy yellow plaid, which they handled as carefully as if it had been a holy relic.

His meditations over, Baronto now rose to his feet with the air of a man inspired, and demanded of the lady of the house a white soup-plate, a jar of pure olive oil, and a hen's feather.

Everything was made ready with feverish haste and care, and duly presented to Baronto who rolled up his sleeves, took up his weird ingredients, and retired to another room, after commanding silence and bidding them leave him undisturbed while he worked out a spell to save the poor little innocent creature.

The peasants gathered round the fire, whispering softly, and anxiously rushing across to put their hands over the child's mouth every time it seems to be trying to emit some feeble cry.

* * *

Still nearly a kilometre away from the Capannacce old Pelagia was dragging herself painfully through the rain. On she went, sometimes stopping to tell the beads of her rosary, sometimes trying to catch up with her Cecchetto— on up the last stretch of the steep and dirty road.

* * *

'Here he is! Here he is!' The peasants had heard Baronto's iron-shod feet scraping their way to the door. Pale and open-mouthed, knowing the life of their little one now hung on his verdict, they all turned towards him.

Baronto was smiling as he reappeared in the kitchen. He made a sign to the peasants at which they jumped up and ran over to him, crowding round him and watching his face, breathlessly.

'The little fellow's going to be all right.'

'Ah!'

Their howl of joy was like the the howl of beasts. The two women burst into tears and dropped on their knees by the cradle, where the baby, already perhaps in its last agony, lay gasping, its eyes closed, lacking the breath to sob.

'The little fellow's going to be all right!' repeated Baronto. He pointed to the soup-plate, the bottom of which was covered by the oil.

'D'you see those seven little bubbles in the form of a

cross?   There's no mistaking them.   Your little fellow has
the Evil Eye upon him, and it's working right through
his veins.'

'Ugh!   Ugh!'

'Your innocent angel, they've put a spell on him!'

'Ugh!   Ugh!'

'Oh, the brutes!'

'I thought as much!'

'The ruffians!'

'Didn't I tell you so?'

'God!   God!   God!'

The men writhed with a savage fury.   Shaking their
fists they strode round the room, their eyes starting from
their heads and gleaming like the eyes of wild beasts,—for
all the world as if they had there, in front of them, all
ready to be set upon and pulled to pieces, the murdering
fiend who had destroyed the Lord's little angel—who had
injected poison into his veins.

'Quiet, quiet!   Just listen to me,' went on Baronto,
speaking in solemn, mellow tones.   'The little fellow is
going to be all right; but there must be judgement, firmness—and no talking.   Those seven little bubbles in the
shape of a cross tell me likewise who it is who has cast
the spell.   But the name of that person it is not for me
to tell you...'

'Tell us!   Tell us!' screamed the peasants, and the anger was blazing out of their eyes.

'I would if I could, but I cannot.   The magic art,
which I practise out of love for my brethren in Christ,
has laid laws upon me that I dare not disobey, lest the
Seven Lamps of the Apocalypse be burning my soul
through all eternity.   Those laws have I sworn to obey,
and, here before you, do I take the oath once more.'

He closed his eyes and stretched out sinewy arms, bristling with long black hairs.

The peasants were watching him with awe.

'Here,' said Baronto, pontifically and frowning in the direction of the cradle, 'here is the solemn truth! The first person who, after the Credo Bell today, shall chance to step on to the threshing-floor, that shall be the person who has cast the spell on your little fellow, and that person alone can cure him...always provided that you can make him promise his own soul to the Demon!'

Half an hour later, with a bottle of Aleatico under his arm, a ten-lire note in his pocket, and an excellent meal in his belly, Baronto made his departure, followed by the blessings of all those good people.

* * *

It was now some twenty minutes since the Credo Bell had rung and nobody seemed to appear on the threshing-floor. Grim-faced and silent, the peasants, gathered on the covered veranda of the building were keeping a look-out across the fields and down the roads, and there was evil in their eyes.

* * *

Old Pelagia had had no end of a struggle but there she was at last. As soon as ever she reached the last turning, which brought her in sight of the house and the veranda with its group of waiting peasants, she sighed her thanks to God and sat down for a minute or two's rest on the dirty rail of a bridge across a ditch. Cecchetto seized his opportunity to dash off and start shying stones at a cluster of chestnuts which were swinging in the wind, right up at the top of a tree, half hidden in the foliage.

As soon as she got back her breath the old woman went

on again, and in a minute or two she arrived, tired out, on the threshing-floor of the Capannacce.

'The witch! The witch!' hissed the peasants, gripping each other's hands, ice-cold with hatred.

The two women left the veranda and went indoors, paying no attention to old Pelagia, who was calling them by name. Meanwhile the men, with scarcely a word passed between them, had become a compact mass that moved down the steps and came grimly towards her.

Cecchetto was some way back, still shying stones at his chestnut tree.

'Isodoro,' called the old lady, smiling as she recognized the head of the household among the men confronting her; 'Isodoro! That little fellow of yours...God bless him and keep you! Can it be true? Oh, poor Veronica! I simply couldn't walk another step...but I just had to come and see for myself...'

Suddenly she shrank back.

'What's the matter? What's making you look so wild? Has something dreadful happened?'

The men pressed round her threateningly, while, being without any clue to the situation beyond an intuition of its seriousness, the old woman looked with terror into their scowling faces.

Seizing her by the arm and stammering out the words, as if they had got tangled in his throat, the head of the household was the first to speak:

'Pelagia...that little fellow is dying. He's all we have, Pelagia. That little fellow is in your hands...you know that...you know it better than we do, Pelagia! A promise, Pelagia...give us a promise and you shall go home alive!'

'A promise!' roared the others, and she felt their hot breath on her face.

'Holy Virgin!' she cried.

'Respect the name of Our Lady, Pelagia! A promise...'

'But what's happened? I just don't understand... Ah, you'll break my arm!' screamed the poor old soul, looking pitifully at them, her eyes streaming with tears. Then, hoping for protection from her friends among the women, she called their names:

'Veronica! Nunziata!... They don't answer.'

'The promise, Pelagia, the promise!'

'But what have I got to promise you?'

'You know that, better than we do!'

'As God sees into my heart, I don't.'

'Ah, so you don't know, eh?'

'No I don't. I swear to you by the life of my little fellow here... Oh, where's he got to? Cecchetto, Cecchetto...'

'Ah, so you don't know, eh? You wicked old monster! What harm did we ever do to you, you murdering old beast, that you should do a thing like that to us? Promise your soul to the Evil One, you foul witch; save our little dying boy; and if words won't do...'

'No, no, you're Christian people...'

'At her! At her!'

'A poor old woman, your friend!... Saints above! O God! O God!'

'At her, the devil's bitch! At her! At her!'

There followed the dull thudding sound of blows and kicks falling on the poor old body.

'Cecchetto! Cecchetto! Oh, you're killing me! O God, God! O Most Holy Virgin! I commend my soul to you!'

'Put her in the oven! Put her in the oven! Make it hot!' screamed the men, whom her entreaties had only served to madden the more. And ten evil hands redoubled their ferocity against the unhappy old creature; she was on her knees now, and her voice was getting fainter and fainter, but she went on commending her soul to God and

calling for her small grandson till she fell senseless to the
ground amid the howling maniacs.

The women emerged on to the veranda cheering on
their menfolk and yelling:

'Finish her! Finish her! Hit her hard, the sorceress,
the damned soul! Cut the heart out of her!'

From every window in the buildings came screams of
uncontrollable savagery, curses, and the brandishing of
fists. And, in the midst of this devil's work, along came
poor little Cecchetto and saw his grandmother lying there
with her clothes all ripped off her and her face and eyes
little more than a bloody, lifeless mask. Screaming with
panic he hurled himself on the group of peasants:

'Don't kill her! She's my Granny! Don't kill her!'
He kicked, bit, and scratched at the ruffians, but they
were quite oblivious of him. They had lifted the old woman from the ground and were carrying her towards the
building, crying:

'Put her in the oven! Burn the witch! Make it hot
for her!'

The rain was falling in torrents. Mad with fright Cecchetto ran round and round the threshing-floor, his eyes
watching the windows and the street in turn, in case help
might be forthcoming. But from the windows nothing
was to be heard or seen but ferocious shouts and faces;
from across the fields and down the roads came the howling
of the wind and the gurgling roar of the water in the
over-swollen ditches.

Suddenly the boy gave a piercing yell. He paused a
moment to make quite sure, then he was off like the wind
down one of the roads. 'The police!' he shouted, 'the
police.'

Two Carabinieri, caught by the bad weather in the
open country, were quickening their steps towards the Capannacce to seek shelter from the sudden downpour.

THE MONUMENT

RENATO FUCINI

Translated by Neville Rogers

'The issue, dear Signore Annibale, is a simple one, perfectly simple. It's up to us to put this matter right; and if we don't do so, we shan't be able to put our heads outside our doors without feeling ashamed to admit that we're dwellers on this rich, productive, and splendid soil!'

'That's the truth, the Gospel truth!'

'Why, a wretched little place of barely two thousand five hundred inhabitants, a starveling, beggarly little spot like Nebibano, *they* have to have a grand marble statue in commemoration of a distinguished citizen of theirs—distinguished, I ask you! And we, who number three thousand one hundred and six souls, haven't as much as a single blue-grey slab to show a stranger who may happen to be passing our way!'

'It's disgraceful!'

'We shall continue to be objects of scorn, and rightly so. We'll be called 'uncivilized', and none of us'll be able to deny it. They'll point us out as people who don't appreciate their great men, and we simply shan't have a leg to stand on. They'll call us, my dear Signor Annibale, just about everything under the sun and we'll be obliged to put up with it because...'

'As for such aspects as glory, honour, and all that stuff we hear about from poets and the gentry, I myself, dear Falsetti, don't care two hoots about them. Take 'em for granted, and that's that. What I'm thinking about, however, is something entirely different: I'm thinking of the practical value that the thing might have for this beloved place of ours. I'm thinking...But am I wrong? Just think, my dear sir,—supposing we *did* get to the point of putting up in one of our piazzas a monument that caused a stir, can't *you* see the advantage that hotels, restaurants, and cafés could get out of it?

'The cab-drivers too?'

'The cab-drivers, of course.'

In the burning zeal of their local patriotism acquaintance passed into a conviction of friendship, and thence their discussion further warmed to a point of affectionate unanimity at which it was decided first that, like other places, their town should have a statue and, secondly, that that statue should be an equestrian one.

'Yes, gentlemen, equestrian!' cried Signor Annibale, looking fearfully and threateningly across to the Nebbiano Hills. 'Yes, gentlemen, equestrian! And all those who aren't friends of ours let 'em just go on envying us till they bust!'

'Equestrian or nothing! We'll have what we want!'

'Life-size or bigger?

'Heavens, a lot bigger than life-size!'

'Twice as big?'

'That's nothing much.'

'Four times?'

'Agreed!'

'Fine.'

'My hand on that!'

'Here's mine.'

In the heat of their discussion, they had not noticed Signor Leopoldo who, having followed close behind them and taken in every word, was loudly enthusiastic, and solemnly promised that, if they opened a subscription, he would put down his name for five lire.

'Bravo, Signor Leopoldo!'

'Thank you, Signor Leopoldo. And now, if I may say so without presumption, once *we* three have really got down to the matter it's as good as settled.'

* * *

Now people had begun to feel like that it was no time for beating about the bush.

On the next morning a Committee of seven members was constituted; and, by the evening, a meeting was in progress in the study of Machioni, the accountant, whose young son was a lawyer and who, shrewdly calculating that one thing leads to another, had generously put himself at their disposal.

The agenda being read out and the discussion opened, they proceeded, straight away, to pass an unanimous resolution that the statue should unquestionably be an equestrian one, and of bronze, if possible; it was resolved, likewise, that the monument should be set up on the Piazza del Plebiscito, despite a few dissentients who adduced good arguments in favour of Piazza Cavour. Hymns to Italy were chosen, hymns to the progress of humanity, and hymns to the local glories, and means were prescribed for the collection of the necessary funds. Subscription lists were accordingly, sent round. But as their principal source of revenue, they relied on public raffles, dances, free loan of the town bands from the academies of music, Benefit Performances, the amateur performances of the Ernesto Rossi Society and, above all, on the proceeds of a special show, which gave promise of the most marvellous results if only Signora Malvina would render that wonderful sonnet of hers about the chastity of Lucrece, and if the barber would give those seventy-five stanzas of *ottava rima* of his on the subject of last year's pilgrimage.

Meanwhile, following the example of Signor Leopoldo,

and after four members of the Committee had had it explained to them that 'equestrian' meant 'on horseback', they all signed an undertaking to give five lire.

'I do believe', said the Chairman, rubbing his hands with pleasure, 'that we're through with the worst part. And now, before I close the meeting...O Lord, I *know* there's something else I wanted to say! It's gone clean out of my head! Ah, yes! As I was saying, this monument—to whom are we erecting it?'

The silence that fell on the group round the table showed that they felt the query to be a shrewd one and deserving of attention. They might have been a series of poses for a 'Twilight' in the style of Michelangelo as they sat there, dead still, all lost in thought.

A good quarter of an hour later Professor Banderuoli, a man of great learning, combined with unusual modesty and exemplary character, asked leave to speak.

'Please go ahead'.

'Among the many glories of the place, among the most pure and shining intellectual jewels of the second half of the last century, I do not hesitate, gentlemen, to mention one name—the name of Canon Palandri!'

Loud bursts of laughter cut short the speech of Banderuoli. A venomous glint showed in his normally honey-sweet eyes. He thumped on the table and demanded a hearing.

'But no, no, dear Professor!'

'*And* without his horse! That'd be a big laugh in itself!'

'Never mind the horse idea,' shouted Banderuoli, un-coiling like a spring. 'Never mind the horse idea! Before a nome like Agostino Palandri's, one abandons any pre-conception. And the laughter, gentlemen, is an unseemly piece of irreverence, a wicked profanation. It's...oh! I'm resigning.'

'No, no, Professor!'

'Please, Professor!'

'Listen, listen! Do hear me, Professor!'

'I'm not going to hear or listen to anybody. Cross off my name and cancel those five lire. I'm resigning!'

And out he walked.

But, next day, the place vacated by Professor Bande-ruoli was filled by Celestino Chivacci, the chemist; a name dear to the Health Goddess by reason of his inimitable imitations of Gerodel Pastilles. I should love to take this occasion of spinning him a well-deserved encomium; however, his well-known modesty, together with a con-sciousness of my own inadequacy, must constrain me to forbear.

* * *

There passed three months of fruitless endeavour. By no means whatever could Professor Banderuoli be brought back to the fold.

'We'll go ahead on our own!' said the Chairman. And he summoned a new meeting of the Committee, at which the three members who alone put in an appearance felt a return of their enthusiasm, and a conviction that they would triumphantly reach their objective.

The bandmaster sent to say that he would accept the invitation of the Committee provided they made themselves responsible for the illumination and the incidental expen-ses. The Director of the Ernesto Rossi Dramatic Society wrote his acceptance, deeming himself honoured, though he was unable, he said, to meet the cost of production. A group of the most socially important ladies had writ-ten a nice letter expressing their admiration for the noble project, and promising that they would at once set about collecting gifts and organizing a Benefit Performance. To

12 T.

crown everything Signora Malvina had promised to render on this special occasion that wonderful sonnet of hers about the chastity of Lucrece, and the barber had already sent in his seventy-five stanzas of *ottava rima* on the subject of last year's pilgrimage, together with a further six entitled *Hosanna! Hosanna!* or *The Return.*

All these announcements by the Chairman were received with enthusiastic applause. The meeting was closed amid lively hand-shakings, mutual congratulations, and allusions of thinly-veiled disgust to Professor Banderuoli and the Nebbiano heretics.

A couple of months later the idea of an equestrian statue had gone up in smoke. As they went about the district the Committee members and their supporters could have been recognized, even where they were not personally known, by the distress that appeared on their faces.

A sculptor friend of the Chairman had written to say that, thanks to his giving his services practically for nothing, the inclusive cost of the monument would amount to something in the region of fifty to seventy thousand lire.

'Needs his head cuffed!' said Falsetti, fingering the wallet in his breast-pocket.

'Sheer robbery!' cried Signor Annibale, cracking a woodlouse, when Machioni went to tell him in his garden after luncheon.

'I couldn't be more pleased,' growled Professor Banderuoli, reflecting that, now the horse had been got rid of there might be a crevice of possibility for his Canon Palandri.

Throughout the district there was general dismay. And deep was the distress of the ladies, more especially those who had already given orders to their dressmakers or tailors in connexion with the business of canvassing for donations.

* * *

'Well then, gentlemen, what are we going to do? It seems that all hesitation is useless.'

'I'm afraid so.'

'We must bow to the inevitable and just boldly give up the idea of a horse.'

So said the Chairman, one evening, to his Committee, the members of which sat glumly listening to him. The meeting broke up in melancholy silence.

* * *

As time went on the big question had attracted the interest of the whole population. In all the shops, and in every haunt of evening amusement, there were discussions in which the asperity and noise varied in accordance with the class of place concerned.

The Socialists maintained a threatening silence, the anarchists got ready stones to throw at the statue as soon as it was in position, and the priests, ever since the idea of an equestrian Canon had been laughed out of court, had been fanning the flames of discord on all sides; meanwhile the cab-drivers, café owners and hotel proprietors were grumbling over their lost hopes of some such stunning monument as might bring hordes of English tourists flocking into the district, and the more civilized and better-balanced people...well, nothing was heard from them because there just weren't any.

I mean to say...No, it's not true. I exaggerated when I said that there weren't any. There were, actually, three. But all three of them took scrupulous care never to let their thoughts be known, lest they should find their customers dropping off.

* * *

The same sculptor had written to the Chairman that for a statue alone, standing on its feet and of natural size, the cost would be about twenty thousand lire.

'Too much! Still too much! Good heavens, yes,' observed the Chairman to his Committee, who heard him with their tails between their legs. 'It's still too much, after the defection of those who had so emphatically guaranteed us their support... I don't know! The sculptor is a good fellow, that I can assure you because we address each other as *tu**. I'll make further inquiries, I'll ask somebody else instead. But, in my opinion, with all this going on in Africa, there must have been a rise in the cost of marble.'

The municipal band was in the early phases of internal disruption and, just as a worm can become two worms when you cut it, so, out of its rent bosom, there arose a whole fanfare of brass-players. The Ernesto Rossi Society had gone into dissolution when the Chairman backed up the people from Nebbiano after it had been found that no more than four of them were prepared to risk the hazards of a journey into town on a wheelbarrow. The ladies said that to go and get mixed up in such squabblings was not quite the thing as far as people in their position were concerned, and they declared that those who wanted a Benefit Performance were welcome to run one for themselves.

When the Mayor was sounded, in an attempt to enlist his help in getting a subsidy from the Council 'towards

---

* The Italian expression *dar del tu*, like he French verb *tutoyer*, is untranslatable in languages which have no linguistic and social equivalent of this familiar and intimate use of the second person singular. See also p. 170. *Edd*.

the erection of a monument in commemoration of (name
to be the subject of later consideration),' that official replied that he'd be delighted 'once the proposal had reached
a definite shape.' The Member of Parliament together
with a certain County Councillor, who were anxious not
to lose votes in possibly forthcoming elections, promised
their warm support, and praised a patriotic initiative so
well befitting the noble constituency and ward they were
so highly honoured to represent.

But despite the universal expressions of goodwill, things
were by no means going well. The Chairman was obliged
to resign when a grave split in the Committee arose over
a wretched dispute between the Brethren of Pity and the
Public Assistance. What a row that was, too! We had
better not go into it now.

Another Chairman took over; Trabalzi, the veterinary
surgeon. 'A stuffed dummy,' thought Falsetti and Machioni. But the good Trabalzi had views of his own and
could uphold them. He accepted the office only on condition that a bust and not a statue was proposed. Playing
the stuffed dummy was not a customary role with him,
and he was by no means the sort of man to undertake
an enterprise and then allow himself to be turned from it.

Under an iron hand like the new Chairman's it seemed,
after a couple of meetings, that things were taking a turn
for the better, but all the new plans went up in smoke
when another sculptor wrote to say that a marble bust
on a little blue-veined column would cost about two thousand lire.

'What robbers these sculptors are!' said the Chairman,
Trabalzi, as he violently slapped the letter down on the
table.

'As to what you term "a marble tribute of some kind"',
went on the sculptor in a postscript, 'I should be glad to
have a little clarification. If you were thinking of a plaque,

that would cost, according to the size, between five hundred and a thousand lire. But if you have something else in
mind, do please let me know and I shall be most happy
to place myself at your service.'

'What shall we decide, gentlemen?' asked the Chairman, addressing his question to the raised eyebrows all
round him.

In a twinkling everything was decided and, this time,
once and for all. They had found the man to honour
with a monument. The bust should be erected to the
memory of Trabalzi, the grandfather of their Chairman,
to that great benefactor who, seventy years before, had
set up the flourishing factory where tiles of polished,
waterproof asphalt were made for open verandas.

When it came to the vote three were in favour and
three against, the grandson of the great industrialist, with
a delicacy which did him honour, having abstained from
voting himself. A second vote was taken, with the same
result. A third likewise. The idea had to be abandoned.
Once again the name of Canon Palandri came up, but,
in opposition, that of Garibaldi was put forward. The
suggestion was duly carried and won the day, not so
much out of a wish to spite Professor Banderuoli, as because they had been reminded that a stone-mason in a
place named Fiesole above Florence had, among remain-
dered stock dating from the days when Florence was the
capital, a Garibaldi bust of blue-grey stone, and that he
would be able to part with it, dispatch it and set it up
for thirty-five lire, the precise sum which the Committee
had already placed in their Treasurer's hands. The inaug-
uration ceremony would take place on the birthday of
Garibaldi, and the place for setting it up would be in a
niche in the face of the Town Hall.

Next evening the business of the Committee found
itself back at starting-point, for the Mayor strongly oppo-

sed the project of making a niche such as would disfigure
the historic façades of the Town Hall, and nothing would
make him budge an inch.

'Let's put it opposite, at the Tempesti's.'

'Do you think I'm going to let you knock down my
wall? Whatever do you take me for?' replied Tempesti,
when the Committee, represented by its secretary, went to
ask him.

'Very well, then, in the *piazza,* in the Pierotti Porch!'

'You know perfectly well', said Pierotti, growling
grimly when the plan came to his ears, 'that I wouldn't
normally hurt a fly. But if any of these half-wits comes
round asking for trouble he'll find himself going up in
the world—I'll make him a Knight with my first kick, a
Knight-Commander with my second and, with my third
—well... the sky's the limit.

After violent protestations which involved, indirectly,
the inhabitants of Nebbiano as well, the Committee disban-
ded, and it was unanimously decided to spend the thirty-
five lire on a good dinner, and to hell with all those who,
out of public spirit or patriotism, might set out to do good
to their home-town.

'A good dinner at the Golden Stag, Beppe's place!
Here's the menu.' Here Bavetta was the accountant, Machioni's young office boy. 'Here, take him that, and say
we'll be round tonight on the dot of nine o'clock.'

Very soon Bavetta returned to say that all was well
and that they might go there at nine. But half an hour
later, Beppe of the Golden Stag, who, in the meantime,
had been doing some rather more cautious calculations,
sent a boy over to the Chairman to say that they must
either cut down the menu or increase the price of the
meal, as he simply couldn't let them have all that stuff for
five lire a head.

MATILDE SERAO

Half Neapolitan and half Greek, Matilde Serao was born in Patras in 1856 and died in Naples in 1927. She was the major novelist of the 'naturalistic' period after Verga, and in her day a famous literary figure both in Italy and abroad. Her production was large and varied; it fills some twenty volumes, includes novels, stories, criticism and journalism, and was influenced by most contemporary styles. As time went on her characters became socially 'grander', more mystical, and less authentically her own. But she never entirely lost a sense of human quality, even when she reached the status of a popular literary figure. Her best writing came at the beginning and end of her career, when she concentrated on the petit-bourgeois world she knew so well, usually in Naples. (Some passages in her novels are classics such as the description of the Miracle of St Januarius and of the State Lottery in *Il paese di Cuccagna*, published in 1891). Her best characters are the women she describes from that world, standing out as though spotlighted in a crowd; or when she can understand, sympathize, and smile, as with Checchina.

Matilde Serao's books were much translated at the turn of the century, though never since. Her best books are perhaps: *Cuore infermo* (1881), *Fantasia* (1883), *Il paese di Cuccagna* (1891); *Castigo* (1893), *La Ballerina* (1899), *Suor Giovanna Della Croce* (1901). Among volumes of short stories. *La virtù di Checchina* (1884) supplies the title for one; and others are: *Piccole anime* (1883), *All'erta sentinella* (1889).

Though the present story is set in Rome it is sufficiently typical, and its selection for this volume is due in part to the praise and recommendation of such modern masters of the short story as Alberto Moravia and Mario Soldati.

A. C.

CHECCHINA'S VIRTUE

MATILDE SERAO

Translated by Angus Davidson

One day, a Friday, Doctor Toto Primicerio, just as he was going out, said to his wife Checchina, who was brushing the shoulders of his overcoat:

'I say, I've invited the Marchese di Aragona to dinner.'

She stopped her brushing, immediately.

'You see,' went on her husband, without turning round, 'he was so very polite to us at Frascati; we must show him some civility, now we're back in Rome. He sees all the noble families, he's on familiar terms with all the Roman princesses; he'll be useful to me. He's coming on Sunday, at seven o'clock, the time when we usually have our supper: that's the time when *they* have dinner. For once *we'll* have dinner at seven, too.'

When he turned round, he saw that his wife had turned rather pale and was looking very serious.

'Does the idea of this dinner worry you, my dear Checca? But the thing's done now and it can't be undone.'

'A Marquis? Here, in our house? A person who goes out to dinner with all the Princesses?'

'Oh well, he'll be quite happy here, and certainly he won't die of starvation. You arrange things with Susanna,' concluded Toto, with fine Roman serenity, as he started off for the San Spirito Hospital, to repair dislocated arms and treat festering wounds. The doctor went away, but a record of him, an invincible smell of carbolic, lingered on inside the cramped flat.

Checchina did not arrange anything with Susanna. The maid was in the kitchen, skimming the broth and muttering to herself about the ungodliness of her master, who ate meat on a Friday while she, Susanna, was content with a piece of fried dried cod. Checchina sat in the bedroom, beside the wide, high double-bed, her hands in her lap, completely absorbed in her own thoughts, not noticing that she was still in her slippers and with a linen handkerchief round her neck. A Marquis who went to the houses of Princesses and embraced them and addressed them with the familiar 'tu'—coming to dinner with *them*! Why in the world had Toto invited him? How had it entered his mind to do such a thing? At Frascati the Marchese di Aragona had been spending a summer holiday with Prince and Princess Altavilla; he used to go out driving every day with the Princess in her carriage and accompanied her to Mass, and they went out on horseback together, she closely sheathed in a black riding-habit, a black veil twisted round her top hat and a tea rose in her buttonhole, he with an olive-green velvet suit, a black satin cravat, steel spurs and a black riding-whip. Checchina had seen them two or three times as they went past like an apparition. He was a handsome young man, the Marchese di Aragona, tall, with curly hair and melancholy, expressive eyes. One day, in dismounting from his horse, he had slightly twisted his foot, and Toto Primicerio had been called to Altavilla to attend to this trifling injury. But from then onwards, each time the Marchese di Aragona happened to meet Checchina Primicerio, he took off his hat to her with a deep flourish, in the grand, aristocratic manner of greeting which is so flattering to women of the middle classes. Three times he greeted her in this way: one Sunday, in the piazza, where

---

[1] See page 162, and note. *Edd*.

the municipal band was playing between the church and
the café, while the beautiful women of Frascati were walking up and down, their heads and shoulders veiled in
white woollen shawls; one Thursday afternoon, when she
was sewing behind the window-panes of her balcony, mend-
ing the cuffs of one of her husband's old shirts, and the
Marchese di Aragona greeted her as he passed along the
street; and one Monday morning, when she was with Susanna in an out-of-the-way lane in the town, negotiating
the purchase of some baskets of tomatoes from a peasant,
with a view to making tomato paste for the winter, and
the Marchese di Aragona, as he went past, again greeted
her: and this time she blushed, as she well remembered,
but she did not know why, perhaps it was because Susanna was quarrelling loudly with the peasant over the
price. And now this Marchese was coming to dinner,
and she did not know what to give to eat to this nobleman
who was accustomed to the culinary fancies of grand cooks.
They had a dinner-service for six people only, which had
been bought at a sale and lacked both sauce-boat and salad-
bowl; would that be adequate? And the salad—for you
must have salad at a dinner-party—what could she put it
in? Well, she could give him *gnocchi* with a meat sauce:
the *gnocchi* she would make herself, and Susanna, who
was especially good at that, would make the sauce. Then
would come the meat with a surround of potatoes cooked
in gravy; then a dish of fried fish. But what was to be
done, when Susanna was always complaining that the
frying-pan was high in the middle so that the oil ran
down towards the sides and the middle part of the fish
became scorched and black? A new pan was needed or
she would have to give up the idea of fried fish. There
were six sets of knives, forks and spoons, but one fork
had two bent prongs; Susanna would have to wash them
very quickly in the kitchen, and the plates and dishes too,

if there were not enough. And the roast, there must be
a roast! Wasn't it usual to have chicken in aristocratic
houses? How was she to roast it when there were two
stoves in the kitchen but no roasting-jack? This dinner
was going to cost a great deal of money; and how was
she to tell Toto what a number of things were lacking
in the house? A Marquis, with such a serious, such a
grand, lordly air about him, with a ring on his finger that
had a diamond, a sapphire and a ruby in it—she had seen
it quite clearly; a Marquis with whom numbers of princesses must certainly be in love: of course she must give
him a sweet course as well. What kind of a sweet could
she make, what could she remember from the time when
she was a girl? A tart with black cherry jam? How
many eggs used she to put in with a kilo of best white
flour, half a kilo of finest sugar, and half a pound of
butter? And how about an oven to cook the tart in?
Really the best way would be to send it downstairs to the
porter's wife, who had an oven; she would have to ask
this favour of that spiteful Maddalena who was always
quarrelling with Susanna on the subject of confession, for
Maddalena was positively a heretic; then, next day, if any
of the tart were left, she would send her a small piece,
to give her a chance of tasting it and to thank her for
her kindness.

And coffee? It was served at table, wasn't it, after
the table had been cleared? Susanna always made the
coffee in the morning, on the fire, with the coffee of the
day before boiled up and a little fresh coffee added; whereas it was clear that these grand people, with the smart,
lively look they always had, drank coffee made in a little
machine over a spirit lamp, and consisting entirely of
fresh coffee, three or four teaspoonfuls to the cup, without
any boiling up. Only the week before Bianchelli's had
had a great display of coffee-machines, all glossy and flam-

ing and looking like gold and silver. Once of those was what she needed; and then Susanna would have to learn, in two days, how to use it. Fifty *lire* would be needed for this dinner. Toto would never give it to her. He allowed her three *lire* a day for the household expenses; but then they had a stock of wine in the house and from time to time there was some little present from one of his patients, a cheese, a *salame*, a few baskets of fruit. Toto grumbled at giving her even these three *lire*; while, in the kitchen, Susanna would swear in the name of St. Ursula, patron saint of all virgins, that she couldn't make both ends meet, it was impossible to make both ends meet, and the butchers were nothing but dogs and the green-grocers no better than pickpockets. How could she bring herself to ask Toto for all this money for the Marquis's dinner? It so happened that she had just lent the six *lire* she had saved, with great difficulty, to that giddy creature Isolina; with six *lire* something might have been managed ... And, at this last thought, she blushed as she remembered.

Finally she rose, went into the kitchen, and stood looking absentmindedly at Susanna as she cut a turnip into minute pieces to put into the soup. Completely absorbed in her thoughts, she said nothing. Two or three times the maid started grumbling about the coal-merchant who had neither conscience nor fear of God, selling watered char-coal, as he did, so as to make it weigh heavier; but her mistress paid no attention. At a certain moment Chec-china, as though suddenly reawakening, said to her:

'Susanna, d'you know how to make curls on the fore-head?'

'What sort of curls?' asked the maid in bewilderment.

'Curls like Isolina's,' murmured her mistress in a low voice.

* * *

When the Marchese di Aragona arrived at ten minutes to seven, as social custom demands, Checchina was still in her bedroom, dressing. She was red in the face, with two fiery patches on her cheeks, so fiercely had the flames of the cooking-stove sent the blood to her head. And she was dead tired, for she had had to do everything herself since Susanna, annoyed at this dinner-party, sourly declined at intervals to have anything to do with it. Already, that same morning, she had not been able to go to Mass at Sant'Andrea delle Fratte; and when she had been unable to hear Mass, Susanna was implacable. And now, at this moment, what with heat and fatigue and the idea that everything would go wrong, a great confusion reigned in Checchina's head: her eyes were glittering, as if with fever. Four times she had washed her hands, for fear there might be the smell of fish upon them; and she sniffed at them automatically, as though she were moving in her sleep. When she went out into the sitting-room, the Marchese paid her a compliment on her healthy looks, and Toto Primicerio chuckled with pleasure. The Marchese was wearing a buttoned-up frock-coat and a white satin cravat with a diamond pin in the form of a horse-shoe; slowly he took off his gloves, revealing his hands, which were white and soft like those of a woman. As she stood there, ill at ease in her new, dead-leaf-coloured woollen dress with the lace ruffle that tickled the back of her neck, she thought, desperately, that it might perhaps be better to give him soup instead of the *gnocchi*.

Toto Primicerio kept repeating and insisting that it was to be a simple little informal dinner in an unpretentious house, that it bore no relation whatever to a princely banquet; the Marchese gave the subtlest possible smile and said nothing. When Susanna announced, in a sharp tone of voice, that the *gnocchi* were on the table, he bowed and offered his arm to the lady of the house. She became aware of the faint perfume that he used—possibly on his hair, or on his handkerchief—a soft, agreeable scent which seemed to linger on her lips, like the taste of a sweetmeat. At the beginning of dinner, to tell the truth, she suffered torments because everything seemed to be going wrong. Susanna kept casting suspicious glances at the Marchese, and her waiting at table was clumsy. The plates and forks took an age to come back, newly washed, from the kitchen; and Checchina sat silent, not daring to call, staring at the tablecloth in deep embarrassment. Toto Primicerio displayed the gross gaiety of a doctor on holiday, risking little jokes and talking in a familiar way to the Marchese, as though they were boon companions; he told him a lot of stories of legs sawn off, of intestines sewn up and fitted back into the belly, of carotid arteries shortened, and of tumours that made people's arms swell up like balloons. The lamp started to smoke, and when it was turned down the light was too feeble. At one moment Checchina's husband remarked:

'My dear Marchese, these *gnocchi*, and the tart we're going to have at the end of dinner, were made by this dear wife of mine, who has a very light hand.'

The Marchese paid her an exquisite compliment. In truth, he was extremely polite. He appeared not even to notice a number of vulgar little incidents, he never looked at Susanna, just as though she did not exist, he took two helpings of fried fish, and talked all the time with the greatest freedom. He spoke in a rather low voice, with a very light, almost aspirated *r* and a very gentle, lisping *s*; his voice had soft, caressing intonations, and the simplest words seemed to rise and fall on breaths

13 т.

of warm air, on compelling gusts of tenderness. As he
spoke, he looked straight into the eyes of the person he
was talking to, with a serious, thoughtful gaze; a slight
smile would appear beneath the blond arch of his moustache, and his smooth hand would be playing with his
knife. Checchina, relieved of her nightmare, took courage
when she saw the lordly composure with which the Marchese di Aragona failed to notice anything: her red face
became pink, and the ruffle which tickled the back of her
neck now teased her agreeably instead of distressing her.
Every now and then, beneath the gaze of the Marchese,
her eyelids would flutter, as though the light in the room
were too bright; but she also smiled, silently, nodding
her head at what he was saying. Apropos of the tart,
which was perhaps slightly overcooked and a little scorched
round the rim, he made some very delicate remark referring to the sweetness of the woman who had made it.
Checchina did not quite understand the full meaning of
the words, but the voice caressed her like the sound of
music. The Marchese refused the coffee, which quite
likely was very bad, and she was grateful to him in her
heart: she had not had enough money to buy the coffee-
machine. Instead, Toto Primicerio insisted on opening a
bottle of *vieux cognac* which a patient of his from France
had given him. Then the Marchese raised his glass and
proposed the health of Signora Primicerio; and she, re-
plying to the toast, drank off a glass of *cognac*—a drink
she had never tasted before—at one gulp.

In the sitting-room, they were all three silent for a moment. It was cold in the poorly furnished, carpetless little
room with its sorry curtains. As though the room could
be warmed by lamps, Checchina had the only other lamp
in the house brought in; but it had no shade and it blinded
you to look at it. She sat down, bolt upright, on the
sofa, conscious for the first time of the wretchedness of

the room and suffering acutely from it: she scarcely heard the harmonious voice of the Marchese di Aragona giving her a sad account of a holiday in Scotland, where the Altavillas, his cousins, had a castle. It had been cold there, and she was shivering here; the tears rose to her eyes. Toto Primicerio allowed himself to be overcome by the irresistible sleepiness that comes to stout men who have eaten and drunk a lot. She cast a few timid glances at her husband as though imploring him not to fall asleep; Toto, like all fat men, snored. Toto did not understand; lying in his armchair, he closed his eyes from time to time and let his head fall forward on to his chest. But at last one of Checchina's glances woke him up, like an electric shock; he rose to his feet, went over to the window, and looked out into the street in order to appear unconcerned, then walked straight out of the room without turning his head. He always needed to sleep for an hour or so after dinner.

The admirable Marchese di Aragona pretended not to see his host leave the room. Leaning back in his armchair with one leg crossed over the other, he displayed his aristocratic foot in its red silk sock and patent-leather shoe; one hand curled and twirled the fair moustache and the other rested on the arm of the sofa upon which Checchina was sitting. Checchina was breathing more easily now, knowing that her husband was asleep stretched out on the double-bed. She dared to raise her eyes and look at the Marchese, her big Roman eyes, unmoving, it may be, in expression, but nevertheless profound. Again she was aware of that soft scent of violets which affected her nerves. The Marchese di Aragona had further lowered the tone of his voice: he was telling her now about his own home, his small bachelor flat where he spent long, lonely hours.

'Why don't you get married, then?' she said ingenuously.

Then she repented of her excessive familiarity. He did
not answer her question; and there was silence.

'The place is lonely', he murmured once again, looking
at Checchina, 'in that melancholy Via dei Santi Apostoli.
Do you know it? Yes? I'm glad you do. Not the
palace belonging to Balduccio Odescalchi, Prince Odescalchi, a friend of mine; no, the house next to it, on the
other side of an archway. I'm on the first floor: twenty-
four steps to go up. I detest long staircases: they are bad
for my heart. In my family, disease of the heart is here-
ditary: we all die of it very early. What does it matter?
Life should be brief and good, but mine is too long; and
it's certainly not a happy one. There's never anybody in
my home. There are two doors to the flat, and in the
morning my manservant gets everything ready that I may
want during the day. Then I am left alone. The place
has triple curtains of yellow silk, of white lace, and of
brocade which protect it from excessive light. What I
like very much is a half-darkness in which one can doze.
There are carpets everywhere, and the whole flat is, as it
were, lined and upholstered against the cold; there is
always a bright fire burning in the fireplace in my sitting-
room. I feel the cold very much; when it's warm, I feel
happy. I am always alone in that house. To amuse
myself, I burn an Oriental pastille to scent the room, I
smoke a cigarette, and I wait for somebody to come...
who? A dream, a phantom, a beautiful woman, simple
and good, who would love me, whom I would adore...
Would you like to come?' he added quickly, kissing her
suddenly on the neck.

'No, no,' she said, putting up her arm to defend
her lips.

'Come on Thursday, between four and six ... Do come, Fanny.'

'Not on Thursday,' answered Checchina, conquered by his use of her name.

'On Friday, then, at the same time.'

And, after making her a deep bow, he went away. Susanna showed him downstairs by the light of a small oil lamp.

* * *

But in the silence of wakeful nights, lying beside Toto as he slept and snored deeply, in the long hours of light, brief drowsiness, of sudden nervous tremors, of sleepless intervals, watching the streak of light coming through the half-closed shutters (which Toto always left like that so that he should wake very early in the morning), sometimes stifling with heat beneath the cotton coverlet stretched flat as a board on top of her, sometimes unable to get warm between the icy linen sheets, Checchina was conscious once more of a strong, lively, growing desire to go, that Friday afternoon between four and six, to the flat in Via Santi Apostoli. In the night and the solitude, as she stared into the darkness with burning eyes wide from sleeplessness, she felt herself filled with courage. The big man snoring, first on one note then on another, and turning from time to time under the bedclothes with a single rapid movement, as though worked by a spring, no longer frightened her now; and, however carefully she listened, she was unable to hear the breathing of Susanna, who slept in a poky little room next door to the kitchen. Her two enemies no longer seemed to her formidable. She must go, indeed she must go, for she had said yes, that evening, when he had kissed her. After all, how long did it take from Via del Bufalo to Via Santi Apostoli?

It would take perhaps ten minutes, on foot. No, a little more: it would take twelve minutes. From Via del Bufalo to Via Santi Apostoli you could take a short cut, zig-zagging from one street to another: you go up Via del Nazzareno, down Via della Stamperia, past the Trevi fountain, through the narrow Vicolo San Vincenzo e Anastasio, then down a short piece of Via dell'Umiltà, along Via dell'Archetto, and, in a moment, there you are at Via Santi Apostoli. For this you would take, perhaps, a quarter of an hour, going slowly so as not to attract attention. Going the longer way round, by Via del Pozzetto, along the Corso and through Piazza San Marcello, it would take you half an hour; there are always so many people in the Corso, knocking against you, bringing you to a halt, getting in your way, holding up your progress. Better to go by the side streets. And, with the clarity of vision of a brain stimulated by wakefulness, she saw herself leaving the house, at four in the afternoon, smiling a little to herself at the trick she was playing on Toto and on Susanna, the maid who prided herself on being so clever, walking along very slowly, looking at the shops, Pesoli the confectioner in Via della Stamperia, the stationer's in Piazza di Trevi, and at the pigeons fluttering high up over the fountain; she saw herself walking faster, now, since she was already some distance from home; she saw herself slipping round the corner into Via Santi Apostoli, looking vaguely at the numbers of the houses; she saw herself going into *his* house, where he was waiting for her...at this point every nerve in her body seemed to tremble and vibrate, and she hid her face in the pillow.

Yes, indeed, at night, at that time when the energies of phlegmatic temperaments are aroused—at night everything seemed easy, everything seemed simple, everything seemed imminent and practicable. She started making plans. To-morrow I shall have a great scene with Toto and wring some money out of him, so that I can at least buy some gloves, some shoes, a muff. Or perhaps I shall go to-morrow to see Isolina and make her go with me to Madame Coppi, who allows me credit, and there I'll buy a hat; later on, when the bill has to be paid, Toto will make an outcry, but he'll have to produce the money. Or again I might go to Isolina to-morrow, throw myself into her arms and tell her the whole story, and then get her to ask that woman who lends money to lend me some; I can think about paying it back later, somehow or other. Or again—I wonder whether perhaps Isolina would be good enough to lend me some things of her own, just for one day? It's true, I'm fatter than she is, but our shoulders are just the same width, and all that would be needed would be to let out the dress at the waist and on the hips. Our feet are just the same size, I think; per- haps mine are a little smaller, but as her shoes are always rather tight for her, they would fit me very well. To morrow, I'll go to-morrow and tell her everything... She felt, now, that she had a new strength in herself which she had never known before, a great courage, a boldness which would help her gaily to overcome every possible kind of obstacle, a will-power so unshakable that nothing could defeat or shatter it. She laughed from sheer pride, in the middle of the night, lifting her shoulders as if she wanted to test her ability to raise an immense weight, just for fun, just to try her strength. Then, after re- examining and amplifying the same plan twenty times over, when she saw that it was completely in order, completely ready and perfect in every way, she arrived always at the final point of her dream, where she went into *his* house, where *he* was waiting for her...And then she plunged headlong into a confusion of fantasies that summoned up dreamy sensations of a gracious half-light, of softness and warmth, of a deep silence, of the voluptuous caress of rich and beautiful things.

But dawn threw her into a leaden sleep, from which Toto's cries and grumblings vainly attempted, for half an hour, to awaken her. She would get up exhausted, with a bitter, sticky mouth, worn out with sleeplessness. Every morning, Toto invented some new explanation.

'It must have been that pork chop that didn't agree with you, my dear Checca.'

'If you feel ill, why don't you take some effervescent citrate of magnesia? It's a pleasant drink, and it sweeps out your stomach like a broom.'

'My dear Checca, the more I look at you the more sure I am that you must be constipated: why don't you make up your mind to it and take some almond oil? Freshly squeezed, from Garneri's, it's a splendid thing.'

'Yes, yes, very well, I'll take some,' she murmured, bowing her head.

And so her will-power, her strength, her courage would slowly wane as the morning went on. In vain did she try to recapture the boldness of the wakeful hours of night. The idea of asking Toto for money became unbearable to her, for she would not know where to begin and he would end by not giving her a penny; she sought to revive her courage, to pull herself together in order to speak to him, but the words died on her lips and she let him leave the house without saying anything. Susanna appeared to her as the other insurmountable obstacle; she was sure she would not be able to deceive that distrustful, suspicious servant with her prying, bigoted eye. As for Isolina, she was filled with deep shame at the idea of confessing everything to her, for no other reason than that it seemed to her highly distasteful to tell the story of her poverty, her incompetence, her lack of experience. And how would she have the courage to present herself at Madame Coppi's in order to buy a new velvet hat? Supposing she refused? That would be a mortification she could not endure. She had never in her life run up debts with a milliner or a dressmaker, having the instinctive horror of debt that exists in all quiet middle-class consciences. And that other woman, the money-lender — Isolina had told her that she was a wicked woman and one couldn't have any satisfactory dealings with her. There was nothing to be done, nothing. While, in the sitting-room, she mechanically dusted the set of cups and saucers, the sweet-dishes and the plate of artificial fruit, while she helped Susanna to wash the vegetables for the soup, while she renewed the muslin lining round the bottom of a petticoat which was all frayed at the edge, while she poured some hot water on the marble top of the washstand and rubbed potash on it to remove the stains—all this time, within herself, she was silently demolishing all her plans of the previous night. They appeared to her now as a dream, as a fit of madness. Even the route by which she would go, which by night had seemed to her so simple, now, by day, was nothing but a confusion and a muddle; she would certainly have lost her way. By the time evening came, everything had collapsed, had fallen into dust, had vanished; she had not dared to pronounce one single word, to perform one single act, to do anything at all that would bring her nearer to the accomplishment of her plans. She became convinced, too, during the day, that she would never achieve her desire. By the end of the day she was suffering acutely from the pain of her own inertia, she was feeling all the bitterness of an inglorious defeat in a battle in which she had had the courage neither to attack nor to defend herself. In her own mind she laid the blame, ingenuously, upon events that had occurred, upon her own circumstances and the people amongst whom she lived, as well as upon herself for not knowing how to achieve anything, for being helpless in every way.

This was the state of affairs—at night, feverish excitement of the imagination, by day, utter lack of will-power—when Friday morning came. She had still come to no decision. At four o'clock she would have to go, since she had promised to do so when he kissed her. How she would go, in what manner, she knew not. That morning, Toto seemed to her noisier, more irritable, more miserly that ever: he wanted to leave only two *lire* fifty for the household expenses, with the excuse that he had no more small change. When Susanna reminded her master that it was Friday and that he must therefore leave a further twenty-five *soldi* for the washerwoman who would be bringing back the clean clothes that day, a quarrel started between the two of them. Toto was annoyed, seriously annoyed, she must understand, at these continual extra expenses: every day there was something new; she must ask the permission of the lady on the second floor to hang out their washing on the flat roof: there was the cistern and water-supply downstairs: henceforth the laundry must be done at home. Susanna replied that she was not accustomed to standing about with her hands in the water all day long, and that it was hardly worth while risking her health for eight *lire* a month.

'Eight *lire, and your keep*!' Toto kept shouting.

'Fine sort of keep!'

After he had gone away, having disgorged the twenty-five *soldi* one by one, Susanna added in conclusion:

'To-day's Friday the thirteenth: on this day Christ died on earth for our sins!'

Checchina, who had not opened her mouth, gave a start. The date, too—she had never given a thought to the date—was a fatal date, a strange combination of day and number. A fear of the unknown rose up within her, with this appointment that had been made precisely for Friday the thirteenth, the day when, as the saying goes, you should neither marry nor start on a journey; and Friday is established by religious practice as a day of mourning, in memory of the death of the Redeemer. She went into the kitchen and wandered aimlessly round for a moment.

'An unlucky day,' she said.

'May God save us from temptation,' answered the maid. 'Shall we recite the little rosary of the souls in Purgatory, the one with three sets of ten *Avemarias*, with the *Requiem aeternam* instead of the *Gloria Patri?*'

'Yes, let us do that.'

And so, while Susanna poured out the lentils for the soup into a dish and blew on them, at the same time shaking them to get rid of the dust, and then separated them with her finger so as to remove any little pebbles or bits of straw; and while Checchina placed a little heap of bicarbonate in a piece of linen and tied it up with thread into a little bag to be put to boil with the lentils so that they should cook quicker—the two voices rose monotonously, without special intonations or inflexions, following the established mode of prayer and with the indifferent sound of a prayer that is recited every day. At the end Checchina gave a sigh of relief, as though her feeling of superstitious fear had been dissipated. Christ must now have been appeased, on this dangerous day, since they had recited the rosary: Christ must now help her, throughout this Friday, towards the thing that she desired. From this inner conviction she derived a little courage, enough to say to Susanna:

'Will you clean the lamps to-day—would you be so kind?'

She felt disgusted, now, at the idea of touching the dirty rag and spending half an hour turning and twisting the little round brush inside the tube. Susanna consented, without saying a word. Checchina, disheartened by this, said, as if she were talking to herself:

'I want to go and see Isolina to-day. She's been three or four times to see me.'

The other woman, busy washing pots and pans, made no reply.

'I might go when Toto goes to the hospital for his evening visit ... about four o'clock ...'

'If I were you, you know, I shouldn't go there,' said the maid, turning round suddenly.

'And why?'

'Because that woman, as everyone knows, is a wicked sinner, both in the eyes of God and of men.'

'No, no, really ... poor Isolina ...'

'Yes, poor Isolina! Poor indeed, she who is sunk deep in sin from morning till night! As though everyone didn't know all the horrible wicked things she does! That blockhead of a husband of hers is the only one who doesn't know anything about it; some Christian soul ought to tell him.'

Checchina glanced at the maid with a frightened look on her face.

'She's paid me three or four visits,' she repeated a moment later, stubbornly. 'I ought to go and see her to-day.'

'All right then, go, if it gives you so much pleasure. But I'm willing to bet that, if you confess your friendship with Signora Isolina to Father Fileno, he'll forbid you to see her, on pain of refusing you absolution.'

'To-day, just this once ...' said Checchina, compromising.

After lunch, there was an unusual occurrence. A new patient arrived, a man who lived in the provinces, suffering from a feverish complaint; he had been sent by the Marchese di Aragona. Toto made a great fuss; he closed the door of his study, questioned the man at great length, wrote him out a long prescription, kept him there for an hour. Checchina was walking up and down, dying with impatience. The man from the provinces left five *lire,* an unheard-of amount for Dr. Primicerio, to whom people usually gave two *lire.* Toto came out in a state of enthusiasm, holding up the dirty five-*lire* note.

'He's a fine fellow, my dear Checca! This Marchese is really a fine fellow! You'll see, you'll see, more of them will come, more patients and more five-*lire* notes. It's what I always said—these noblemen always make a point of repaying a civility. Well, it's three o'clock, I'd better get dressed to go to the hospital. You see, there *are* satisfactions in being a doctor.'

While he was undressing in order to change his clothes, she followed him about, step by step, as if she wanted to help him.

'Are you pleased, Checca?'

'Of course I'm pleased.'

'I must try and see him, this Marchese, to thank him. Goodness knows where he lives! Anyhow, he's a real gentleman. Don't you think so?'

'Yes, indeed.'

'If I see him, I'll tell him to come and see us here again, one evening after supper.'

'Yes, do tell him.'

The doctor went off whistling a tune, delighted with the profession he had chosen, feeling sorry for all the other unfortunate men who had become lawyers, engineers, professors. Then Checchina took out her dead-leaf-colour dress, her hat, her coat, her gloves, took a clean handkerchief, a linen one, and laid them all out on the bed. Susanna had brushed and combed her hair that morning; now she ran a comb through it again, to smooth it down a little, not wishing to call Susanna to do it again—she hadn't the courage for that. Then she began slowly dressing, looking at herself constantly in the glass and discovering that she had three freckles below her left eye; but from a little distance they were not visible. She loathed all these ugly things that she was putting on; there now, the top part of the dress was too loose round the waist and so tight round the chest that she couldn't breathe! She had never noticed it before, but to day she noticed it. One glove had come unstitched, she wasted time stitching it up again and she had no black thread; so she mended it with grey thread; it didn't look too bad, it would do. She tried on the hat two or three times, tilting it differently each time; but in the end she put it on as she always wore it. She looked at herself for a last time in the looking-glass and it seemed to her that she cut a very mean, poor figure; but what more was there she could do now? Slowly she moved away, gathering her coat around her; she went into the kitchen.

'Are you going out?' asked the maid.

'I'm going to see Isolina.'

'It's raining,' said the other woman sharply.

'What? It's raining?'

'Hadn't you noticed? It's been raining for half an hour.'

Checchina went to the dining-room window: the courtyard was all wet. But that might perhaps be from the water-taps; so she went to the window of the sitting-room, the only one which looked on to the street. Certainly it was raining, not in a downpour but very finely and continuously. She opened the window and put her hand out, as though she did not believe her eyes: her glove was soon speckled with little drops. She sat down for a moment, as though her strength had failed her. Then she got up again.

'I'll take the umbrella,' she said to the maid.

They both hunted everywhere for this umbrella, the

only one in the house—the kind of umbrella that costs six *lire* fifty.

'It was behind the wardrobe,' Checchina kept repeating, like a parrot.

'It *was*, it *was*, but it isn't there now.'

And they went on rummaging, looking everywhere, even in places where it could not be, under the bed, in the sideboard, in the wardrobe drawer. Nothing; it was not there.

'Let's have another good look,' she said, obstinately.

'It's no good looking, it's not there. The Doctor must have taken it, seeing that it was going to rain. D'you remember if the Doctor had the umbrella under his arm when he went out?'

'I don't remember, I didn't look.'

'Well, he must have taken it, it's no use worrying any more.'

And she went back to the kitchen. But, with the nervous stubbornness of one who is determined to find some lost object at any cost, Checchina went on looking, casting bewildered glances into every corner where the umbrella might possibly be. There was nothing, nothing. She went back to the window; it was raining harder now; the basin of the little fountain at the corner of Via del Pozzetto was overflowing; she saw open umbrellas going past, their tops gleaming with rain, and underneath them moving legs were visible with trousers turned up and muddied shoes. It was raining, and there was no going out without an umbrella. It would cost sixteen *soldi* or even a *lira* to take a cab, for the Roman cab-drivers, in bad weather like this, were terrible robbers. It went on raining and the window-panes became dimmed, and she could no longer see the people passing along the street.

'D'you think Maddalena has an umbrella she would lend me?' she asked the maid, going back into the kitchen.

'Maddalena? I'm sure she has one; but *I'm* not going
to ask her. For two days now she hasn't said good-morn-
ing to me when I've gone past her door, ugly slut that
she is.'

Turning her back on her, without another word, Checchina opened the door and went downstairs like an auto-
maton. In truth, tears of humiliation had come into her
eyes and she was trying hard not to cry.

'My dear Maddalena, I've got to go out to see a friend,
Signora Isolina, about some business; it's raining, and
Toto has taken the umbrella. I wonder if you would be
so kind as to lend me yours?'

'Of course, of course, with all my heart, dear Signora!
If it were that pious hypocrite Susanna, I would say no,
for *she* wouldn't give a sip of water to a dying man. But
for *you,* my dear Signora! But the trouble is, the umbrella isn't here; my husband took it away with him this
morning. I wanted to go out too, and I wasn't able to.
But if you could wait till he comes back, at *Avemaria*
time...

'Thank you, Maddalena, but it doesn't matter.'

'He can't be long now, about half an hour.'

'Never mind, it doesn't matter.'

'There's nothing I can do, dear Signora; I'd help you
if I could...'

Checchina looked out into the street. It was still raining, but less than before. She went upstairs again, very
slowly, having decided to wait till the rain stopped. After
all, she ought not to be very late; he had said between
four and six. But she had no watch. She stood at the
window, in the damp, enveloping twilight, looking straight
into the dark space of the window-pane to see if the raindrops were thinning out. She no longer had any idea of
what time it was. And then, finally, little by little it
stopped raining, and she moved away. Someone rang the
door-bell.

'It's the washerwoman,' Susanna said.

'I've got to go out now,' answered Checchina.

'What about reading the list, then? She won't go away without her money.'

But the thing took a long time. The washerwoman began by complaining of the bad weather which prevented her from drying the clothes, then she had to shake out her coat which was wet with rain. Checchina, standing at the dining-room table, fumbled at the laundry-book with trembling fingers, unable to find the right day, while the washerwoman divided the linen into separate groups, one group of sheets, another of shirts, another of table-napkins, a bundle of handkerchiefs and stockings. They started checking them, but the list did not tally. Checchina had taken the wrong page: it was an old list, and they had to begin all over again. The final result was that one sheet was missing and one handkerchief had been substituted for another. Here a dispute arose between Susanna and the washerwoman, for the latter said she had never had the sheet, while Susanna maintained that she had delivered it to her with her own hands.

'Is it written down?' demanded the maid, shouting at her mistress.

'Yes, it's written down,' replied Checchina automatically.

'Well then, it ought to be there.'

The washerwoman shook her head, unconvinced. She never lost anything, she said, she only washed for four families, everyone was always satisfied with her accuracy, she had already delivered the other three lots and there had not been too much of anything.

'Have a good look in the cupboard. I expect the sheet's there; *I* never had it,' she went on.

At last, after they had looked carefully, the sheet was found, rolled up in the grey ironing-cloth.

14 T.

'How did you come to write it down?' the maid asked her mistress, thoroughly mortified.

'I don't know.'

Then came the question of the handkerchief. Checchina had never had handkerchiefs with the letter *R* on them, said Susanna. She had a great deal of difficulty in persuading the washerwoman to take back the handkerchief so as to see whether it belonged to someone else to whom she had given the handkerchief belonging to the Signora. The washerwoman said she never lost anything, they had seen that over the sheet which, after all that discussion, had then turned out to be in the house: there must be some mistake also about the handkerchief. In the end she said she would take it away; she would see about it, she wasn't at all sure; she would take back this one, which was by no means a bad one, it was large and pure linen throughout. When the moment came for payment, more difficulties arose: the list added up to thirty-two *soldi* and Susanna had only twenty-five. The washerwoman wanted the whole amount, naturally; she had to buy soap, she said, and anyhow it was a miserable thing to have to do washing in the winter, in icy water. Checchina stood motionless, her eyes wandering, listening without intervening, trying to calculate in her mind what time it could be. So aloof did she seem that, when at last the washerwoman had gone away, still grumbling, Susanna started complaining to her mistress that she always left her to deal with these questions and to fight for the interests of the household which, when all was said and done, ought not to have concerned her at all, and that nobody paid any respect to her, not even the master of the house—he less than anyone, in fact. Checchina, paying no attention to her, went to see if it was still raining. It was not raining now, but it was already dark and they were lighting the lamps. She hesitated for an instant, then made up her mind. It couldn't be really so very late, in winter the days are so short! She could still go.

'Are you going alone?' asked Susanna.

'Yes, alone.'

'At this time of day?'

'It's not late.'

'It may not be late, but it's dark.'

'What does that matter? It's so very close, Via di Propaganda!'

'Excuse me, but it's not at all suitable for an honest woman to be walking about alone at this time of day. There are so many evil-minded people in the streets. Besides, it's just the time of day when you might be mistaken for one of those women.'

'When a woman goes her own way, nothing happens to her.'

'I know, but if the Doctor comes to know that you went out alone at this hour of the day, he'll certainly be angry, and *I* shall get into trouble for letting you go.'

'I promised Isolina...'

'Well, this is what we'll do. I'll get dressed in one minute and go with you to Signora Isolina's. If we're two together, no one will say anything to us. Besides, I know how to answer these impudent men.'

'And who's to look after things in the kitchen?'

'Everything's ready. I'll bank up the fire with ashes and be with you in a moment. While you pay your visit, I'll wait in the hall; I'll say another rosary, so as not to have to talk to that wicked Teresa—for that's all she is, may Our Lady protect her!'

Checchina sat down forlornly in the dining-room, not knowing what to do. She heard Susanna moving about in her little room, knocking into the walls in her haste as she put on her cheap woollen dress. It was not possible now to stop Susanna going with her. Now she would have to go to Isolina's, to Via di Propaganda, and to stay there and pay her a visit. She was caught, it was impossible to get rid of Susanna. They went out, pulling the door shut behind them. Checchina walked flaggingly, as though the muddy ground were holding her back. In front of the church of Sant'Andrea delle Fratte Susanna crossed herself. Isolina was not at home. Checchina breathed again.

'So much the better,' murmured the maid. 'Let's go back.'

They walked all the way home in silence. Maddalena stopped Checchina at the entrance door.

'If you want the umbrella, Nino's back from the workshop.'

'It's no use now, thank you,' replied Checchina very gently.

'In any case, the Doctor's back too; he's upstairs.'

'Ah!' said the other woman simply. And she did not hurry upstairs. Toto had come back, letting himself in with his own key, and was now changing his shoes.

'You've been out in this weather, Checca?'

'It wasn't raining when I went out.'

'Where have you been?'

'To see Isolina.'

'And what was she doing?'

'Nothing; she wasn't there.'

'You could go back.'

'Yes, I could.'

'I've been at the hospital. Not much to do; just a dislocation and a broken leg, nothing else. I took advantage of that to go on to the *Caffè di Roma*—you know, in the Corso—to see whether by any chance the Marchese di Aragona was there...'

'In the rain, you went?'

'I had an umbrella. I remembered the Marchese di

Aragona telling me that he sometimes dined at that café. I had a cup of coffee; confound it, it cost me five *soldi*, and one for a tip to the waiter, who put on a disgruntled face into the bargain. I didn't find the Marchese.'

Silence followed, while she slowly undressed, putting away her things one by one. As she started buttoning up her overall she asked:

'What time is it, Toto?'

'Six o'clock.'

She turned her face for a moment to the wall.

* * *

Susanna was taking the things she had bought for dinner out of her big red cotton handkerchief, and saying as she did so:

'Here are the *cannelloni*, handmade ones, two pounds of them as you told me; here are the pilchards, to be cooked in the pan with oil, breadcrumbs, and marjoram: they were being sold at sixteen *soldi* the kilo, and I had to make a great fuss to get them for fourteen; here's a jar of tomato, to make the sauce for the *cannelloni* ...'

'And this—what's this?' asked Checchina, who was watching and listening, her hair not yet done, and so pale that she looked yellow.

Then Susanna pulled out something white, a piece of paper, a letter which had become wet and stained with red juice, having lain between the bottled tomato and a bunch of garlic.

'It's a letter,' said the maid. 'The postman gave it to me for you.'

On the envelope of best English writing-paper was written: Signora Fanny Primicerio; there was a dirty mark right on top of the name. Inside it said: 'How cruel you

were to-day! What have I done that you should make
me suffer so? I waited for you, in an agony, from three
o'clock till seven. Will you come to-morrow? Be kind
to me, I am so unhappy. You promised me you would
come; come, then. I will wait for you again, alone, and
calling upon you with longing, O beautiful creature destined to be loved. I implore you on my knees, do not fail
me.—Ugo di Aragona.'

In a flash, after reading the letter, Checchina seemed
to see him kneeling in front of her—the handsome Marchese di Aragona himself, in that damp, dark kitchen;
and she began trembling all over, and everything went
whirling round her, the saucepan on the fire, the gridiron
hanging on the wall, the flat-irons resting on the hood
over the fireplace; and the sound of gushing water in the
sink seemed to her like a thunderstorm.

'I'm going to fall down,' she said to herself, and leant
against the table.

'Are you cold?' said the maid, hearing her mistress's
teeth chattering.

'Yes, I'm cold,' murmured Checchina, instinctively
pushing the letter into her pocket.

'It's not so very cold outside, it's *scirocco* weather.
Is your stomach upset, perhaps? Would you like me to
fry you a couple of pilchards, done quickly?'

'No, no.' And she went off slowly into her bedroom,
her hand still in her pocket, holding the letter. But for
a long time she did not dare read it again, fearing lest
Susanna might come in unexpectedly and catch her. The
maid was sweeping in the dining-room, and Checchina
was afraid even of her hearing the rustling of the paper.
Then she had an idea; she took her prayer-book, placed
the letter inside it, turned over two or three pages, then
opened it and read the letter, as though she were reading
a page of the book. Oh, that lovely letter, with the Mar-

chese's coronet on it, such a very simple letter, written in such a fine, gentlemanly handwriting, with its blue ink dried with golden sand! The words were spun out languidly, voluptuously, linked—hand in hand, as it were—by very fine little lines; and, below them, the big signature, clear and ample, like ringing, sonorous music. She repeated the words two or three times, in a whisper: Ugo di Aragona. Then it seemed to her that the expressions he used in the letter composed a sorrowful melody, a melody which made her melt with compassion, as though some great disaster had befallen him. She seemed to hear his voice pronouncing those melancholy words with a deep sadness in its tone; tears rose to her eyes. But soon her impression became less agitated, and her mind retained only the figures: he had waited for her from three until seven.

While she was brushing her hair Susanna, contrary to her usual habit, remained silent, and Checchina was frightened by her sulkiness. What could be the cause of it?

'Isolina has written to me...' She dropped the hint without making any display of the matter.

Susanna did not answer.

'...just to tell me that she wasn't at home yesterday because an aunt of hers was ill.'

She breathed again, once this complicated untruth was out.

'I expect it was a male aunt,' muttered the pious Susanna.

But she did not put off her sulky looks; in vain did Checchina hover round her, obsessed with an uneasiness such as she had never felt before. Susanna would not be drawn into conversation. Then Checchina's uneasiness was increased: if this bigoted woman mentioned the letter to Toto, what was she to do? And she grasped the letter convulsively between her fingers inside her pocket, as if she wished to crush it; but she had not the courage to tear it up. She read it a third time, opening it out inside a drawer in the chest-of-drawers, on top of a pile of table-napkins; she intended to learn it by heart and then destroy it, but she became confused and the sentences were jumbled up inside her head. For a moment she thought of hiding it somewhere—but where? The chest-of-drawers and the wardrobe were useless, for Toto was perpetually asking her for the keys so as to fetch something or other from them; the dining-room table had drawers with wooden handles but no locks, and the card-table in the sitting-room had no drawers at all. It was no good, she had better keep it in her pocket, it would be safer there; but at lunch, owing to her increasing anxiety—seeing that Susanna still preserved her angry expression and her scornful silence— Checchina ate hardly anything. Nervously, from time to time, she put her hand into her pocket to make sure the letter was still there, but not once did she take out her handkerchief for fear she might accidentally pull out the letter with it. The maid, how-ever, said nothing, and Toto, for a wonder, did not start an argument. He was tired as a labourer who has been lifting bales of goods at the docks, and after lunch he went to sleep at once on the bed, fully dressed and wrapped up in an old shawl, snoring like a pair of bellows. At half past three they had to call him four times, and then, clearing his throat and spitting, he grumbled that he had a poisonous mouth and a headache.

'Are you going to Isolina's again, to-day?'

'Yes,' she said resolutely.

But after her husband had left Checchina, as she was dressing, grew worried again at the thought of Susanna. Could she have suspected anything? That would be the last straw. She paused as she was buttoning up her dress, seized by a sudden weakness and uncertainty: then the sad music underlying the words of the Marchese's letter touched certain fibres in her heart and startled her and made her hurry on with her dressing.

'Good-bye, Susanna.'

'Good-bye,' said the other woman, in a hard voice.

But she did not add: 'May God go with you,' as she always did. Checchina again felt frightened as she went downstairs, but the light outside and the clear way ahead brought back her courage as she walked up Via del Naz-zareno—very slowly, for it was early and she did not wish to arrive too soon. But, when she came in front of the stationer's shop in Piazza di Trevi, she turned cold with fear. She had left the Marchese's letter in the pocket of her overall, and Susanna could read handwriting, not only print. She fumbled in her pocket, automatically, two or three times, praying secretly that the Lord would make her find it, as though a special miracle might occur. And, still searching, she turned homewards again, saying to herself:

'Holy Virgin, may she not have read it! Holy Virgin, help me!'

It seemed to take her an age to get home again. She was praying quietly to herself.

'Open the door, Susanna, it's me!'

'Oh, it's you,' she replied drily.

As fate willed it, it so happened that she was holding the overall on her arm. Checchina stopped short, aghast.

Then she said quickly: 'I came back because I left Isolina's letter behind and there was something important in it that she wanted me to explain. Is the letter in that pocket?'

Susanna held out the overall. 'I was just brushing it,' she said.

Checchina took the letter without opening it and went off again, saying to herself: Did she read it or didn't she? In the street, as she turned again along Via del Nazzareno, she glanced back at the window of the flat: Susanna was standing there, looking at her.

'Oh my goodness,' thought Checchina, 'now she's seen that I didn't turn into Via Sant'Andrea.'

But she continued on her way, incapable of doing anything else, her will-power paralysed by the idea that Susanna might have read the letter. In Via San Vincenzo a man stopped her:

'Hallo, Signora Checca, nice to see you, where are you off to?'

It was Alessandro Pontacchini, a friend of the family, who kept a little tobacconist's shop.

'I'm going this way, Signor Sandro,' she said, shaken by this sudden interruption, 'I'm going...on a matter of business...'

'Do *you* have business affairs, Signora Checca? Well, well. I'll tell Signor Toto that he'll have to look out,' he said, with gross Roman archness.

She smiled feebly. 'Just to the dyer's,' she explained; 'I'm just going to the dyer's, about a dress...'

'Ah, you're a good, careful person, Signora Checca! Not many women like you to be found in this place! And that's why I've given up the idea of getting married. When I thought of it, it was already too late, my dear Signora Checca; Signor Toto had got in before me.' And he laughed.

Overcome with embarrassment, she made no answer.

'One of these evenings, when I can leave my nephew Cencio to mind the shop, I'll come along to you and have a good gossip. I'll bring some roast chestnuts and you can provide some cheap white wine, Signora Checca. How about it?'

'Yes, by all means.'

'You tell that lucky rascal Toto, and give him my greetings.'

She started on her way again, feeling more and more agitated. Now there was Signor Sandro too, who would come and start talking and would tell a story and make more jokes—and at home there was Susanna, who had perhaps read the letter and who had seen her, from the window, turning into Via del Nazzareno instead of Via Sant'Andrea. And goodness knows how many people she knew had met her on the way and taken note of her, and she had never noticed them! And supposing that one of Toto's colleagues at Santo Spirito had seen her and immediately went and told him about it, at the hospital, and Toto, his suspicions aroused, went off to Isolina's and failed to find her there? And, not finding her, went home, and Susanna told him the whole story, from the arrival of the letter to her coming back and then going out again, and which street she had taken? But she walked on, she still walked on, no longer seeing anybody.

'Where are you going?' said a well-known voice.

It was Isolina: she was standing outside the café of the Quirino Theatre, leaning against the wooden balustrade; she was badly dressed, with an old hat and gloves that had been mended.

'Where are you going, my dear Checchina?'

'I was coming to see you...' stammered Checchina, flabbergasted at this further encounter and no longer knowing what to say.

'To see *me*? In *this* direction? What's come into your head? But what's the matter with you, my sweet? Are you feeling ill?'

Taking her by the hand, she dragged her into the doorway of the big Palazzo di Sciarra, where building operations were going on and stonemasons were coming and going, and piles of rubbish and wooden rafters blocked the way.

'There's nothing wrong with me, nothing at all,' replied Checchina, trying to recover herself, 'but for some days I've been feeling upset, I don't know why...'

'Perhaps you're going to have a baby, my dear Checca.'

'What an idea! I don't know what it is, it comes over me from time to time...'

'O my dear, darling child, *I* ought to be staying in bed, I feel so ill. What a dog's life this is! What a lot of vexations we have to put up with! If you only knew, if you only knew...that scoundrel Giorgio, my own sweetheart, if you only knew what he's doing to me...'

'What's he doing to you?'

'Things you'd hardly believe possible, my dear Checca. Enough to make me weep all the tears in my body. No less than this—that I know for certain that he's making advances to one of the young women here, one of the waitresses at the café, a dark girl, and that he's here every evening, drinking beer and punch and giving her tips of a whole *lira*, to ingratiate himself, of course; why, it's a thing so horrible and filthy that one can scarcely believe it.'

'Is it really true?'

'What? The person who told me about it can't possibly be lying, he's such a fine, charming young man, a student of literature, who writes poetry too and publishes it in a Sunday paper, and lives next door to us; he's such an honest young man, and he comes here in the evenings to make a study of things that he'll put into his books afterwards; and it's he who told me about Giorgio's disgraceful behaviour.'

'You believed him?'

'I would much rather *not* believe him, my pet, but Giorgio has always been such a terribly thankless sort of man. And as fickle as can be. Now to-day, just to spite him, I'm not going there; and I came past here to see if I could pick her out, this waitress—she'd be painted up to the nines, I imagine. But I haven't been able to make out anything; it's too far off and the window-panes make a reflection ... However, it's cold here. Let's go; I'll come with you and tell you the rest of the story on the way.'

'No,' said Checchina.

'Don't you want me to come with you?'

'No.'

'Ah!' was all the other woman said.

The flames of bashfulness were burning in Checchina's cheeks; her voice was strangled in her throat.

'So you're in a hurry, are you?' went on Isolina slowly.

'Yes.'

'Are you going there for the first time?'

'Yes.'

'And is he a good-looking young man?'

'Yes.'

They stood there, close together, at the corner of Via dell'Archetto, stepping back from time to time to make way for the carts of bricks and stones that were constantly passing along the street.

'Well done, Checchina! And you told me nothing about it! Really, I see that you don't care about me in the least, and you don't trust me, whereas I've always told you everything. I see you're just a great big hypocrite...'

'Oh, Isolina!'

'Well, it's a question of temperament, and I'm not finding fault with you; when one loves, one is afraid. Yet I might have been able to help you, to give you some advice. Where does he live?'

'Along here ... quite near here ...'

'Where?'

'In Via Santi Apostoli.'

'A dreary street, and dangerous too: too close to the Corso,' remarked Isolina with her air of experience. 'Tell him to move, to take a room in a more distant part of the town: it would be better...'

'He wouldn't go to a room in a more distant part; he's a nobleman, a Marchese...'

'A Marchese? Which Marchese?'

'The Marchese di Aragona.' The name was sighed rather than spoken.

'Aragona? Yes, I've heard him spoken of, a very grand nobleman. Has he given you fine presents? A bracelet?'

'No: he's sent me flowers.'

'Has he written you wonderful letters?'

'Only one.'

'You have it in your pocket, of course? Do let me see it.'

Checchina showed it to her. As always, she submitted to the will of the person who was with her.

'It's lovely! How lucky you are, my darling Checchina, to be truly loved! Oh, the virtuous little person who never said a word!'

'I've told you everything.'

'Go on, my dear, go on, and God bless you! Be prudent, I do implore you; you're new to these things, and a mere trifle can betray you; you don't know what a risk you're running, you must be cautious. I know what it means, and what palpitations of the heart I've suffered. Go on, I won't keep you any longer, you lucky creature; if I see Toto, I'll tell him we've been together for two hours. Two hours will be enough, will it? Or...d'you intend to stay longer?'

'Oh, Isolina!'

'Don't be shocked, there's no harm in it. Give me a kiss, my dear; we're more than friends now, we're sisters.'

And off she went down Via delle Vergini, with her tripping step like a frivolous little bird. Checchina walked slowly on, again disheartened by the shame of having been forced to tell everything, feeling that it was all finished

now, since another woman knew about it, since she herself
had had the weakness to pronounce that name. As she turned into Via Santi Apostoli she glanced at the church, and,
as she passed it, tried the gate, but it was closed. In front
of the great Odescalchi palace stood a carriage with armor-
ial bearings; it was empty, waiting for somebody. Then,
from the opposite pavement, Checchina saw the archway,
and, beyond the arch, two shops, and then the small door
with steps leading up to it. But on the threshold, leaning
against the wall and blocking half the entrance, stood the
porter, a big, tall man with a coarse face bristling with
grey hairs, a red woollen scarf round his neck and a peaked
cap set rather crookedly on his head. He was smoking a
pipe and looking up into the air. Checchina at once stopped dead on the pavement facing him, unable to cross the
street. In order to enter the doorway, she would have to
ask the permission of the porter, inquire of him whether
the Marchese di Aragona was at home, and then walk
past him. She summoned up all her energies for this effort, but half way across the street she stopped again. The
porter had an ugly, brutal face, one of those irreverent
faces that dishearten the timid. She walked on as far as
Rèanda the upholsterer's, trying to rally her courage, and
then crossed the street. She went past in front of the door
without looking up at the porter: and yet she could see
that he was looking her up and down in an impudent
fashion. She arrived back again at the church, and turned
round to look up at the windows of the house, despairingly,
as though asking for help. The green shutters were closed,
as the Marchese had told her, because he preferred a sub-
dued light. Then she went back again, from the Palazzo
Odescalchi as far as the café at the corner of Via Nazio-
nale, passing slowly in front of the door. The porter was
reading a lottery ticket, an angry look on his face, but he
did not move. She did not go in. Going back towards

the Palazzo Odescalchi, she passed the door again, for the third time: he was slowly refilling his pipe, pressing down the tobacco with his thumb—and he was still standing in the doorway.

So Checchina gave it up. Bowing her head, she turned homewards.

EDOARDO SCARFOGLIO

Scarfoglio, half Abruzzese and half Calabrian, was born at Paganica near Aquila in 1860 and died at Naples in 1917. In a country where most writers are :ournalists of some kind, Scarfoglio was considered the finest journalist of his day, one of its *più belle penne* (as the phrase then went): literary critic, writer on travel, politics, and polemics in general.

The only fiction he ever wrote was around the age of twenty, all contained in a volume which has the same title as this story. These tales belong in some ways to the 'naturalist' cycle of Verga and Capuana; but there is a firmness of outline and of effect which differentiates them, as it does from the earliest stories of D'Annunzio, written at the same time and about the same district. Scarfoglio's stories are not so imaginative as those of his fellow Abruzzese, but they are less strained and have a pleasant and genuine rustic quality of their own.

Il processo di Frine (published, with other stories, at Naples in 1884) has not been translated before. It was included in a charming film made up from short stories of the last century called *Storia d'altri tempi*, directed by Alessandro Blasetti, and with the chief parts evocatively played by Gina Lollobrigida and Vittorio de Sica.

W. J. Strachan's use of a modified English west-country speech is an original attempt to deal with the perennial problem which dialects offer to the translator.

A. C.

THE PHRYNÉ CASE

EDOARDO SCARFOGLIO

From *Il processo di Frine*

Translated by W. J. Strachan

The indictment states, though not without a touch of
legal pomposity, how on the morning of 23 May 1879
Mariantonia Desideri, aged twenty-six, wife of Giatteo Baciccia, nicknamed 'The Good-for-nothing,' aged thirty-two,
a peasant born and resident in Guardiagrele, entered the
local chemist's shop, and, seeing that it was full of customers, deposited in a corner a small basket covered with
newly gathered vine-leaves which she had brought along,
and sat down to wait for the shop to become empty.

The chemist, who noticed that she was looking fresher
than ever, like a plant still moist with dew, felt a return
of his old gallantry, and as he pressed a label round the
neck of a bottle, he thrust his head between two peasants
who stood there with their hands, holding the money,
stretched out ready to take their purchases, and questioned
her with a glance. Mariantonia responded with a sign on
her part, indicating that she wished to wait; and since
the chemist, who interpreted it his own way, smiled, Mariantonia, misunderstanding in her turn, smiled back.
Then she wiped her nose on the corner of her apron and
and stayed there, patiently contemplating her beringed
fingers, creasing the folds of flesh above her generous
bosom with her lowered chin. The various male and
female customers left the premises in turn as the chemist
hurriedly served them; and when the last one had been

handed his dose of quinine and had turned to go out, Mariantonia picked up the basket she had previously put down and stood it on the counter in front of the chemist. He, surprised by this unexpected gift, lifted up the leaves and looked questioningly at the donor, and remarking that they were cherries, covered them over again and laid the basket on one side.

'What do 'ee want?' he asked, not knowing what to think.

There seemed nothing odd in Mariantonia's appearance as she stood erect at the other side of the counter; she was the same handsome, silly creature that she had always been.

'A little poison.'

The chemist, who was in fact more taken aback than suspicious, stared at her face; but the harmonious features before him were so serene and unspoilt by the increasing opulence of her flesh that Guardiagrele's purveyor of public health was amused at his own surprise and failure to realize at once that it was a pretext on her part for coming to terms of surrender. And with a laugh and in a light-hearted tone as if to keep up the jest, he asked:

'An' what do 'ee intend to do with it?'

'It's for killin' rats.'

This natural enough reply, uttered in such calm tones, upset the chemist's sly and egotistical calculations and dealt a blow at his vanity.

'Come, come! What rats be 'ee talking about? Aint'ee got a cat?'

But Mariantonia insisted with such quiet sincerity that the chemist thought he would take advantage of her needs to dictate the conditions of its sale while she argued away with reasoning that was inspired more by imagination than logic:

'But they be eatin' all the corn...' He interrupted her with a laugh intended to be Mephistophelian.

'I can't give it 'ee.'

'An' for why?'

'Because I can't, that's for why!'

'Well, thee's given it to Graziella, the road-sweeper's girl an' won't give it to me? I'll pay 'ee out!'

'Look 'ee 'ere. I'm not goin' to give it 'ee.'

And they went on like this, she pressing her demand, he persisting in his refusal to the accompaniment of sly grins and evil leers. Then he left the back of the counter and closed one wing of the door so that the full light of the sun which had hitherto flooded the whole shop, rebounding from the glass cabinets and refracted by the bottles, was cut off. A discreet shadow spattered them rather meanly and seemed as if it were advising them to hurry. In fact, the chemist, seeing that Mariantonia was unaffected by the smooth talk with which he was endeavouring to inveigle her, approached her closely from behind and whispered: 'If th'll let me 'ave ee, I'll give 'ee the poison.'

Mariantonia, without a hint of embarrassment, indeed quite simply as if it had been a threepenny piece they were talking about, replied: 'All right, thee can 'ave me.'

The chemist glanced at her again, this time with more suspicion than surprise. He had usurped a husband's rights on more than one occasion and he had frequently induced some of his wretched female customers who were impecunious to pay him as it were in kind. But Mariantonia's surrender seemed too good to be true; this willingness to part with her virtue without any show of resistance, revolt of modesty, or apparent sensual desire, was truly an odd business, for she had always ignored the blandishments, promises and jeers of this rustic Don Juan. However, her outward appearance was so calm and ingenuous, in those beautiful shining eyes her natural stupidity slumbered so undisturbed, that our preparer of drugs, in his masculine vanity, attributed everything to himself and spared no grateful thought for the rats.

They then had an argument; the chemist insisted on immediate payment. But Mariantonia declared that it was impossible; they were expecting her back home; someone might come in.

'Let's close the door,' he said.

'Be thee mad? Old Gammy-leg saw I come in an' not come out!'

She arranged a future assignation, however, with such apparent artlessness that he had to give way. But the chemist, annoyed that she had partly gone back on her word, or so it seemed to him, intended to go back on his, at any rate to some extent. He began to quibble.

'I'm not goin' to give 'ee straight poison; I'll give 'ee poison-baits like I've given Graziella.'

Mariantonia calmly returned to the attack.

'Poison baits! Oh, no 'ee does'nt. They bain't no good. Proper poison, or I bids 'ee good-day!'

Finally they came to terms. The chemist, whose mental faculties were beginning to be clouded by sexual excitement, asked: 'And where do 'ee propose to put the poison?'

'In cheese.'

'Well, run and fetch cheese and bring it here.'

And he flung open the wing of the door which he had previously shut. Mariantonia dashed out, and as his lust died down in the interval of waiting for her return, fresh doubts began to torment him; but the return of that magnificent wench with a bowl of bluish earthenware full of grated cheese suddenly interrupted his lewd thoughts. He opened a glass cabinet, took out a little bottle full of arsenic, and dropped a pinch of it on to the cheese.

'A bit more,' coaxed Mariantonia, and the chemist

obeyed. But before letting her go, he exacted an instalment of what she owed him.

Mariantonia entered the kitchen, put the cheese away in the larder and poked up the fire; then she took off her dress and stood there in her petticoat and blue bodice. She next removed her red scarf with its yellow floral pattern, withdrew the slightly sweat-covered medallion of the Madonna from between her breasts where it reposed, kissed it piously as if to invoke its aid for some great undertaking, and began to cut the macaroni out of the *pasta* which, after first spreading it out in a thin sheet, she had rolled and left to dry on the big wooden tray.

Mariantonia's arms, bronzed in the sun, but none the less handsome in their Bacchus-like robustness, and dusty with flour, purposefully cut up the pasta into the requisite shape, and her limpid eyes calmly contemplated the little heap of macaroni as it rapidly increased in size. When she had finished she took it from the tray to separate the pieces, and as the water in the pot was boiling, she threw the macaroni in. Then, all powdered with flour, she asked her mother-in-law:' Do 'ee want the macaroni wi' oil or peppers?' 'Wi' oil.'

Mariantonia, who had expected this reply since it was a fasting day and the old woman did not eat things cooked in meat fat on those occasions, went back to the kitchen. From the *mesa,* as they call the food-chest in Chieti, she took a small hunk of cheese made from ewes' milk and began to grate it. Next she unhooked a frying-pan from the wall, poured some olive oil into it, added a few cloves of garlic, and put it on the fire. She then lifted the lid of the pan to see how the macaroni was getting on. It was done. She removed the pan from the chain and emptied its contents into a colander. Leaning forward thus, with her ample hips taut like a mare's crupper and her body thrust into the steam arising from the macaroni, she looked magnificent. When she had drained the water off into a basin put there for that purpose, she straightened her torso, still holding the colander in her hands, and served some of the macaroni into a bowl and some on to a large plate, lifted the medicated cheese from the sideboard, opened the food-bin, and took out the other lot of cheese which she had grated. She remained as composed as ever; her handsome moon-face wore all the serenity of innocence. She served a mixture of peppers and tomato preserve on to the large plate; into the bowl she poured the cooked oil and sprinkled the poisoned cheese over it. And with her two beautiful Bacchus-like arms, which showed not the slightest tremor, she transferred it all to the table.

Giatteo, who had a large appetite and little desire to speak, helped himself generously from the large plate and immediately started to eat; but the old woman who sat all day long in the porch like a sentry and saw a good deal and who, furthermore, suffered from dyspepsia, feeling unable to start a conversation with her son, began mumbling a prayer before she touched the food. Mariantonia was gazing at her; her fork held upright in the air reflected her inward suspense, though she betrayed no exterior sign of emotion. She was filled with that nervous expectancy with which a novice sportsman, gun in hand, watches a flock of larks flying above his snares. And when at last the old woman put in her first mouthful, Mariantonia too plied her fork frenziedly between her teeth and did not lift her eyes until her plate stood empty before her. Then once again she looked at her mother-in-law who was calmly chewing away, and it seemed that the macaroni was more to her taste today than usual. Giatteo, who had now appeased his hunger, began to chat and the old woman answered and ate at the same time.

But Mariantonia was beginning to shift about on her chair as if she was sitting on thorns; she would like to have been miles away. If only that cursed old bitch would stop eating! A vague terror arose in her mind and shaped itself into this thought; 'Let it kill 'ee'. Look, 'er never stops, look!'

But the old woman was eating the doctored food, mumbling it between her gums with that strange ecstasy which the toothless appear to find in eating pap. When at length the macaroni was finished, she mopped up all the gravy from the plate with a piece of bread and put that in her mouth too. At this point Mariantonia rose to clear the table. Giatteo went to fetch his pipe from his jacket pocket, and the old woman who felt heavy with food, went upstairs to have a sleep. By this time Mariantonia was as nervous as a boy who has committed some misdemeanour and feels the moment of discovery approach. The old woman had enough arsenic in her body to finish off a herd of cattle.

'Who can get that lot out of 'er?' thought Mariantonia who felt more and more panic-stricken every moment. For a short while she hoped that the poison would not kill the old woman, that it would merely cause a passing sickness, a violent fit of colic maybe, but a horrible voice from upstairs called out twice: 'Marianto! Giatte!' and set her trembling. She stayed still for a moment, waiting, hoping that she had imagined it in her panic, but once more the cry came from above in such a terrible tone of threat or entreaty that Mariantonia could not stay still and ran upstairs. And when she arrived in the doorway and saw the old woman lying in the middle of the bed, purple, and her face horribly contorted, pressing her hands against her stomach, an uncontrollable terror and nausea flung her back and, leaping downstairs, she dashed into the kitchen, mad with fright. Giatteo, his pipe in his

mouth, was standing outside by the door; at the sight of
his wife, his eyes and lips opened wide with curiosity, and
he asked:

'What's amiss?'

Mariantonia who by now was relieving her emotion
in a fit of weeping was at first unable to speak; she leaned
against the larder door with her apron held up to her face,
murmuring between sobs and moans:

'Mamma...mamma... O my God! O Jesus Christ
and Blessèd Virgin!'

Giatteo, still tired from his heavy work in the fields
and conscious of the agreeable weight of food on his
stomach, started up, displeased by this interruption and
nervous about the annoyance and expense of an accident,
again asked:

'Look, what's amiss? Can't 'ee say what 'ee wants?'

'O Christ! an' now what'll I do, what'll I do?'

'What's amiss? Can't 'ee tell I?' cried Giatteo brus-
quely, going behind her and snatching the apron away
from her face. Then another howl from the old woman,
accompanied by ominous groans, sobs, and retchings, came
from above. Giatteo left his wife and moved towards
the stairs, but Mariantonia clutched him by the shirt and
dragged him back.

'Don't go up! Don't go up for Christ's sake!'

'Why not? What's 'appened to mamma? What 'av 'ee
done to 'er?'

'I've give 'er poison,' cried Mariantonia, letting go of
him; and a fresh frenzied burst of weeping choked her
eyes and her voice. For a moment Giatteo was stunned;
his flesh seemed to freeze; then he crossed the kitchen and
strode out. Mariantonia was left alone, albeit slightly
calmer for having confessed; but she was still in a daze.

At that moment, the sun which had climbed above
the wall of the house opposite flooded the doorway.

Upstairs the dying woman's groans rattled in her throat.

Shortly afterwards, the police magistrate entered with the maresciallo of the carabinieri.

'Good,' said the magistrate, greeting Mariantonia with a sly smile. 'You've made a job of it!' And he turned to see if someone else whom he expected was coming along.

'The registrar isn't in sight yet,' he added, addressing the maresciallo. And he asked the woman, this time in a dry, grim tone: 'Where's the body?'

Mariantonia did not reply. She was in the grip of a cold terror and her teeth were chattering as she propped herself up against the wall, drawing herself close to it as though she hoped to hide there.

'It must be upstairs,' the maresciallo replied for her.

'Let's go then,' concluded the magistrate, inviting the poisoner to precede him.

'I bain't goin' in there!' retorted Mariantonia, but the maresciallo gripped her arm and dragged her in.

By this time the news had spread through the market-town, and all the inhabitants began to hurry to the house where there was now a crowd and a confused shouting round Giatteo who did not dare enter. He just stood there outside, pale, abject, but yet with a lighter heart than a few minutes before, like a man who has miraculously escaped being buried alive in a landslide and stands dazed watching the rocks which have just fallen in front of him and are still sending up clouds of dust. Strange rumours were running through the crowd; from the fantasies stimulated by the emotion of horror the Mariantonia legend was suddenly springing to life. Mariantonia's love-affairs and the circumstances of the crime were the themes they were elaborating. The names of the various lovers were being passed from mouth to mouth. Everyone was looking for an accomplice; but who could it be? At length someone reported that Pasquale Spatocca had told him that Mariantonia had asked him about a method of poisoning rats and he had advised her to mix the poison with cheese. At this juncture, the registrar arrived with two carabinieri and entered the house. Then the maresciallo appeared at the door, exhorting the crowd by voice and gesture to disperse; in the rear Mariantonia could be seen, held by carabinieri. A threatening voice cried out:

'Bitch! Whore! Hang 'er!'

And in the midst of this outburst of popular conscience Giatteo clung to the maresciallo, ingratiating himself:

'Taint nothin' to do wi' me, officer, I've done nothing'.

* * *

Because of the commonplace nature of the crime, the stupid imprudence with which it had been carried out, and finally because of the criminal's confession first to her husband and then to the magistrate, the case was expeditiously concluded. The examining magistrate of the Assizes of Chieti, who could not find any opportunity for the prosecution of his investigations, since everything was clear and plain, and Mariantonia's way of life, about which all the witnesses were in agreement, explained the motives of the crime, confirming as they did the prisoner's statements made to the Guardiagrel magistrate, was far from pleased. For an examining magistrate who has held that tiring office for some little time and has given further proof of his wisdom, however tame he seemed among the piles of law-cases bound in green or red, is governed by two ardent and successive passions at every new crime or scandal. The first is to find out their author, the second to throw light on all the shady parts. The court of law with its great paraphernalia of carabinieri, ushers, gowns, advocates, male and female witnesses, oaths and jurymen, the prisoner's stand, with its admonitory inscription stating that all men are equal in the eyes of the law, might appear to be the most thrilling centre of the eternal drama of justice; but it is merely a pompous rehearsal of the parts. The Judges slumber, the President yawns as he shifts on his seat, the Public Prosecutor rolls his eyes heavenward as he prepares to pour forth his sonorous eloquence, the jury scrawl or carve on the desks or benches, the public come and go as if they were in the market square, the prisoner with clear, calm reasoning assesses the sentence he will probably get. Nobody pays any heed to the arguments for the defence or prosecution since everyone knows that it is merely a gymnastic contest between a man paid by the Crown to indict and a man paid by the accused to defend him. The case is not tried as in England in the open court, where two barristers produce their witnesses and accumulate proofs for and against the accused. The proofs have already been collected, the case is already completed. It only remains to show the facts to the jury, those twelve good men and true, chafing under the right which they must exercise under duress and upon whose judgement the ultimate excitement of the drama depends. But the real dramatic development is enacted behind the scenes in the chambers of the Examining Judge, those tiny ill-furnished rooms which for the most part do service as an antechamber for usher and witnesses, a refuge for the clerks of the court, a study for the judge and a store-room for the material evidence. And the true dramatist is the Examining Judge, that modest man, bourgeois in dress and appearance, who bears no sign of authority on his back, who, boxed up in his little room with a stove burning in the winter, venetian blinds closed in the summer, half buried among heaps of papers, half choked by the smoke from his cigar, calmly

continues to write one order after another, always with
the same formulas that vary only with the different crimes
and penalties; that man who presents the aspect less of
a magistrate than of one of those hundred thousand re-
cluses who serve their country for forty years, penning the
records of some branch of public administration in a
minute-book. A first glance into this room throws light
on the genesis of each drama, for here and there, on the
desk, seats, the top of the stove, in fantastic disorder lie
the strangest tools of the trade—clasp-knives, sheathed
daggers, rusty pistols, hatchets with chipped edges, bun-
ches of skeleton-keys, blood-stained clothes, water-meters,
glass vessels containing human organs, metal-plated guns,
loaded sticks, everything sealed and labelled with the
owner's name together with a description of the nefarious
use to which it was put and the case for which it served
as evidence. Then, if you could spend a few hours inside, a strange sight would meet your eyes: advocates,
deputy Public Prosecutors, carabinieri, witnesses constantly
going in and out; clerks compiling records or sealing
indictments in the office; hanging round the usher in the
antechamber, as if he were some arbiter of human destiny,
the witnesses awaiting their call, bunched up by the
windows or in the middle of the room in a state of
suspense, grave, muttering in low voices, as if the mere
sight of the judge struck terror into their hearts.

This dignitary himself passes from one business to
another, from the examination of a witness to an argument
with counsel, a confrontation of two people charged with
crime to a medical report, from a search of premises to a
prison visit, spying and smelling out, divining matters
relevant to the crime in the slightest clues, moving from
one crime to the next, slowly accumulating the evidence
for the drama of the public trial. In Italy where, especially in small towns, the strength, acumen and diligence

of the police leave much to be desired, the judge has to
supply this deficiency, combining his own office as a magistrate with that of an investigator, rectifying the mistakes
committed through excess or lack of zeal by those responsible for public security. He is therefore constrained to
develop a truly canine sense of smell. He must visit the
scene of the crime, nose out the truth from conflicting
evidence and the incoherent statements in dialect of the
witnesses, he must pounce on clues in the words and confusion of the prisoner. His work is great and enduring;
his fantastic powers are fortified by his concentration, and
the continual piecing together of minute details develops
his sixth sense. Gradually the rigidity of his mind, already crystallized through his systematic, almost mechanical application of the code of law, becomes flexible;
his brain undergoes a progressive change; he becomes a
trustworthy observer, and before his inquisitorial activities
have declined and deteriorated into a mechanical habit, he
acquires—thanks to his clairvoyant spirit—all the intuitive
faculty of the artist or scholar. In this way he inevitably
becomes devoted to his work; he loves his case as an
author loves his book; he loves it as a criminologist or a
tragedian. He seeks out its causes and its climate, not so
much in order to earn by honest means the four hundred
lire per annum which the State allows him over and above
his stipend as a judge, as for the satisfaction of his craving
to investigate, newly awakened in his mind. He treats
the most brutal offenders with kindly affability, collects
witness's evidence with all the rapture of a geologist discovering some mysterious fossil; he undertakes a fatiguing
journey on horseback in mid-winter or high summer to
ascertain whether a certain window was accessible without
a rope and whether a musket shot could hit a man at a
given distance. And yet he falls a victim to the maladies
that all investigators contract: he gets to love problems,

derive satisfaction from painful inquiries, take a strange delight in monstrous crimes; and when the crime is a commonplace one and proofs crowd in on every side and the accused's confession leaves no scope for his subtle wisdom as examining magistrate, he is as put out as a doctor curing a case of bronchitis that yields to treatment and promises no dangerous complications.

The Mariantonia case belonged to just such a category. At first it seemed possible that some welcome obstacle might arise, since Mariantonia had denied her guilt at the magistrate's preliminary examination. The magistrate had looked at her with obvious satisfaction and said in a gentle voice:

'But how? Haven't you already confessed before the police magistrate? Would you care to have your statement read out to you?'

Mariantonia was disconcerted. Twice or thrice she repeated: 'I don't know nothin'.

When she finally admitted her guilt, the judge wanted to know the motive for the crime. The wretched woman, who had not yet recovered from her terror, drifted from one subject to another, falling into a hopeless confusion. But her interrogator patiently, almost paternally, searched her mind with his calm voice and brown eyes. He knew that her mother-in-law bullied her, turned her husband against her, but he failed to discover from her the reason for it. He did not even ask her if she had any accomplices; the matter was only too clear, since a host of witnesses had testified to the cause of the dissension between mother and daughter-in-law. He therefore confined himself to asking her who had supplied her with the poison. She began by hesitating; then she said she had obtained it from a certain goldsmith on the pretext of cleaning up her gold. That was all. Mariantonia was taken off to prison by the two carabinieri who had brought her, and as she crossed the antechamber she found it full of witnesses who were discussing with the usher what penalty the prisoner incurred.

'The death penalty,' Domenico d'Addesso, the usher, was saying as the door of the clerk's room opened and they caught a glimpse of Mariantonia. All the witnesses turned their eyes to the doorway to see her. They were peasants from Guardiagrele and Pretoro, some gentry, and the parish priest of Guardiagrele.

Shortly afterwards occurred two other incidents which seemed to confuse the issue. The goldsmith mentioned by Mariantonia swore that he had never supplied her with any arsenic. He, in his turn, required a statement from the chemist as to whether he had enough arsenic in stock to have been able to supply Mariantonia. The chemist admitted that he had and suspicion once more fell back on him. But he denied everything. All the witnesses agreed that he had never been known to supply poison without a doctor's prescription, and that for the destruction of vermin he sold small rat-baits, incapable of killing a woman, since rats not infrequently ate them with gusto and suffered no ill consequences; furthermore the amount of arsenic found in the old woman's intestines was too large to have come from rat-baits. It was therefore presumed that Mariantonia had either bought arsenic in Chieti herself or through some third party. And as in cases where the offence is not flagrant and there is lack of sufficient evidence, justice leaves the purveyor of poison in peace, no one gave the present matter another thought.

But another fact came to light; a large number of witnesses stated that a certain Pasquale Spatocca, a small Guardiagrele landowner, had knowledge of the crime. The said Spatocca was called. He was a degree superior to the other peasants, with his gold earrings and a dark check jacket of woollen material over his unstarched shirt. In a tone of sincerity sufficiently convincing to destroy any previous misgivings about him, he admitted that two days before the crime Mariantonia had inquired from him how to poison rats, and he had advised her to mix the poison with grated cheese. Pasquale Spatocca was immediately released.

Thus, during these first two summer months, the case was speeded up and, after many journeys between the rooms of the Examining Magistrate and the Public Prosecutor, the reports were finally collected in a large volume bound in red and tied with a red tape.

Meanwhile in the cells of the San Francesco di Paola prison among a crowd of thieves, child-murderers and abortionists, Mariantonia was gradually recovering her composure. The heat was suffocating, the insects left them no peace, and the board fixed in front of the window-bars cut off any view of the country. Mariantonia found a strange form of relief. She got the job of cleaning the room in which Donn' Angelamaria Chiola, who had had a nephew of hers murdered, was kept prisoner. In return Donn' Angelamaria passed on to her the remains of the good dinner which was sent her from outside. This food was a consolation to Mariantonia and restored her quiet stupidity.

When her counsel, Don Pietro Saraceni, came to see her, he watched this amazing woman with all the satisfaction of a connoisseur in human nature: this fantastic delinquent whose pleasure in food caused her to forget the fate in store for her and soothed her conscience.

And when she wanted to know what penalty was in store for her, he shrugged his shoulders: 'What can I do for you? You gave her a kilogram of arsenic! The penalty for poisoning is the same as for parricide, death; and you have to go to the execution with a black cloth over your head. But they'll allow the plea of extenuating circumstances and commute the sentence to penal servitude for life.'

Then he looked at Mariantonia again. This woman in her silly impassivity, pale from confinement, was so serenely beautiful that he could hardly bear to leave her and in her presence his thoughts were wholly aesthetic; the Code had vanished from his mind. Suddenly he asked her: 'You're from Rapino, aren't you?'

'Yessir, yes, Mr. Advocate.'

'Have you got a silk dress?'

'Yessir.'

'And a nice silk scarf?'

'Yessir. I've a scarf wi' a flowery pattern on't.'

'And have you got ear-rings, necklaces and rings?'

'Yessir; I've all them things.'

'Well, d'ye know what you must do, girl? When the day of the trial comes, deck yourself out like a bride; put on everything you've got; make yourself as beautiful as you can; your best lawyer is yourself. Got me? Well, look after yourself!'

And Don Pietro went off cheerfully, as if he had found inspiration for the end of a novel or a play rather than a loophole in a tricky case.

* * *

The Mariantonia case was heard at the Chieti Assizes in the first fortnight in December. The President, a justice of the Aquila Court of Appeal, was a strict judge who in the course of years had acquired a somewhat chilly and pompous manner as the result of constant legal argument. One of the judges was a lean little old man, sallow, stringy, a mummy covered with a gown of venerable antiquity; the other was a handsome, muscular man with a soft, luxuriant chestnut beard. The Public Prosecutor was a young man of thirty, fair, myopic with thick lips and an amiable expression.

The Court was unusually crowded; the notoriety of the case and the woman involved had spread through the town, and many fine ladies adorned the gallery. The jury occupied their double row of benches and did not appear particularly pleased with the temporary authority which conferred on them the power of life and death. There was a continuous traffic between the office and the court. The public filled half the room. Don Pietro sat alone at Counsel's table with a few sheets of paper and some books in front of him, and, without a thought for what was going on round about him, was composing the last alexandrines of a play. Mariantonia stood completely self-absorbed with a white handkerchief pressed to her eyes. Before the President was a glass vessel containing the old woman's poisoned intestines. After the citation of the witnesses, the reading of the indictment, the President's address to the jury and the other legal formalities, the cross-examination of the prisoner began.

The President said: 'The accused, Mariantonia Desideri, stand up before the Court.'

Mariantonia calmly rose, removing the handkerchief from her face; a sudden murmur ran through the room.

'Christ, dont 'er look lovely!' whispered one of the jurymen into his neighbour's ear. Don Pietro glanced at the prisoner in the dock and then turned back to his alexandrines with a satisfied air.

Mariantonia was an amazing creature. Her healthy, opulent form, still unspoilt by any hint of obesity, dressed in a light brocatelle material with a yellow floral pattern, looked as if it had been moulded in clay by some sensual sculptor. The whole of her bosom was covered with gold necklaces with large pendants hanging from them, and her red fichu, patterned with black, was knotted under her chin according to the custom among married women, but it unsuccesfully veiled the upper past of her breast which rippled with every movement like a heifer's dewlap. Her round face, pale from her long confinement, possessed in its harmony of feature a perfection of beauty unknown among the citizens of Chieti. The eyes of this country Locusta, large, limpid, languid, were filled with tears. Long earrings of unusual pattern hung by her cheeks below the fichu. Below the necklaces three large brooches like the emblems of some barbaric order of chivalry were pinned in a row, and her fingers were covered with rings.

She gave confused replies to the questions put to her. She admitted the crime, but when she was cross-examined about the motives which led her to it, she gave a few dull glances in the direction of the President, then suddenly renewed her weeping, turned to sit down, and hid her face again. Nothing more could be got out of her. But she had made a favourable first impression on people's minds for two reasons. The charge, based on the guilty woman's confession, was so evidently true beyond all doubt and since Mariantonia had pronounced her guilt with her own lips, the jury would have no difficulty in arriving at its verdict. It would be merely a question of deciding the sentence. And so, as this case offered nothing to excite curiosity or stimulate the vanity of mystery-solvers, the way was open for an appeal to sentiment. When Mariantonia first rose to her feet there was a general wave of sympathy, not unmixed, in some quarters, with admiration. A further circumstance increased public sympathy and plucked the strings of pity, namely the husband's evidence.

Giatteo came out of the witness's room; he too wearing his Sunday best: trousers with brown stripes drooping onto new shoes, coarse cotton waistcoat and jacket, clean shirt, soft round hat which he kept twirling between his fingers displaying the pink lining. He was sallow, mean-looking, ugly. His nose had been flattened by a punch received in a brawl; his face was clean-shaven. He trembled as he spoke, almost as if he was intimidated by the law, and recounted the events in full detail, describing the quarrels between his mother and his wife. When the President asked him the cause of these dis-agreements, he trembled still more, as if in awe of his wife. He declared that Mariantonia's bad behaviour was the reason.

'Of what did this bad behaviour consist? Perhaps she failed in her wifely duties?'

'What did 'ee say? I didn't git your meaning.'

'Had she any lovers?'

Giatteo once more gaped at his questioner as if he had not understood.

'Did she make a cuckold of you?' finally asked the president.

'Yes, y'r lordship.'

Mariantonia had straightened up at Giatteo's first words and stood listening, the tears welling in her eyes. At length she smiled. A second murmur ran through the courtroom. That ugly little man who had coldly turned his wife over to the police for fear of getting himself involved in her disgrace and was now publicly confessing his shame, seemed beneath contempt. The men in the audience could not forgive him the rights he enjoyed over this splendid specimen of womanhood. The cross-exam-ination continued.

'Were you aware of your wife's misconduct?'

'Yes, y'r lordship.'

'How did you know?'

'Mamma told me.'

'And did you never manage to cure her?'

The witness shrugged his shoulders.

'When did it begin?'

'Can't say. I think when we first got wed.'

'Could you tell us the names of your wife's lovers?'

'I dont know. Mother told me she had Ciccantonio Peloso, then Pascala Spatocca, then Dunate Cece, then there was Menanze Croce; but I don't know nothin' about it.'

'Were the quarrels frequent between the two women? Were they violent? Did they ever come to blows?'

'They was always at it, y'r lordship; they'd go for each other, then start blubberin'.'

When Giatteo had been dismissed and before the next witness was called, a few remarks were exchanged and something like a communion of feeling occurred among the jury, in the galleries, and among the ordinary public. The dramatic element in the development of a case which was already quite clear to everybody had now shifted back to Mariantonia, whose life and person were gradually assuming an increasing importance in the eyes of the spectators. As a result of this understandable reversion of interest, the legal drama was smothered by the moral and aesthetic drama. Don Pietro Saraceni had completed his verse play and was now standing, hands in pockets, leaning back against the seat, visibly satisfied.

He was thinking about Piccardo Castelvecchio's *Phrynē*, and to him his own version seemed better. And he was right.

Meantime the procession of witnesses continued. It was a tale of adulterous love-affairs, all flowing from seventy various sources in a large country town and two villages, from Guardiagrele, Pretoro, Rapino, into the Assize court with all the rude freshness of local colour; all the gossip and village rumour which, mixed up with the latest and much exaggerated stories of brigands, were destined to enlarge the narrative heritage of the Commune of Guardiagrele.

Crocifissa Vicoli of Rapino had a curious tale to tell. Mariantonia, who had been born in Rapino and lived there, had got to know Giatteo who worked in Pretoro with a spindle-maker and who had occasion to pay a visit to Rapino to sell spindles. From that time on, Giatteo had gone there pretty often; in short, it became common knowledge that they were to be married. Now, one evening when the banns had been published for the first time, Crocifissa was on her way back from the country carrying a bundle of lupin for the animals, and passing in front of the fountain, noticed Mariantonia who had forgotten all about her copper vessel that was already overflowing and was laughing and fooling round in the shadow of the sunset and under the branches of an elder with Don Giovannino Coletti, the son of the lord of the manor. Then, before starting back for Guardiagrele with her betrothed, Mariantonia herself told her about the encounter and said that Don Giovannino had been hanging round her for some time but that she was still a virgin and wouldn't listen to him; and even that same evening she had resisted the young gentleman's attempts to seduce her by promising him a tryst for the day after the wedding. Don Giovannino Coletti, cross-examined, confirmed Crocifissa's deposition.

Although, outside, the piazza of San Giustino and the roofs of the houses around and, beyond the Tre Porte, the whole valley of the Pescara was under a blanket of snow, in the court room itself the heat was considerable. The ladies were discussing in whispers whether they had not better leave but the men were succumbing more and more to the strange spell that this rustic harlot was exercising over their minds. When Pasquale Spatocca entered the witness-box there was a general stir of curiosity. He was the embodiment of the rural Don Juan, enriched by the virtues or vices of his father, a man who calmly squanders his small patrimony without any thought of trying to increase it, who has discovered the way to enjoy life even in the country, taking his chief delight in eating and drinking and winning the favours of married women and bespeaking those of the as yet unmarried ones for the future. He walked in with his check coat, red woollen tie, gold earrings, and silver watch-chain across his belly. He was strong-limbed, well covered, a healthy colour though a tinge of purple was beginning to threaten the region of his nose. He seemed no whit abashed, nor did he pose as a lady-killer. He spoke rather clumsily in a vain effort to add an Italian polish to his Abruzzi dialect; but he never got confused. He told about his love-affair with Mariantonia with much simplicity; he recounted the arsenic business in precisely the same words which he had used before the Examining Magistrate. He did not appear to have anything else to add. The public were a trifle disappointed; they had expected something more. Suddenly the Public Prosecutor, who had not opened his mouth so far, asked how long his relations with the accused had continued. Pasquale Spatocca replied that they had begun three months after Mariantonia's arrival at Guardiagrele with her husband. Once again he was asked whether his love-making had continued even while Mariantonia, to common knowledge, had other lovers and whether he had been aware of these betrayals.

Pasquale Spatocca blushed hotly and shook his head. Then Don Pietro Saraceni requested the President to put the same question to Mariantonia. She said he had. A murmur arose from the public for the third time. Their Don Juan was turning into a vulgar *Monsieur Alphonse* *

* (Translator's note: a character in a play by Dumas *fils*).

in his check jacket, but when pressed to speak the truth, Pasquale nodded 'yes'. But he was overcome with confusion and his cheeks flushed with shame. He replied for the most part by nodding or shaking his head, hardly knowing what to say; and only with considerable difficulty did the President succeed in making him admit that after a few months' intrigue he had remained in Mariantonia's good graces not by virtue of love or money but through a certain respect or perhaps admiration that she had for his reputation as a libertine; and since he had done nothing either to prevent or discourage her lapses, she even confided in him about them. He was not her lover; Mariantonia never had any, being one of those women who have little use for love-affairs as such, in the way that some wealthy people have little use for material possessions. She surrendered her body without a fuss, as much as to say 'have me if that will make you happy!'

Questioned as to whether he believed that the arsenic could have been supplied by the chemist, he said no; Mariantonia had never wanted to yield to the chemist's advances. As to the cause of this repugnance on her part, he replied: 'Because he was too much like her husband.'

The whole of this deposition, particularly the last reply, won increasing sympathy for Mariantonia. This magnanimous lover, this unwitting Ninon de Lenclos, began to be surrounded with a romantic aura which kindled the imagination of the audience. The President glanced nervously at the gallery, but by this time the ladies had become convinced of the warmth of this human drama and insisted on hearing it to the end. Moreover, what further indecencies might not now be disclosed by further witnesses? Pasquale Spatocca's decadence in the opinion of the public, like Giatteo Baciccia's vileness, turned to Mariantonia's advantage. Two members of the jury, who, whether out of contrariness, lack of aesthetic sense, or zeal for justice, had so far paid little heed to the duel of words, stopped scratching hieroglyphics on the woodwork, and began to listen. More witnesses of both sexes were called. They testified about this or that incident in Mariantonia's life, this or that circumstance concerning the crime; they expatiated on the lack of harmony between mother-in-law and daughter, the continual bickering, the squabbles and scenes of violence. Then the parish priest was called. Don Teodoro Cianci advanced modestly, biretta in hand and greeted the court with a slight bow of his head. His good, honest face almost created an atmosphere of Christian virtue around him. He was grey-haired and wizened, but on his still youthful lips he wore an expression of so much gentleness and in his tranquil gaze, pensive under the shadow of his white bushy eyebrows, shone such mild patience and godliness that his mere presence was enough to purify the erotic atmosphere which was beginning to spread.

Don Teodoro Cianci swore to speak the truth, the whole truth and nothing but the truth, with the reservation that the oath could not compel him to reveal the secrets he had learned in the confessional. When this was conceded, he sat down and, with a notable absence of gesture, told in pious accents how Mariantonia's conduct was known to the whole population of Guardiagrele and how he had tried in vain to heal the breach between her and her mother-in-law and lead her back to a respectable life.

'This woman,' said the parish priest, 'did not sin through perversity of soul nor unbridled licentiousness. She failed in her duties because of her foolish lack of will and intelligence and the undue importance she gave to her stomach.'

At these words a murmur of astonishment once more

ran through the court. The drama was extending; a new emotion had been introduced. Don Teodoro was heard in solemn silence.

'This vice of gluttony,' he went on, 'thanks to the wretchedness of our country districts, makes an easy conquest of our peasants. The scarcity and poor quality of the food, together with overwork, arouses a craving for more copious and appetizing food. The peasant who all his life eats unsalted maize cakes, cooked between two iron grids on his kitchen fire, who all his life feeds on vegetables—broccoli, beans, turnips or peppers—dreams of white bread with salt and meat as the height of luxury. Thus in our rural areas, the pig, in whatever way it is cooked in the form of salame or any other dish, has become the focal point of every vague aspiration towards material well-being. On winter Sundays the roast pork is the symbol and subject for rejoicing, and the whole village assembles in the market place. This woman, for example, has allowed herself be led astray by the sin of gluttony; all her wickedness proceeds therefrom. When some titbit excited her appetite, she could not resist temptation. She did not give herself, she sold herself. It was salame that she found most irresistible; she gave herself up to regular orgies of it with Pasquale Spatocca; and this was the true cause of her quarrels with her mother-in-law, because, as always happens, one sin brought another in its train. Mariantonia had become indolent; she did not want to work; she ceased going to the fields almost entirely; at home she left everything in disorder; she neglected the family cooking. The result was perpetual acrimony. He had fought the evil with all his power; he had preached her a sermon on the sin of gluttony. 'But,' added Don Teodoro, raising his eyes to the crucifix nailed above the president's head, 'human nature is frail and blind, and she did not hearken to the voice of God

that came from above, she yielded instead to earthly temp-
tations that enticed her from below.'

When the parish priest had finished speaking, there
was a general atmosphere of excitement; the romantic aura
which had surrounded the personality of Mariantonia began to evaporate. All eyes were focussed on her as if in
reproach but, once again, she had slumped back on to the
which had surrounded the personality of Mariantonia beringed fingers, and shaken by the violence of her sobs.

Meanwhile the other witnesses threw further light on
this new moral aspect of the prisoner; all the questions
harped on the same note, and the parish priest's words
were fully borne out by many testimonies. Thus, the
Chieti landlords, who are not big landowners, their pro-
perty being broken up into many small holdings which
they let on occasion without a thought that a peasant family cannot derive sufficient sustenance from them, suddenly confronted with so unexpected a problem, heedless
of the cause and concerned only with the effect, were
stricken with a fit of academic piety. Mariantonia now
reaped the benefit of this new phase of public opinion.
From being a woman tempted by a bestial vice, she had
become the victim of bad conditions.

These thoughts therefore claimed everybody's attention
when the lengthy cross-examination of witnesses was over,
and the Public Prosecutor's closing speech misfired in the
general distraction.

He was dry and uncompromising. A young man, as
we have already mentioned, he brought to the first exercise
of his office the youthful zeal and rigid dogmatism of the
missionary who has faith in his mission. For him, doubts
and obscurities did not exist; it was all clear-cut: in the
dock was a woman, a monster who, by a freak of nature,
had been given a beautiful face; a woman who made the
most shameful mockery of her body, a woman tainted

with the most bestial vices and who in cold blood had brutally murdered her husband's mother. Such was the fact as she herself had confessed it and as had been confirmed by seventy witnesses. He therefore could see neither extenuating circumstances nor any excuse whatsoever. His prosecution seemed superfluous and the verdict of the jury was beyond all doubt. The decision on the case was in the hands of the court, which was bound to punish the accused with the utmost rigour of Article 531 of the Penal Code.

The speech produced an unsympathetic reaction. Overharsh zealousness is like white heat; it engenders in the minds of those it is trying to reach a kind of spheroidal phenomenon; it flashes by, leaving things unscathed. Furthermore, while he had been perorating two incidents occurred, trivial enough in themselves, but which in the general atmosphere of excitement contributed not a little to the distraction of the chief actors in the last act of the drama. One of the jurymen had brought along some specimens of grain in a paper bag; perhaps he was intending to sell or buy a stock. To relieve his corn-merchant's boredom during this long session, he was amusing himself by counting the grains one by one. He had already counted them three times when right in the middle of the Public Prosecutor's speech the bag slipped from his hand and the grain spilt out on to the floor with a noise like running water. An exclamation mixed with laughter followed and then suddenly it was quiet again.

Shortly afterwards, the President, who was beginning to think with some anticipation of the dinner awaiting him, was shocked by a strange sight; the old judge who was sitting on his right was cautiously sliding his hand along the table edge. When it reached the president's inkwell, it grasped it, drew it towards himself with astonishing patience and poured all the ink into his own inkwell. Then he quietly picked up the latter, lowered it into his lap and began to transfer all the ink to a bottle which he gripped between his knees. The president, newly arrived from Aquila, was unacquainted with his colleague's vice and, never dreaming that a high court judge could be afflicted with kleptomania, tapped his arm, as much as to ask him what the devil he was doing. The judge, caught red-handed, opened his knees and the bottle fell on to the parquet floor with a terrible crash, and once again, laughter and a general hubbub drowned the orator's voice.

So Mariantonia's cause was perceptibly gaining ground. She had the public on her side; the jury wearied by their prolonged immobility and captivated by the general feeling of sympathy for the accused, would most willingly have shown their indulgence. But how could they ignore her confession? At most they could allow a plea of extenuating circumstances which would commute the death sentence into one of penal servitude for life. The discrepancy between human feeling and the law was distressing to everybody present.

It was amid this general perplexity that Don Pietro rose to speak. The one sensible thing Mariantonia had done among so many pieces of foolishness had been to choose this advocate. More of an artist than a legal quibbler, a story-teller, dramatist, and professor of history rather than a defender of widows and wards, even to the Assize court he brought his warm, animated, spirited eloquence, and what amounted to poetic intuition. Even his person, which was that of a peaceful gladiator, his ample chest and his kindly face possessed those elements of friendly persuasiveness.

Serene, smiling, to all appearance quite confident in his case, he rose to his feet in the midst of all this doubt. It was not his intention to plead extenuating circumstances or seek excuses for the crime; the crime, as the Public Prosecutor had so clearly said, was there in that glass vessel, in those poisoned intestines, confessed by the accused, corroborated by the statements of seventy witnesses. The work of counsel for the defence was like that of the Public Prosecutor, superfluous.

'I have therefore advised my client to call no witnesses for the defence. What purpose could witnesses serve? What could counsel do? My client has committed a crime covered by article 531 of the Penal Code; she should suffer the penalty prescribed by the law. So be it. But are the jury machines of justice deputed to classify crimes in the pigeon-holes of the Code, or do these trustees of a moral mission stand above all human legislation? Should not the jury act in some way as a corrective for the inevitable inflexibility of the Penal Code, taking into account all the circumstances and subtleties, the whole atmosphere of the crime? Should not the jury be both artists and psychologists and get right down into the minds of the offenders over whom they have the power of life and death? Does not the work of the jury resemble that of the artist who, in his scrutiny of the events and human beings that he is dealing with, finds not only the raison d'être, the manner and conclusions of his work, but also the development and healthy interpretation of the moral law, contributing in this way to the progress of those moral conventions which human society imposes upon itself? Forget, therefore, gentlemen, your judicial office, and forget mine; I am an artist, you, men possessed of an artistic instinct. Let us in all calmness examine the moral factor which is involved in this case. And first, gentlemen, allow me to draw your attention to an argument which the pestiferous atmosphere of a Court of Law has so far done nothing to dispel. The Greek system of morality, gentlemen, was based on aesthetics: the beau-

tiful and the good were inseparable, and a Greek court-
esan, Phrynē, famed for her radiant beauty, when brought
before the judges with no other defence than her beauty,
was absolved from guilt. Now the woman before you,
as you see, gentlemen, is extremely beautiful; a Greek
tribunal would acquit her without more ado. But we,
unfortunately, are not in Greece; and our aesthetic sense
here has rapidly deteriorated. I do not therefore plead for
a free pardon for her. What I ask you is whether you
consider this canon of Greek morality wholly false? Do
you believe that a woman of perfect beauty can have
within her the roots and causes of evil, that she can be
actuated by an almost innate wickedness? No, gentlemen
of the jury, ask your beautiful wives who are listening to
my words; they will all, with one voice, answer 'no'. The
physiological reason which often enough proceeds from
the realization and bitterness of inferiority would be lacking. The motive of the crime, therefore, must be exterior
and accidental. Let us look for it. That is easily done;
seventy witnesses have mentioned it. It lies in the irre-
gular or illegal indulgence in love-making brought about
by the sin of gluttony. It is this strange physiological
fact that I once again and more emphatically commend
to your attention.'

And Don Pietro Saraceni with his brilliant and sonorous eloquence, in a series of now scientific, now para-
doxical arguments, presented a vivid and colourful portrait of Mariantonia's character. He showed how the
animal element predominated in her; he depicted her as
a handsome animal whose sensual appetites, because of
her healthy constitution and the wretched conditions of
the peasant class, could not be restrained by moral sanc-
tions. 'But if', he continued, 'there were not other causes,
we should have been unable to explain how this woman,
dominated by her animal appetites as she was, should

have preserved a relative virtue. How was it she was not led on to theft? How was it she made no attempt to hide her habits by means of deceit? Yet she always behaved with strange frankness: she had confidants; she recounted her adventures. Do you not see in this woman who bestows her beauty with such serene indifference, who possesses no sense of shame, who is perhaps even lacking in a sense of affection, and who amid all this passion for fructification appears to be destitute of the power of fertility, do you not see something odd, some malady of the body or soul concealed beneath her outward well-being? Yes, gentlemen, this woman's guilt lies not in the heart, but in the mind. Her appetites are precisely those of cretins and idiots. This woman, and the stupid ingenuousness of her crime proves it, is mentally sick. Like the mask in Phaedrus' Fable, she is as beautiful without as she is empty within. She does not therefore come within the provisions of article 531 but of article 35 of the Code'.

Such was the argument sustained by Don Pietro with all the colour, warmth, and fireworks of sophistry which would have made a resounding success of a final scene in a Dumas play. When he sat down, he smiled as he had done at the beginning, because from every corner of the room he could feel as it were streams of sympathetic understanding flowing towards him. Public and jury alike had, of their own accord, reached the same conclusions as the orator; they were looking for a legal loophole—some article in the Code that would authorize them to exercise their clemency.

Almost without discussion therefore they agreed that it was a case of partial mental deficiency as provided for by article 35, and of extenuating circumstances provided for by article 684 of the Penal Code. The result was that the Public Prosecutor demanded a sentence of five years' imprisonment which the Court reduced to three.

The public applauded. Mariantonia stood dazed, still uncertain whether they had condemned her to death or not. Don Pietro Saraceni met the advocate Carusi on the staircase of the court. He stopped to congratulate him.

'Ah, my dear fellow,' replied Don Pietro with a laugh, 'the world belongs to harlots!'

GABRIELE D'ANNUNZIO

D'Annunzio would make a convenient end to this anthology, as in a way he closed one epoch of Italian writing and opened another. His major work, *Il fuoco*, was published in 1900, and thus marks a neat chronological break. By example or by contrast, D'Annunzio affected the whole of Italian prose for the next thirty years. As he himself remarked to Ojetti, he had as much influence on Italian writing as Chateaubriand had on French; and for once he did not exaggerate. It took a civil war to wrench Italian writing back into the tradition of Manzoni and Verga.

This is not the place to attempt an adequate assessment of one who, however he is considered, was certainly one of the most remarkable phenomena of his age. There was about him some mysterious quality, some spell-binding 'magic' which, like beauty, usually bodes no good for its possessor. Some might explain him in relation to the Abruzzi; for others it might seem impossible to separate the strange mingling within him of Christian and Pagan, genius and self-adoration, savagery and tenderness, sensuality and ascetic devotion.

Here, in these two stories, he is in his uneasy early period; for they appeared in his first book, *Terra Vergine*, published when he was nineteen. They show him trying to conform to the literary canons of his day, to Verga and the *veristi*, while he is already drawing away to his own hybrid world of 'aesthetic sensuality' from which he was to emerge with an international name and as a key figure in Italian life.

D'Annunzio's prose, like his poetry, is so highly charged that it is almost impossible to render in any satisfactory version that is close to the original. Rhetoric is always a sensitive point in translation from Italian into English, and he was master of rhetoric for two or three generations of Italians. Here Anthony Rhodes, author of the best biography of D'Annunzio in English, suggests one feasible treatment of his prose and Adeline Hartcup another.

Novels and stories: *Il piacere* (1889), *Giovanni Episcopo* (1892), *Il trionfo della Morte* (1893), *Le vergini delle rocce* (1896), *Il fuoco* (1900), *Le novelle della Pescara* (1909), *La Leda senza cigno* (1916), are among the most interesting. The whole of his production, poems, plays etc, is now in a National Edition.

A. C.

THE HERO

GABRIELE D'ANNUNZIO

Translated by Adeline Hartcup

Already the great banners of San Gonselvo were out
in the piazza, swinging heavily in the breeze. The bearers were Herculean figures, red in the face, their necks
bulging with muscle, and they were joking together.

After the victory over the Radusans, the people of
Mascalico were celebrating the September festa with special splendour. Their hearts were filled with a wonderful
fervour of devotion. The whole province was offering the
abundance of the recent harvest to the glory of its patron
saint. The women had hung their bridal coverlets from
one window to another above the streets. The men had
festooned the doors with leaves and branches, and covered
the thresholds in flowers. Then the wind blew; there was a
a great dizzy swirling in the streets which went to the
heads of the crowd.

The procession was winding its way from the church
and spreading over the piazza. In front of the altar, just
where San Pantaleone had fallen, eight chosen men waited for the moment to lift the statue of San Gonselvo.
Their names were Giovanni Curo, l'Ummalido, Mattala,
Vincenzio Guanno, Rocco di Ceuzo, Benedetto Galante,
Biagio di Clisci, and Giovanni Senzapaura. They stood in
silence, conscious of the dignity of their task, their heads
a little muzzy. They looked strong enough; they had the
burning eyes of fanatics; in each ear, like women, they
wore a gold ring. From time to time they felt their
biceps and wrists, as if to measure their strength; or else
they smiled fleetingly from one to the other.

The statue of the patron saint was huge, of hollow bronze, blackish, with silver head and hands; and it was exceedingly heavy.

Mattala gave the word:

'*Avande!*' he said. 'Forward.'

Around them people crowded to get a view. The windows of the church reverberated with every gust of wind. The nave was cloudy with incense and gum benjamin. Fitfully strains of music reached the ears of the crowd. A kind of religious frenzy took hold of the eight bearers amid this hubbub. They held out their arms, at the ready.

'*Una! Dua! Trea!*'

Mattala counted:

With one accord the men strained to lift the statue from the altar. But its weight was overpowering: the statue swayed to the left. The men had not yet got a good grip on its base. They staggered as they struggled to right it. Biagio di Clisci and Giovanni Curo, the clumsiest of the team, let go. The statue swung, violently, over on one side. L'Ummalido let out a cry.

'Careful! Careful!' called the onlookers, seeing their patron saint in danger. From the piazza came a mighty uproar which drowned their voices.

L'Ummalido had fallen to his knees, his right hand still under the statue. So he knelt there, his eyes on the hand which he could not free, big eyes full of terror and pain; but not another cry came from his twisted mouth. A few drops of blood trickled on to the altar.

All together, the team made another effort to raise their burden. It was a difficult task. L'Ummalido's lips twisted in agony. The women in the crowd shuddered.

At last the statue was lifted, and l'Ummalido drew out his crushed and bleeding hand, which had lost all semblance of form.

'Go home, now! Go home!' people called, jostling him towards the door of the church.

A woman took off her apron and offered it to him for a bandage. L'Ummalido refused. He said nothing. He was watching a group of men arguing with excited gestures around the statue.

'It's my turn!'

'No, no! My turn!'

'No! Mine!'

Cicco Pono, Mattia Scafarola, and Tommaso di Clisci were wrangling about being eighth bearer in l'Ummalido's place.

He went up to them as they argued. He held his crushed hand to his side, and made way for himself with the other.

He said simply:

'It is my place.'

And he put his left shoulder under the patron saint. Gritting his teeth, he bit back the pain with savage resolution.

Mattala asked him: 'What do you think you are doing?'

He answered: *'Sante Gunzelve's* wishes.'

And, in step with the others, he moved off.

Stunned, the people watched him pass. Now and again someone, seeing the wound bleeding and turning black, called to him as he went past:

'L'Umma, what's up?'

He did not answer. He walked firmly on, keeping step with the music, his mind turning a little, beneath the big coverlets which flapped in the wind, amid the growing press of the crowd.

Quite suddenly, at a street corner, he fell. The saint halted a second and swayed, and there was a moment of confusion. Then it went on its way once more. Mattia

Scafarola took the empty place. Two relatives lifted
the unconscious man and carried him into the nearest
house.

Anna di Ceuzo, an old woman skilled in treating
wounds, looked at the shapeless, bleeding hand; then she
shook her head.

'What can I do?'

There was nothing she could do.

L'Ummalido, who had come to, did not open his
mouth. He sat quietly contemplating his injury. The
hand hung, its bones shattered, lost beyond hope.

Two or three old farmers came to see it. Each one,
with a gesture or a word, expressed the same idea.

L'Ummalido asked:

'Who is carrying the saint?'

They answered: 'Mattia Scafarola.'

Again he asked: 'What's on now?'

They answered: 'Vespers and music.'

The farmers took their leave. They went to Vespers.
From the church came a great peal of bells.

One of the relations set a pail of cold water beside the
injured hand, saying:

'Put the hand in that now and again. We will be
back soon. We are going to Vespers.'

L'Ummalido was by himself. The pealing bells grew
louder, changed rhythm. Daylight began to fade. Whip-
ped by the wind, an olive tree beat its branches against
the lower part of the window.

Sitting down, l'Ummalido began to bathe his hand
little by little. As the clotted blood came away the injury
appeared even greater.

L'Ummalido thought: 'It's quite useless. It's lost.
Sante Gunzelve, I offer it to thee.'

He took a knife and went out. The streets were deserted. All the faithful were in the church. Above the

housetops the lilac clouds of the September sunset scurried like sheep on the run.

Inside the church the packed crowds were singing almost in chorus, with regular responses, to the instruments' sound. Intense heat came from lighted candles and living bodies. The silver head of San Gonselvo shone from on high like a beacon.

L'Ummalido entered. To the amazement of all he made his way up to the altar.

In a clear voice, holding the knife in his left hand, he said:

'*Sante Gunzelve*, I offer it to thee.'

And he began cutting at his right wrist, quietly, in full view of the horrified people. Gradually the shapeless hand came away, amid the blood. For a second it hung, on its last threads. Then it fell into the copper offertory bowl, at the feet of the patron saint.

Then l'Ummalido lifted up the bleeding stump; and in a clear voice he repeated:

'*Sante Gunzelve*, I offer it to thee.'

THE VIGIL

GABRIELE D'ANNUNZIO

Translated by Anthony Rhodes

In the centre of the room lay the body of the mayor, Biagio Mila, fully clothed. A lighted candle had been placed at each corner of the bed, and his face was covered with a cloth soaked in water and vinegar. The vigil for the dead man had begun; his wife and brother were spending the night in the room, on either side of his bed.

His wife, Rosa Mila, who might have been about twenty-five, was in the flower of womanhood, exuding health in a kind of pellucid well-being, her skin fresh with the fragrance of a ripe fruit; her big grey eyes had depths as varied as a piece of agate, and her hair was so abundant that the locks seemed to cascade over one another, concealing and caressing the nape, the low forehead, the eyes themselves.

His brother, Emidio Mila, was about the same age, a cleric lean and tanned, with the face of a man who has spent much of his life in the fields. A soft reddish down covered his cheeks, and the impression of virility was enhanced when he smiled, by his strong white teeth. His eyes had a yellowish tint, and they sometimes shone like bright new gold coins.

Neither of the watchers spoke; the woman was occupied with the glass beads of her rosary, the man watching their movement, both indifferent, with that indifference which certain country folk display before the mystery of death.

'It's warm tonight,' he said at length.

She looked up at him slowly, indicating tacit consent. The room was low, full of the flickering light of the candles, with shadows changing in the corners and on the walls, playing now here, now there, with varying intensity. The shutters were closed, but through the open windows a breath of air came in, gently stirring the muslin curtains. Laid out on the white sheets of the bed, the dead man might have been sleeping.

Emidio's words fell emptily in the silence of the room; the woman bent her head again, and returned to the slow counting of her beads. Her breathing was laboured, and little drops of moisture glistened on her forehead.

After a while, Emidio said: 'What time are they calling for him tomorrow?'

In the most natural tone of voice, she replied: 'At 10 o'clock. With the Congregation of the Sacrament.'

Silence fell again, broken only by the regular croaking of the frogs in distant fields; and the room was filled with the scents and savours of the summer countryside. This bucolic peace was harshly disturbed only once when, from the dead man himself, came a kind of gurgle. Starting up with horror from her chair, Rosa moved away from the bed.

Emidio put out a hand, to calm her. 'Don't be frightened. It's only a passing phase.' She took his hand instinctively, as she stood listening to the dead man's sounds, averting her eyes from their source. The gurgle continued, from the belly of the corpse, seeming to rise up towards the mouth.

'It's nothing, Rosa. Don't worry!' He pointed to a wooden bridal chest with an embroidered cushion on it, suggesting she should move there.

She sat on it, beside him; in her distraction she still held his hand. The wooden chest was not big, and their elbows touched.

In the silence as they sat, they heard now, from far away in the fields, the song of reapers at work. 'They

are threshing the corn at night,' she said. 'By moonlight.'
She spoke partly to relieve her feelings, the pent-up worry
and weariness of the last few hours.

Emidio did not reply, and she removed her hand; the
contact with him now caused her a growing feeling of
uneasiness. For she, too, was obsessed with a thought
which had arisen in both of them, unexpectedly, without
warning—the memory of their rustic, adolescent love.

In those days, they had lived in the Caldore neighbourhood, at the cross-roads, on a sunny hillside. At the end
of the cornfield was a high wall of ashlar stone; on its
southern side, which Rosa's parents owned, and where
the warmth of the sun was more propitious, was a luxuriant fruit orchard.

Here, in spring, the trees blossomed joyfully, full of
the sound of the bees, so many little silver, rose and
violet domes of colour; cut out, waving against the sky,
draping the wall, swaying in the breeze. Rosa would
come out here and walk behind the wall, singing softly
to herself. To the listening Emidio on the other side, a
voice clear and limpid as a fountain welled up among the
blossoms. He often listened to that song. He came here
furtively, to escape the rigours of his diet, (he was conva-
lescing from an illness), bringing with him inside his coat
a large piece of forbidden bread. He would walk beside
the wall, in the last furrows of the corn-field, until he
reached this particular place which now became for him a
haven of delight.

Here he would sit, leaning his back against the sun-
drenched wall as he ate, his teeth biting deep into the
bread, his fingers groping for the tender shoots of corn,
whose every grain, full of earth's fresh flavour, seemed
to exude a milk-like sap. Thus, for the convalescent youth,

the pleasures of taste and sound were exquisitely mingled in one sensation. Lying in the sun, surrounded by the scents and savours of the countryside, which filled the air like heady wine, he listened to Rosa's song. Gradually that song became a natural restorative, a physical nourishment, suffusing his blood and being.

Thus the voice of Rosa came to be a force, an agent in recovery. And when he was restored to health, it still retained something of its sensual, recuperative force. Later, when the two families became closer friends and saw one another more often, there arose in Emidio one of those silent consuming passions which can sap the energy of a lonely and diffident youth.

One afternoon in September, before he left for the seminary, the two families went for a picnic together in the woods, along the river. The weather was mild, and the three waggons drawn by oxen made their way past the great cane shoots which flowered beside the water. The picnic was laid out on the ground, in a glade bordered by tall poplars, where the grass was short, scattered with little flowers, purple and sweet smelling. Through the leafage above, great shafts of sunlight fell around them, and the shallow water at the sides was still. All conspired to create an atmosphere of lacustral calm, pure and limpid; the water plants themselves seemed to be asleep.

When they had eaten, some of them wandered away along the river, leaving the others lying, stretched out on the bank. In this way, Rosa and Emidio found themselves together, walking arm in arm along a well-marked woodland path. She leant against him, sometimes bending down to snatch a leaf, putting it to her mouth, biting the bitter stalk, laughing, throwing back her head, staring high up at the passing birds. Once, when she did this, the comb of tortoise-shell which held her hair was loosened, falling back, and the golden hair spread out in all its richness on her shoulders.

He bent with her to gather up the comb, but as they rose, his head struck her's. Then she raised her hands to hold her head and cried, half-laughing, half in pain, 'Ahi!'

The youth stared, and as he did so, a new feeling, a tremor of excitement, ran through him so that, in his efforts to control this emotion, his blood was drained and his cheeks went pale. She replaced the comb and then, from the bark of a tree, she tore off a long ivy spiral, which she deftly wound around her head, to hold the rebel locks in place. The green and russet of the leaves, the golden hair in disarray, were thus combined. 'You like it? Like that?' she said.

He stared, but could find no words to express his feelings.

'You don't like it then? Or have you lost your tongue?'

He longed to fall upon his knees before her as she mocked his speechlessness. He could have cried with shame.

At one place a fallen aspen blocked the way; using both hands, he raised it for her to pass beneath. Then in a flash, the foliage seemed to frame her, crown her, in its greenery. They came to a well, with a square stone basin set on either side; the clustered foliage threw deep shadows all around it, a leafy cloister in a vault with mirrored waters at the sides.

'How beautiful!' cried Rosa. Bending down, she scooped up water in her hands to sip, then filled them both again, and held out her hands to him while drops of water sprinkled her dress. 'Drink!' she cried.

Half distracted, he still could only stammer: 'I'm not thirsty.'

Pouting, thrusting forth her lower lip, she tossed the

18 T.

water in his face. She then lay down in one of the dry basins, as in a cradle, with her legs hung dangling over the side and she moved them petulantly. Then, as suddenly, she was on her feet again, staring at him blankly. 'Well, shall we go?'

In silence, they returned. Blackbirds sang above them, the sunlight fell across their path, the forest scents surrounded them.

A few days later, Emidio left for the seminary.

A few months later, his brother married Rosa.

During his first year at the seminary, the novice often thought of his new sister-in-law. In class, as the priests explained the *Epitome historiae sacrae,* he gave his imagination free play; and while his neighbours practised their obscenities, he hid his face in his hands, deep in his own eroticism. In church, as the litanies rang out to the Virgin, he was far away, in the company of another *Rosa mystica.*

As he gradually learned about life from his fellow-students, that scene in the woods took on a new meaning. The knowledge that he had failed to profit from it, the bitter feeling that he had not gathered a preferred fruit, filled him with torments of self-reproach.

So that was what she had meant! Rosa had liked him! Unknowingly, he had refused an offer of one of the greatest human joys! The thought obsessed him, becoming daily more painful and insistent, so that, with time, he came to feed upon it, increasing the suffering, until inexorably, during the long monotony of seminary life, it became an incurable depression, an endless melancholy...

If only he had known!

The candles guttered in the room. Although the shutters were closed, the air now filtered through the gaps more gustily, causing the curtains to billow.

Rosa was tired by the long vigil; sometimes she closed

her eyes, and her head nodded till it drooped. Then, abruptly, she would open them wide, and return to life.

'You are tired?' he asked softly.

'I ... no ... no.' Straightening her back, she tried to gather strength.

But in the silence that fell again, a creeping lethargy invaded her. She rested her head against the wall, her hair falling over the nape of her neck as she slept; while from her half open mouth, came the sound of slow, regular breathing. How beautiful she looked! The rhythmical rise and fall of the breast, the outline of the knees beneath the skirt, filled him with desire. A sudden gust of wind rustled the curtains, extinguishing the two candles nearest the window.

While he stared, he was overcome with her sensuality; he thought: 'If I could kiss her!'

The cries of the reapers came in through the June night, with the solemnity of liturgical chant, taken up from afar by other voices in varying notes and tones, in unaccompanied melody; while the pale light of the full moon fell through the shutters and illuminated the room, outshining the candles.

Emidio turned again to the dead man on the bed. His glance ran down the rigid line of the corpse, stopping at the hands involuntarily, yellow, swollen, crooked, furrowed, livid with lines on the back. He quickly turned away, while the head of the unconscious Rosa against the wall slowly drooped towards him. How beautiful her head was as it curved so gently forward! Once, its movement half roused the sleeper, and the eyes flickered, revealing a glimpse of an iris, like a violet tinged with white.

He held his breath so that she should not wake, and he remained quite still, while her head inclined slowly more and more towards his shoulder. He listened, and heard the beating of his own heart, the throbbing of his own pulse, the pounding inside his head, sounds which seemed to fill the room, causing him a profound disquiet. But she went on sleeping, and as the minutes passed, he felt more composed. As he stared at the female throat, that voluptuous 'necklace of Venus', and breathed the warm breath, smelt the fragrance of her hair, he felt himself gradually melting into languor too.

Another gust of air swept through the room, laden with the scents of the night, bending one of the candle flames until it, too, went out.

Then, almost without knowing what he was doing, quite naturally, abandoning himself to instinct, he kissed the sleeping woman in the mouth.

She woke with a start, her eyes wide open as she stared at her brother-in-law. Slowly, she gathered up the hair behind her head and sat motionless, her body thrust forward, alert, staring into the flickering shades.

'Who put out the candles?'

'The wind.'

Neither spoke again, both seated on the bridal chest, next to one another, uncomfortable and uncertain of themselves; for they now deliberately prevented their consciences from judging or condemning their thoughts and actions. Spontaneously, both turned their attention to exterior things as if intent on them, putting on a hypocritical, an assumed mastery of feeling to conceal emotion. But little by little intoxication overcame them again.

The songs of the reapers followed one another in the night, hanging in the air, caressing, reply upon reply in antiphony, male and female voices joining in amorous union. Sometimes one voice would emerge above the others on an individual theme around which the other harmonies surged like ripples on the current of a stream. Sometimes, at the beginning of a verse, came the strumming of a guitar, in fifths; sometimes, between verses, the measured beating of the reapers.

Both listened closely.

Perhaps because of some change in the wind, the incoming scents had changed, too; from the hill of Orlando, or from the Scalia gardens, came the powerful smell of oranges, the perfume of roses, pungent, filling the air with the flavour of wedding sweetmeats; or from the marshes of Farnia, the damp fragrance of gladioli, cool to the breath as a draught of water.

Thus they remained, in silence, seated on the wedding chest, motionless, intoxicated by the sensuous beauty of the lunar night, while the last candle flame flickered, its flame bent, and the molten wax dripped. At any moment it would die. Neither moved as they watched the tremulous flame, waiting, eyes wide open. Another gust of wind extinguished the last flame. Then in the dark, certain of one another, with the same desire, at the same moment, man and woman clasped one another, interlaced, seeking each other's mouths, blindly, desperately, without a word, suffocating each other with kisses.

GRAZIA DELEDDA

This last story is something of an appendix, for Grazia Deledda, born at Nuoro in Sardinia in 1875, died only in 1936, and her best work was undoubtedly done during this century. She won the Nobel Prize for Literature in 1928, and was considered one of Italy's leading novelists.

Her work never quite fits into literary 'periods', the tale given here was actually published in her very earliest book, *Racconti sardi*, in 1892. Later she was to cover a broader field, like Matilde Serao, but she remained soaked in the Sardinian atmosphere in which she had been brought up and to which, in her later writings, returned. As time went on she was to be influenced by many schools, particularly the French realists and the Russian moralists. Here we have a first glimpse of her simple approach to the barbaric, yet oddly sane, world of the Sardinian hinterland. This strange world was to reappear in many of her books; it is said to be much the same even today.

Deledda's production was very large, and much was translated into indifferent English early in the century. One novel was published in The Traveller's Library in 1928, with a stimulating introduction by D. H. Lawrence. Some think her best books were written at the beginning and end of her life: *Elias Portolu* (1902), a novel, and *Cosima* (1934), an autobiography. It is hoped that the first of these will soon be available in English.

A. C.

THE SORCERER

GRAZIA DELEDDA

Translated by George Arthurson

They lived at the far end of the village, one of the most prosperous, picturesque villages in the mountains of the Logudoro, and their little cottage, built of dark stone, was the last of all, and looked down over slopes covered with great bushes of broom and lentisk.

Spinning in her doorway, Saveria could see the sea in the distance on the edge of the horizon, mingling with the sky, platinum-coloured in summer and foggy in winter; sewing by the window, she had a view across a vast stretch of valleys reaching right to the foot of her mountains, and she could smell the warm fragrance of the golden harvests stirring in the sunlight and hear the stream tumbling down and rolling on through the rocks and breaks in the mountains.

In this dark little cottage with its roof covered with red and yellow moss and darkened still more by an old vine-trellis, in such a glory of blue sky and wide, silent horizon, Saveria had spent two years of the most blissful life imaginable with her young husband, a man with great flashing eyes and lips deep red like the fruit on the moorlands over which he led his flocks, his sole wealth. He was called Antonio. He too had been very happy since he had married the girl of his shepherd dreams; yet after two years of perfect happiness a slight cloud had appeared in the serene sky of his life. Saveria had not yet made him a father, nor did she show any signs of doing so; it was a very sad business! He had dreamed so much of a bright little boy, as dark-skinned as himself, who as soon as he could get on his legs would follow him up and down, through woods and valleys, helping him in his heavy shepherd's work, a little urchin who would become a strong young man, the joy and hope of his parents in their old age, who would marry and in his turn hand on their name and the issue of their flocks to another, and so on for ever and ever! All Antonio's forbears had been shepherds and his dream was to perpetuate this glorious state of affairs, but how was he to do so if no heir were born?

They had used every possible means: vows, novenas, pilgrimages. Antonio had walked barefoot and bareheaded as far as the famous sanctuary of the Madonna of Miracles at Bitti, had formed a procession, had had solemn mass sung, and promised to give the Madonna as many pounds of manufactured wax as the baby to be born would weigh; but all was in vain. Saveria was still as slender as slender, elegant in her costume with its yellow bodice and embroidered blouse, and the house was still waiting to be enlivened with the shrill cries of the baby so dreamed of, and the long melancholy lullaby of the mother and the puling in the cradle.

Yes, it was a sad, sad business! He had already given up all hope when one day a friend of Saveria's came to see her and said to her very mysteriously once the first greetings *à la française* were over: 'I don't suppose you know, Sabe dear, that Peppe Longu told me you were childless because...'

'Because what?' asked Saveria eagerly with eyes opening wide.

'Because what?' continued the other lowering her voice. 'May God forgive me, but you do know that Peppe is a first class sorcerer, at least everybody says so... and he himself told me it's because of one of his spells that you are childless.'

'Lord preserve's!' exclaimed Saveria laughing and making the sign of the cross. Like all humble country-women she was superstitious and believed in magic; what is more, she had once seen with her own eyes a white figure wandering about the mountains; but that Peppe Longu, for all the sorcerer he was, could be so powerful, well, that was too much! But her visitor persisted, hurt at Saveria's unbelief, and talked and talked till in the end Saveria was convinced.

After an hour's gossiping by the fire on the embers of which she had put the coffee to bring it to the boil, she was so convinced of Peppe's magic power that she asked her friend thoughtfully: 'But tell me, couldn't he break this power of...of hell?'

'No, he couldn't, he said he couldn't! He seems to have a grudge against your husband.'

At dusk Antonio appeared at the foot of the rocky road on his black pony with his saddle-bag heavy with fresh cheese and butter-milk. While he was taking this out of the bag under the vine-trellis Saveria told him everything; he did not laugh but merely knitted his thick brows and shook his head. And when all was attended to, his pony, his saddle-bag, and what he had brought home, Antonio sat down cross-legged by the fire and got Saveria to tell him the strange news once again.

'But what on earth have you to do with Peppe? What reason can he have for taking a horrible revenge like that?' Saveria finally asked with great seriousness.

'No reason at all! Unless it's because I always laugh at his magic.'

'That's a pity! You remember how he got rid of the locusts that were ruining Don Giovanni's vine? And Jolgi Luppeddu's too?'

'Yes...true enough...but...well, we'll see! I'll speak to him to morrow.'

'Oh, if only he could undo the spell!' exclaimed Saveria.

That night both husband and wife dreamed once again of a beautiful, dark-skinned little baby, but on the morrow, though Antonio begged him repeatedly, the village seer absolutely refused to undo the spell.

He was a rather mysterious fellow, this sorcerer; he lived as well as anyone else but never did any work. Besides the magic deeds he did openly and of which he boasted, such as killing locusts and curing sick ewes with simple mysterious words, things for which he accepted no payment, he did, it is true, have many midnight visitors. Yet no one thought anything of that and it was generally believed that the spirits he had at his command gave him the money and the supplies which were in such plenty in his ramshackle cottage. But perhaps Antonio thought differently because, seeing that his entreaties and his threats were all alike coming to naught, he betook himself one night to Peppe's and promised him a shining gold franc provided he would eventually undo the spell.

At first Peppe turned a deaf ear on him, pretended indeed to be shocked, like an artist to whom someone was suggesting a transaction that would defile the poetry of his ideals; then, actually seeing the glitter of the gold franc—and who knows where the shepherd had got it?— he gave way bit by and exclaimed:

'Well, yes. I'm doing it out of kindness and pity for Saveria though; you don't deserve it, always laughing at me!'

Antonio protested; then Peppe instructed him to turn up the following night at a lonely spot on the mountain, with rifle unloaded, a large white cloth, and two candles. Antonio left the money with the seer and promised everything; yet, once he was back on the dark road again, he shook his first at the tumble-down hovel he had just left and sneered: 'We'll see!'

The following night he was the first to reach the appointed spot: it was a horrid place, on a steep slope and looking still more eerie in the pale yellow light of the setting moon. Not a breath of wind stirred in the calm night, and the flowering brambles, dark creepers, and moss smelt sweet in the mysterious silence of the moonlit rocks.

The shepherd placed on a rock the large cloth and the candles, and the rifle which in accordance with Peppe's instructions he had not loaded, and then he waited. Peppe was not long in coming. His first words were: 'It's just on time: midnight.' He spread the cloth out over a great bare stone a bit away from any others, stuck the candles in the ground and made the shepherd lie face down for a moment.

When he got up again Antonio noticed that the candles were alight and the rifle was on the cloth. 'Let's begin!' said Peppe.

And there he began performing a thousand fancy tricks which Antonio watched with frowning brow and a smile of contempt on his lips. More than ever he felt like laughing at the sorcerer, but what was his horror when Peppe turned towards the stone covered with the cloth and asked it questions in a strange language which was probably meant to pass for Latin, and the stone made answer in the same language in a plaintive, mournful voice which came up out of the earth... At the same time the candles went out of their own accord without either puff of wind or Peppe's bending over them. As a matter of fact Peppe turned again to the shepherd, who was trembling like an aspen leaf, and said to him: 'The stone answers that the rifle will tell us whether the spell is broken or not!'

'How?' asked Antonio who felt more normal again on hearing the seer's voice.

'Have you left your rifle unloaded?'

'Yes, indeed!' cried the shepherd.

'Well, take it and shoot into the air; if it goes off, it's a sign that the spell is broken.'

Antonio, who was by now prepared to witness all the miracles of creation except this last, took the rifle and fired... Peppe fell to the ground, emitting not one groan, his heart pierced by a bullet. Instead of shooting into the air, Antonio had aimed at him.

* * *

After his accidental crime the shepherd first decided to take to his heels because, in spite of everything he had thought the rifle would not go off. Then it struck him that no one knew anything about the whole affair and... he folded up the cloth, took the candles and his rifle and walked back to the village by way of the rocks so that he would leave no trace behind him; and in perfect peace of mind he spent the rest of the night with his beloved Saveria.

Still an unbeliever where magic was concerned, this hardy shepherd with the big flashing eyes could never understand how the stone had spoken, how the candles had gone out, and how the rifle had gone off; nevertheless nine months later he had the joy of taking up in his strong arms a beautiful little baby boy of whom Saveria had made him father. Then he bitterly repented that he had not shot into the air; but unable to restore the seer to life again, he contented himself by having a requiem celebrated in the old chapel up in the mountain.